JUSTICE FOR RADAR

THE VIRTUES BOOK V

A.J. DOWNEY

COPYRIGHT

Editing & book design by Maggie Kern @ Ms.K Edits
Cover art by Dar Albert at Wicked Smart Designs

DEDICATION

To Bryan for taking me to Florida and inspiring this book in so many ways. I'm grateful. I love you. Hell of a way to admit it, huh?

PROLOGUE

*J*ustice...

"K, I'm going to take this stuff and grab the truck and I'll be around to pick you up." Billy leaned down to kiss me, and I smiled, kissing him back.

"Sounds good," I murmured, and he gave me a wink before heading up the sidewalk.

This whole trip had been one big fantasy, I swear to God!

It felt like I had been single for like forever, even though it hadn't been long at all... such was my last relationship. I had been lonely and had dared to try a dating app on my phone and I have to say, it was the best decision I had ever made.

I had met Billy on the app several weeks back while he was on a job in Houston, Texas. We'd talked for weeks and weeks before he had come to my town. We'd hit it off so well, that I had done something I *never* do, which was having sex on the first date. Let me tell you, it had been incredible!

About two weeks later, he had asked me to fly down to Florida to join him, because let's face it, I can work from anywhere and worked from home, anyway. If I had the money I would have said yes in a heartbeat and then he'd said, *"Who said anything about you paying for it? No, I want you to join me. I'll pay for everything… just say 'yes.'"*

I'd taken the leap and had said "yes." I mean, I had never been to Florida, and it sounded like an adventure. He'd flown me on a one-way ticket and now we were supposed to drive back. I was so excited to be here with him and to see different parts of the country. It was like a dream come true.

I waited for him to pull around in his truck. A few minutes stretched into ten, then into close to twenty… I tried calling him but there was no answer…

Suddenly, I couldn't breathe.

What was going on?

What had I done?

1

*R*adar...

"Papá."

I turned around on my barstool at the lunch counter, away from my laptop, at my youngest daughter's call.

"What's up, baby?" I asked her.

Lucia had turned eighteen, had graduated from high school, and was just slumming it around Ft. Royal for the summer before she started classes at one of the local community colleges. She was a smart girl, taking the next year to get some prerequisite basics done before deciding on what she wanted to do for the rest of her life... which that wasn't always how things went. Still, she was a planner, my youngest, and she got that from her older sister, who had been a planner too. I think they ultimately got it from me once I'd gotten my act together. They certainly didn't get it from their mother; either their birth mom or the woman I'd been with who had been around to raise them.

While I didn't miss their junkie birth mom, the loss of their step-mother still hurt. Both me and them.

Lucia came up in her cute little apron and jerked her head back behind her. I followed the nod of her glossy black hair, and my eyes went right to the subject.

Another thing my kid got, that I was sure came from her step-mamma and how she'd been raised by her while I worked too many goddamned hours, was a heart of fucking gold.

My eyes fell at one of the two-seater tables in the front window, to the rolling carry-on suitcase tucked under it, and the backpack taking up one seat. They finally drifted up the toned and pretty nicely tanned leg of the woman sitting opposite the backpack, and the muddy tracks of makeup on her face that she wiped at with a napkin as she silently cried. Her hands were shaking.

"What's the story there?" I asked, as Lucia slipped around the lunch counter to set her pitcher of water down.

"She's been here a week, week and a half," Lucia said. "Her name is Justice, but everybody calls her Jussy. She's a real sweet lady."

"So, what's with the waterworks?" I asked, frowning slightly.

"That's a long story, but to sum up, she met a guy on one of those dating apps, a contractor type. They hit it off, and he flew her down here. They were supposed to leave today and he's left her."

I blinked at my daughter.

"I'm sorry, you wanna repeat that?" I asked, shocked, in disbelief, like I was really fuckin' sure I hadn't just heard her right.

"You heard me," she said, and she looked across the dining room with a concerned frown furrowing her brow.

"What're you thinking?" I asked. She tore her deep brown eyes off of the woman across the diner and put them firmly on me.

"I'm thinking we ought to help her," she said with a shrug. "She's a nice woman. I've talked to her a lot this week. She came in for lunch while that asshole was working. I hate to see her like this."

"Baby, she's a citizen. How do we know this isn't some kind of grift?" I asked.

Lucia rolled her eyes at me and said, "I'm your daughter. I would know, and honestly, you should go talk to her. She doesn't know anyone here. She's pretty broke at the moment, and will you just look at her?"

I turned back and took her in. She had long dark hair, but she wasn't Latina. No, she was a white girl and I hated to say it, but most

4

white girls were trouble. Still, she looked so pathetic over there it certainly tugged at the heartstrings a bit.

She wasn't old, but she wasn't exactly young, either. I would have to place her in her thirties somewhere, but low or high? That I couldn't quite tell just by looking at her from across the diner.

"*Please*, Dad?"

I turned back to my daughter and the pleading on her face and in her eyes did me in.

"Alright," I grumbled. "Let's see what's up."

I pushed to my feet and went across the diner, Lucia hurrying around the counter and catching up to me.

"Jussy," she said gently, and the woman looked up, startled out of her silent, tearful staring out the front window.

"Yes?" she asked softly. She had a nice voice.

"This is my dad. Everybody calls him Radar," she said, and I gave a bit of a neutral nod.

"Hi, Justice. Mind if I sit?" I asked.

"He can maybe help you figure some things out," Lucia offered, and Justice smiled up at her.

"Thank you," she murmured. "And yes, of course." She gestured at the seat across from her and I moved her bag off of it and under the table, taking a seat.

I studied her a moment, and she was beautiful now that I got a look at her up close. She was definitely on the low end of her thirties. Her hands were elegant, and her nails manicured, but natural, and I liked that, too. Her makeup, though streaking, wasn't caked on and I could appreciate that. She was a natural beauty and didn't feel the need to play it up to excess.

"Want to tell me what happened?" I asked, and her expression became guarded in an instant. I held up my hands and said, "I'm not here to judge. I promise you that. I'm just here to listen and to maybe come up with a way to fix the problem."

She bit her lips together and rolled them back and forth, trying to decide. I waited her out patiently because I could tell, she'd been through it and was running seriously low on trust like a scared cat.

Although, luring a person out of their mistrust and fear was a lot harder than just waving some food at them. The waiting them out part still rang true for any creature, though.

"Um, I don't know where to start," she said with a nervous laugh.

"How about at the beginning?" I suggested.

She took a deep breath and let it out slowly and said, "Um, I recently got out of a really bad relationship, and, um, I started dating again sort of – er, I picked up one of those dating apps on my phone…" she nearly ducked as though she expected yelling or even a blow to come out of me. I held still. I didn't want to cross my arms or give her any kind of indication that I disapproved or any such shit. That wasn't going to get me what I wanted, which was her story.

When all she got out of me was careful neutrality, she cleared her throat and went on, "I started talking to Billy, but he was, um, far away."

I smiled encouragingly and gave a nod. She went on. Her nervous use of the word "um" was endearing and almost cute to be honest.

"He was on a job in Las Vegas, and we started talking, like a lot. Every day, in fact, and agreed to meet up when he came back in my direction. We, uh, did and…" She blushed, and I had to guess she'd probably gotten freaky with him on the first date. But hell, who didn't when the circumstances were right? Still no judgment here.

She took a sip of her drink and swallowed hard and wrong. She almost choked, but pulled out of it after a moment.

"You alright?" I asked her.

She nodded and held a napkin to her mouth.

"Take your time," I told her. "It's all good. I get it – strong attraction, it's hard not to be when you talk to someone for so long before meeting them. There's a certain amount of comfort there. It's not really like meeting them for the first time. You've got an established rapport like that. Certainly not like this here," I said, gesturing back and forth.

"Yeah," she murmured, nodding without looking at me. That was okay. If it helped her to get the story out, she didn't have to look at me. Truth be told, her body language had my senses tingling. She reminded me low-key of Faith – certainly not as bad as when we'd first gotten a hold of Faith, but some of the same traumatized mannerisms and shit were there. Made me want to ask *"who hurt you?"* but I was sure all that was going to get me was Justice shutting down and not wanting to talk anymore about it or about anything. I didn't like being counterproductive when I could help it.

Damn, kid... I thought of my girl, Lucia. *You got a radar for shit just like your old man.*

"Um, he had to go... on to a job down here the next day. Two weeks later, he asked to fly me here to join him with the plan to drive me back through Texas where l live. Today, we were supposed to head back but..." her face scrunched, and the tears began to flow. "He, um, he left me."

She wrung her hands and sniffed hard, trying not to fall apart. She said, "I don't have any money. I, um, only get paid once a month and that isn't for three more days. He knew that and..." She cleared her throat and got herself together and said, "So here I am and I don't know quite what to do but I'll figure it out."

"Okay." I nodded slowly and asked, "Can I ask a few questions?" She nodded. "What is it you do?"

"I'm a subcontracting graphic designer, a sort of ghost writer if you will, only for cover designs for books instead of writing them, you know?"

I gave a small laugh and said, "I don't, but I assume that means as long as you have your laptop or access to a computer, you can do your job from anywhere?" She nodded and patted the side of a large tote-looking bag down on the floor between her leg and the window.

"That's why Billy and I were supposed to, um, work... you know, as a couple or whatever."

I nodded.

"Okay, so in a few days you get paid, and then what was the plan?" I asked.

"Buy a ticket home from the same airport, same cheap airline, hope I have enough after rent and bills to get a hotel, and when I get home, do the whole ramen diet and never trust anyone ever again?" she cringed adorably, and I chuckled.

7

"Well," I said with a deep breath, sighing out on the end of it. "I know you're low on trust and believe me, you have every fucking right to be by the sound of it, but I think I got a way to fill a few gaps in your plan if you think you can trust me and my kid over there."

I jerked my head back in the direction of my daughter, who was serving another table. Curiosity swirled in Justice's brown eyes, and she swallowed. I could see she already did trust Lucia, I think just by virtue of her being female, which, believe me, I both understood and wasn't offended by at all. After all, catching criminals was my trade. I didn't overmuch pay attention to what they did – a bail jumper was a bond jumper was another skip trace to put food on my table to me, but some of those captures? Knowing what they did and knowing I was putting them back behind bars definitely put a little sugar on top of the cheddar I earned for doing it. Which sounded weird putting it that way, but it makes sense, you know?

"I'm listening," Justice murmured and sat back in her seat.

I nodded.

"This is what we're gonna do…"

2

*J*ustice…

"It's up to you," he said, leaning back in his seat, crossing his arms over his chest. I eyed him from across the small table.

He was a compact individual, and all of it was pure muscle, from the sleeveless white tee showing off muscular arms that belonged on a carved statue, to his long tan cargo shorts that practically hugged equally muscular thighs. The man introduced to me as Radar looked dangerous. Like he'd hurt people before, or maybe even for a living. He fixed me with a patient but kind gaze, his deep brown eyes almost black, smoldering but naturally so. No, his emotional state was calm – incredibly so. Calm and smooth as glass, which I could tell. I'd had a lot of practice reading moods. From the way I'd grown up to… to living with Rodney… before Billy.

I swallowed hard and said, "And your oldest daughter, you're sure she won't mind?" I asked softly.

"Mariposa?" He shrugged. "One, she's at college, up the coast in Tampa, and two, it's my house. What I say goes."

"And just like that?" I asked. "Just like that, you'll invite me, a woman you don't even know, into your house to stay?"

I was having a hard time wrapping my mind around it. It was so bizarre. *No one was ever this kind...*

"Just like that, if you want to," he said and held up his hands. "Only if you're comfortable with the idea."

"Wait, only if *I'm* comfortable?"

"Yes, that's right."

I sat and mulled it over for what was probably too long, but still this was kind of a big ask of somebody I didn't know. But honestly, what exactly did I have to lose of any value here? My life? Didn't seem like too much was there to be honest.

I heaved a sigh and nodded for Radar's benefit.

"Yeah?" he asked, his gaze sharp and intelligent.

"Yeah," I affirmed. "Yeah, okay... I mean, I don't have anywhere else to go."

"Well, you do now," he said. "You comfortable coming with me or you want to wait for Lucia to get off work?"

"Oh, no, I don't want to put anybody out. I can come now," I said, adding hastily, "If that's convenient for you."

He gave me a crooked smile and nodded slowly, as though he thought my stumbling over my words and rushing them out was adorable or something and not the ingrained fear response they actually were.

I tried not to sigh in frustration with myself and instead plastered on a fake, but hopefully convincing smile of my own.

"What can I help you with?" he asked me gently, and I swallowed hard.

"Um, nothing. I've got it," I answered, hefting my laptop bag onto my shoulder after looping my purse over my head and settling the strap crossways over my body.

He telescoped the handle to my rolling hard-sided carry-on and handed it to me, and I nodded.

"Thank you."

"You sure I can't take anything?" he asked.

"No, no, you're already doing so much. I can handle it."

Standing, I realized he was shorter than me, though not by much, maybe five-foot-six to my five-foot-eight. Still, what he lacked in height, he made up for in presence.

"Lucia!" he called out across the diner and his daughter turned with a raised eyebrow, pen poised as she'd been about to take an order. He rattled off in Spanish that was at once the same and yet completely unfamiliar to my rudimentary understanding of Mexican Spanish from living in Texas. The pronunciation of his Spanish a completely different animal from what I was used to, but being in Florida, I had to consider it wasn't typical Latin American Spanish but potentially Cuban Spanish that I was hearing.

I was curious about that, and when he turned back to jerk his head that I should follow him, he did so with a bit of a rakish grin. I realized my wide-eyed expression in a bid to keep up with the differences in his Spanish perhaps made him think I didn't know the language at all – which was fine. I could appreciate the value of having a hidden advantage.

I would be lying if I said I didn't have any apprehension or anxiety following him out of that diner and into the oppressive heat and beating sunrays of Florida. The sunshine was deceptively cheery for how dark the day had turned for me and I cleared my throat.

"I walked this morning," he said, pausing.

"So, it's not far then?" I asked and he smiled, turning, and coming back to me.

"Just around the corner and like three houses down," he said. I nodded slowly. "Would you like to phone a friend back home?" he asked.

I shook my head. "No, I'm fine… it's fine," I said, and he cocked his head.

"Nothing about a man abandoning you several states from where you live is 'fine,' honey. It's okay to be scared. It's okay to be sad, and angry, and nervous and your mind going a mile a minute. It's okay to not be okay right this second. I know you don't know me, and that you're taking a huge leap of faith. I know it doesn't mean a whole lot, but it's going to be okay. We'll get you set up, let you breathe a minute, and get this all figured out. The important thing is that even though you don't feel safe, you are. I promise."

I blinked and nodded mutely. I mean, what did you even say to that? I wanted to believe him, but somehow, I just couldn't and yet... I swallowed hard and dragged my carry-on a step and with a smile he dropped back a step beside me so we walked together and I wasn't following anymore.

"So, we covered your name and what you do, but where are you from originally?" he asked.

"Um, Iowa originally. Got married at eighteen to my high school sweetheart. He joined the military, and we were stationed at Ft. Hood, in Texas. Things fell apart." I laughed a bit nervously. That was the understatement of the century. He was still in prison for what he'd done to me. "I stayed in Texas and that's pretty much all she wrote."

"It's a start," he said with a nod.

"What about you?" I asked, and he smiled, bowing his head.

"Took a bit of the long way around," he said. "Got married young, like you. Thought she was the love of my life, had Mariposa and Lucia. She got tied up with drugs and it got bad. Divorced, fought for my girls, won... their mother died. OD'ed when they were seven and five. Met Marisol. We were hot and heavy and got hitched... then she got cancer. She died while the girls were in high school. I sort of gave up trying after that. Threw myself into work and stayed there."

"I'm sorry," I murmured. "That's a lot."

He barked a short laugh and looked over at me. "Impressive."

"What is?" I asked.

"You're going through it, and you still got a spot of empathy for things that happened years ago and are done and dusted."

I swallowed hard and said, "It was my own stupidity that got me here."

He shook his head. "None of that, now. You weren't driving out of town one passenger light. Only stupid motherfucker in this scenario is the guy you were with, honey."

We were silent for a time as we drew up to the house he'd described, sure enough, only a few houses in from the corner and across the narrow residential street—a cute little single-family hacienda-style home, the white stucco gleaming, the reddish clay tiles undulating along the roof a beacon among the surrounding roofs that were just plain shingles.

I smiled at it. The only thing remotely like it was way down the block on the opposite side, but wasn't quite so nice as this one.

"You have a beautiful home," I murmured, taking in the three arched windows in the front, looking in on a clean and tidy living room.

"Thanks," he said and hit the button on a key fob, the garage door trundling up on its track, revealing a white Escalade on one side and a motorcycle on the other.

"Come on in," he said. "Let's get you settled."

I followed him into the garage and up the two steps into the house. He left the garage doors open behind us, unconcerned about the creeping heat, as he closed the door leading from the house into the garage behind us.

"You can close it," I murmured and with a smile, he clicked the remote in his pocket. I was surprised it worked through the door, but it did. I could hear the hum of the garage door opener's motor as the door shifted down into its closed position.

"Kitchen is through there." He pointed. "Den, where I'm usually working, is through the living room just that way, but the bathroom and bedrooms are back this way," he said, pointing down the hall in the opposite direction. I followed him that way.

"Bathroom," he said, pointing.

"Lucia's room," he said, touching a door. "And this one will be yours. Mine is just there at the end." He opened the closed bedroom door to the room that would be mine and stepped aside.

"I'll let you get settled. Find me in the den if you need me."

"Okay, thank you," I murmured.

"It's no problem," he said. "Make yourself at home."

I nodded. He left.

I looked around at the room, which was obviously at one time a teenage girl's, but with some serious taste and style. The colors were bright and cheery, but also subtle and lovely – yellows, pinks, and turquoise in tasteful patterns that reminded me of hand-painted and decorative tile. A picture of a street with its old-fashioned cars and brightly colored buildings that could only be Havana hung over the bed, bracketed by sheer curtains held back to the wall was the room's centerpiece and the colors made sense, reflecting the bright paint jobs on the buildings.

I went to the small white desk and set my laptop tote down on the floor beside it and sighed. I wheeled my little suitcase aside to where it would be inconspicuous and sank into the chair at the desk and looked around.

I would need the Wi-Fi password to work or to explore my options for flights etc., but first, I just needed to take a minute.

I closed my eyes and let the apprehension go and the gratitude fill me.

I was feeling fortunate. Fortunate, but also scared… no one did something for nothing. That wasn't the way the world worked. Still, for right this moment, I could try to breathe.

Except breath wasn't coming, my throat and chest growing tight and my eyes beginning to burn until I just gave in and cried, thinking thoughts of Billy…

Why?

Because I had really begun to love him, and I had no idea what I'd done to deserve this. None. Nothing. I just didn't know why he could leave me like that, and it *hurt*. God, it hurt, and I didn't know quite what to do, how to get around that hurt. So for a time, I let it consume me. Let it burn me up from the inside out until I felt hollow and all but ash remained.

I couldn't cry anymore. I couldn't hurt. I was just… numb.

3

*R*adar…

I cleared my throat and sat down in my chair, pulling out my cellphone and clicking a few keys at what I affectionately referred to as my battle station in my den. I pulled up the listings for the hotels on the boulevard and picked the one that Lucia had mentioned when she first told me about Justice.

The line rang and the voice on the other end when it picked up was a familiar one.

"Rosa," I said.

"Oh, hey, Radar. How are the girls?" she asked, and I had to smile. Rosa had babysat for me more times than I could count. That was small-town living for you.

"Good, good. Actually, that has nothing to do with why I called."

"Oh?" she asked. "What's up?"

"You have a guy named Billy that was staying there, checked out this morning?"

"Hmm, you know I'm not supposed to be doing this," she said and clicked her tongue as she clacked along some keys. Finally, with a sigh, she said, "Nope. No Billy, no William… what can you tell me about him?"

"Had a woman with him, Justice something or other," I said and sort of kicked myself for not getting a last name.

"Oh, yeah. Sweet woman, always pleasant, always said please and thank you when she would come to the desk for more towels or whatever. He was in room two twenty-three with... ah, huh. Yeah, says here the room was checked out under the name of Travis Morrison."

"Hmm, interesting. You guys take down vehicle information or anything like that?" I asked.

"Dodge Ram fifteen hundred, Texas license plate..." I wrote the number she gave me down on one of the legal pads I kept nearby.

"So, what happened?" she asked after I'd finished scribbling down all the pertinent information.

"Left the girl he was with behind. Said he was getting the truck to bring it around and ghosted her."

Rosa gasped on the other end of the line. "She alright?"

"No, but she will be. You know how I feel about shit like this going down in our town."

"Now that I surely do," Rosa said, and she sighed. "Well, hope what I gave you helps. It's about to get busy in here. I've got to go."

"Thanks a million, Rosa. This is all I'll need."

"Give him hell, Radar."

"Copy that, darlin'."

The line went dead, and I leaned way back in my seat before calling up the captain of our little outfit.

"Radar," Cutter greeted me. "What's up, buddy?"

"Just giving you a heads-up that I picked up a stray," I told him.

"You? How's that now?" he asked.

I told him what happened, and he gave a low whistle. "Fuckin' citizens, man. And they want to call *us* the animals."

I heard Hope in the background ask him what was up. His voice grew distant as he held the phone away from him and said, "Radar's dealing with a townie situation. I'll fill you in later."

"Yeah, that's all this is right now," I said. "A townie situation. Just wanted to let you know."

"Nah, you're good, man. You do what you need to do…" he trailed off, then asked, "She pretty?"

"Not bad at all," I confirmed with a grin. "But I'm not about to go there. That's not my speed."

"No," Cutter said thoughtfully. "No, it's not. God speed, man. Let me know how things shake out."

"Will do, Captain."

I ended the call and sighed, pushing to my feet before going on a deep dive through my resources to find out more about this Billy who wasn't really a Billy and what the fuck his deal was.

I wanted to check on Justice, make sure she was up and running, but the sound of her racking sobs through Mariposa's bedroom door stalled me out in the hallway. If it had been one of my daughters weeping like that, I would have killed a son of a bitch – but as it was, I held no attachment to this woman. I didn't know if my going in there would make things better or worse, so I erred on the side of caution and silently backed off, away from the door, edging back down the hall where I'd come from to do what I did best.

I stopped in the kitchen for a soda and cracked the top on the can, taking a drink and heading back to my desk. I stood and stared at the legal pad some and finally, I dropped into my pilot's seat and stayed staring at it, brooding for a while.

What dude did was fuckin' *dirty*, but I didn't know this chick from Eve. How did I know she didn't flip her shit or do something crazy to get her ass left behind?

I mulled it over, thinking about Lucia. My kid, much like myself, had a sort of sixth sense for these things. Unfortunately, it was a skill we'd both learned through trauma. She and Mariposa both went through it with their bio mom and Lucia, my sensitive little flower, had been bullied in school until I'd finally put a stop to it. Of course, by the time I'd found out what was up, it'd been going on for a while.

And no, I hadn't whooped the kids' asses. I sure as fuck kicked the shit out of their daddies' asses, though. You wanna raise little fucking crotch goblins, you can reap the consequences.

I sighed and took another drink of soda and brought myself back around to the problem at hand, which was damn sure *not my problem* until I'd gone ahead and made it my business by bringing her under my roof.

I set it aside for now, figuring I could come back to it. I tended to trust my gut more often than not, but this time I denied it. My gut had told me she was alright enough to help, but I didn't need to go too far too quick. That in and of itself could spell disaster.

No, best to see how things shook out before I took any extra steps in that arena.

I'd dove in headfirst a few times with these kinds of things and had been burned accordingly. I would like to think I was older and wiser at the ripe old age of forty-five. Hell, I'd like to reach something like eighty with enough time to really enjoy any grandkids if my girls decided to go that route. Of course, that was presupposing I let any boys close enough to 'em to knock 'em up. Pretty sure Mariposa was going to go lesbian anyway. Just a gut feeling, and it had nothing to do with her being a radical feminist before anyone gets their panties in a wad.

"Eh-hem…"

I sat up sharply and spun in my chair at the light, feminine sound of my houseguest clearing her throat.

"Yeah, what's up?" I asked, looking her over.

She was barefoot and she'd used the bathroom, her face freshly scrubbed of tears and makeup, the long lacy skirt of her country dress grazing the tops of her feet, her short jean jacket over the thing with its sleeves rolled back neatly above the elbows giving her a decidedly country feel. Quintessential Texas standing in a Florida home, the hushed vibration of the running AC filling the silence between us.

The polish on her toes was chipped, same with her fingernails, but it was readily apparent why as she chipped at her nails out of nervous habit.

"I was wondering if I could get the Wi-Fi password, so I can send a few completed projects out."

"Yeah, yeah!" I grabbed a post-it off the stack I kept convenient under the edge of my monitor and wrote it down for her, holding it out.

She stepped down into the slightly sunken den off the hardwoods onto the gigantic area rug I had down here and padded forward on silent feet. She had grace with how she moved, and I was having a hard time not taking notice. She was beautiful, and I had a renewed itch to find out just what the fuck dude had been thinking.

She plucked the note with the password from my fingers, sticking the adhesive strip to her index finger and looked down at it. She snorted a laugh.

I grinned. Her smile transformed her face, and I'd be lying if I said it didn't make her an absolute knockout.

"Big files?" I asked casually, and she looked a bit guilty.

"Usually. I can zip them down."

I nodded. "Internet isn't the best around here lately. Last big storm did some serious damage to the lines that the companies still haven't sorted out yet."

She smiled and gave a little shrug. "Can't be worse than hotel internet," she murmured.

"Now there's the truth." I nodded.

"Thank you," she said, drifting back to the doorway.

"No sweat," I told her. "Make yourself at home."

She nodded and disappeared down the hall, back toward the bedrooms.

I shook my head and turned back to my bank of monitors and pulled the radio down from its bracket nearby, queueing it up.

"Scarlett Anne, this is Radar – come back."

"Yeah, Radar, this is the Scarlett Anne – what's going on?" Marlin's rough voice came back over the airwaves.

"Yeah, Marlin. You got my partner out there with you?" I asked.

The mic must have changed hands because the next voice to crackle to life over the airwaves said, "Yeah, bud, this is Atlas. What's up?"

"We got a mystery to solve, buddy. Come to my place when you get back in?"

"Sure thing. Can you give me the preliminaries?" he asked.

"Not on this one. Just come on in and bring some Scooby Snacks – I'm almost out."

"Copy that, brother." He disappeared off the mic and then clicked back on. "Marlin says a couple hours or more yet."

"It's no rush," I told him. "Just need your eyes and reason on this."

"You got me curious," he came back, laughing. "I'll be there, with beer. You're cooking."

"Fair trade. See you when you get in – over and out."

I hung up the handset and sighed. Staring at the legal pad and switching screens, I started to hunt.

4

*J*ustice...

A light knock fell at the door, and I sucked in a long shuddering breath as though breaking the surface after a long, deep dive. I took off my glasses and sat up a bit straighter as the door opened and Lucia poked her head in.

"Hi," she said, and I smiled and knew it was a bit wan, but it was the best that I could muster.

"Hi," I murmured back.

"Dad's cooking dinner," she said, jerking her head in the direction down the hall where the kitchen resided. "Told me to come get you, said that you couldn't hide in here forever."

I folded my hands in my lap and looked back to my laptop's screen and the sleek lines I'd been drawing on my drawing tablet, restating things for this historical epic's cover.

I cleared my throat and stared at the screaming confederate soldier on my screen, finally making a face. It just wasn't coming out the way I wanted it to. He didn't look angry. He looked like he was having an orgasm or something. I sighed and realized lunch had been a long time ago and eating would probably be wise. I would either get a second wind or I would be done for today and either way was honestly good with me. This was the third cover I was working on today and honestly; my creative reserves were running on empty. Emotional trauma did that to a person, I guess.

"Yeah, I should probably give it up," I said, and she leaned down and looked at the screen over my shoulder and laughed.

"Yeah, I don't think that's the look that you're going for with his face."

"Not at all." I sighed. "Maybe I just need to find a different head altogether."

"Sounds a little morbid when you put it that way," she said with a slight giggle, and I smiled.

"I Frankenstein's Monster these things all the time." I gave a stretch and winced as stiff muscles protested, and things acted like they wanted to pop but just wouldn't give.

"You've been sitting way too long, and this chair sucks," Lucia said judiciously, and I smiled.

"Beggars can't be choosers," I said gently. "I can't tell you how grateful I am to even just be here right now. What you and your family are doing for me…"

"Pssht!" She waved me off. "It's nothing, really. It's nice not being just me and my dad for a minute."

I smiled, nodded, and pushed to my feet, wincing some more.

"You need to move more," she said. and I nodded.

"Apparently," I agreed, following her out into the hallway, closing the door behind me out of a habit borne of living in a hotel for the last couple of weeks, the slight pang of anxiety of *do I have my room key*, hitting and fading almost immediately.

No need for a room key here, dummy, I thought to myself. The ingrained habit of incessant berating over the smallest mistakes follows me, a demon on my back, up the hallway.

I wonder if Billy noticed… if that's why he abandoned ship just as soon as he could?

"Hey! There she is!"

I flinched at the boisterous greeting and shrugged my shoulders, ducking my head, forcing a laugh.

"Sorry," I apologized immediately. "I get in the zone and lose myself for a while."

"Nothing to be sorry about," Radar said, slicing through some bell peppers at the cutting board with both speed and precision. A born cook. I pressed my lips together and realized I knew nothing about the man whose house I inhabited... not even his real name.

"Grab a seat," he said, pointing at the opposite side of the counter. "Lucia, get our guest a drink."

"Oh, I can do that," I said quickly. "Lucia just got home from serving people all day. She shouldn't have to do it at home."

Lucia made a noise like that was hilarious and rolled her eyes at me, popping open the fridge door.

"What's your poison?" she asked me. "Soda, milk, water, got some sun tea in here, orange juice..."

"The tea sounds lovely," I said, and she smiled back over her shoulder, her large dark eyes expressive as she tossed her long, straight black hair over her shoulder.

Her mane was impressive, falling well past her waist, almost, *almost* to the tops of her thighs. I used to braid my best friend's long red hair every morning before school when I was a teen and really got into learning different braiding hair styles and the like. My hands very nearly itched to do Lucia's now and to dust off those old skills.

She filled a glass with ice out of the fridge's door dispenser and brought out a pitcher of tea. She poured me a glass and handed it over. I paused before drinking, breathing in the fruity and slightly spicey scent.

"Ooo, what is this?" I asked, taking a sip. *Wow*, it was good.

"Ginger and pear white tea," Radar answered.

"Sweetened with honey," Lucia added.

"My bro Stoker's ol' lady makes it," Radar declared, tossing onions into a skillet on the stove.

"Serenity is cool," Lucia said. "She's got this little goth rocker-chick aesthetic, but she's super, super chill."

"Ah, goth I'll agree with you, kid, but I think the rocker aesthetic is pure Stoker," Radar said, adding bell pepper slices to the onions.

Lucia rolled her eyes. "Stands to reason, Dad. Stoker *is* a rocker."

"He plays bass in a garage band, sweetie. I love the guy – he's one of my brothers – but it's a hobby not a lifestyle."

"Duh, that's because the club is all your lives," Lucia said, getting herself a glass of tea.

"No, *you're* my life, *preciosa*. You and your sister, and don't you forget it." He pointed the tip of his knife at his daughter and gave her a baleful look.

She rolled her eyes, but her blush gave her away. I couldn't help but smile at the sweet exchange.

"Yo, yo, yo!" a masculine voice called from the front, the front door clapping shut behind it.

"Yeah, in the kitchen!" Radar called out.

"Oh, *hello*." A man entered the kitchen with two plastic grocery bags lined with paper ones in each hand, the familiar rattle of glass bottles coming from within them.

He was handsome, I guess. Forties in the face, but the silver frost along his temples and along the tips of his goatee put him maybe at fifty's door. I couldn't honestly tell. He was fit, the arms hefting the bags onto the counter near me sleek and toned with muscle.

He wore a leather vest, a pair of cargo shorts, and some flip-flops. The look very rough and tumble beach bum – his skin a red-kissed bronze from the sun, freckles standing out along the tops of his shoulders and his trim chest. His eyes were a vivid bronze color except for half of the iris of one of them, which was half blue.

"Heterochromia," I muttered, and the new man grinned, his teeth very straight and very white.

"That's right. Most people don't know the name for it."

"What?" Lucia asked, kind of rearing back in confusion.

"The thing going on with my eye, kid." The guy stuck out his hand to me and said, "I'm Atlas, and you are?"

"Sorry, I'm Justice," I said, shaking it.

"Nice to meet you, Justice. You a friend of Lucia's here or...?" He trailed off and I sort of didn't know what to say, eyes widening and taking a big sip of my tea to buy myself time and promptly choking on it as I tried to swallow and inhale at the same time awkwardly.

"Whoa, easy! You alright there?" Atlas clapped me on the back over my denim jacket as I tried not to let tea spill out my nose.

Lucia ripped off some paper towels from the nearby holder and handed me a wad of them.

"Easy." Radar was suddenly there, taking the glass from my hand and facilitating putting paper towels into my hands which I shoved against my face and streaming eyes as I coughed and sputtered, trying to regain my composure.

"You okay?" Voices started to raise in concern and I waved them off, getting to my feet and making a dash for the bathroom to get it together and to try and figure out how to answer the question without humiliating myself further.

The bad decision that was trusting Billy was just the gift that kept on giving, apparently.

By the time I had relearned how to breathe, my throat felt raw. I had to wash my face *again* from my eyes watering uncontrollably, and I was just done with today. Just *done*, but embarrassment aside, I had to go back out there, and I figured the best way was the truth – I mean, it always was, right?

With a sigh of defeat as I stared at my reflection, I ditched the paper towels in the bathroom trash and squared my shoulders. I went back out to the kitchen, blushing with embarrassment to a trio of waiting and concerned looks.

"How you doing?" Radar finally ventured.

"I am so sorry. Wow, not sure today can possibly get any worse but then… yeah… there was that." I tried to laugh and the newcomer, Atlas, smiled at me and shook his head.

"Radar filled me in right quick," he said, scratching his jaw with his middle finger. "I'm sorry you're having a rough day."

"Thanks," I murmured, retaking my seat. I picked up my glass, widened my eyes and with a gusty melodramatic sigh said, "Let's try this again," to a track of some light laughter. I took a drink and didn't die – yay, progress.

"So, it sounds like you're going to maybe be here a little while yet," Atlas declared, taking one of the two final seats at the counter on the other side of Lucia.

"Close to a week more," I murmured. "First flight I can get is Monday." It was Tuesday, so… yeah. I wasn't all that thrilled. I was sure I would overstay my welcome, but the good news was I got paid on Thursday – so at least there was that.

"Book your ticket yet?" he asked. I swallowed hard and nodded.

"I could either afford it or a hotel. If I waited any longer, the flight would be out of reach with climbing prices so…"

"No, that's good," Radar said, back at the stove, shaking the pan over the flame the chicken and vegetables within hissing and sizzling, the mixture growing fragrant with seasonings and spices.

"Fajitas." Atlas clapped his hands and rubbed them together. "Alright!" He reached into the top of one of the bags and pulled out a beer, twisting off the top and passing it to Radar who took it and a drink in one smooth, slick movement.

I met Radar's intense gaze over the beer and startled slightly, averting my eyes immediately.

"So what are your big plans since your vacation got so rudely extended?" Atlas asked.

"Oh, I don't know that I can call it a vacation," I said. "I mean, I've still been working this whole time."

"Aw, yeah? What do you do?" Atlas asked.

Boy, wasn't he just the King of Small Talk?

I shifted on my seat and said, "I'm a graphic designer. I design logos and stickers but most of my business is designing book covers for various novels nowadays."

"Oh, wow, what'd that take to get there?" he asked.

I cleared my throat and said, "I got lucky. I don't have any formal training. I'm all sort of self-taught."

"Wow, you go, girl!" Atlas leaned back in his seat and looked impressed.

"Her stuff is really good. She let me see a bunch of it," Lucia declared.

"The Wi-Fi at the diner was better than the hotel's." I blushed.

"I believe that," Radar said with a smile, chuckling. "Food's on," he declared, and he effectively shut down the chitchat for a time by serving Atlas up first with a wink behind the guy's back at me. I blushed and tried not to giggle.

It was hard for me to trust and to warm up to people, but apparently, Radar was as good as his nickname because he seemed to get that. Lucia smiled at me encouragingly and winked at me too at one point as we all four sat at the counter along stools and stuffed our faces.

Radar was a talent in the kitchen. His fajitas were really good. After dinner, Lucia got up and started cleaning up without being asked and I got up too.

"Where you going?" Atlas asked jovially, and I flinched at being called out and blushed.

I said, "I thought I would help."

Lucia looked back over her shoulder from where she rinsed dishes at the sink and said brightly, "You don't have to!"

"I would like to," I said. She nodded and I went to the open dishwasher, taking a dish from her and loading it neatly. I felt the eyes of Radar and Atlas along my back as they sipped beer and the small talk continued.

"Feel like going for a walk?" Radar asked.

Lucia shook her head and said, "I've been on my feet all day. I'm just down for some Hulu and to call it a night."

"I would, actually." I cast Lucia a smile and said, "I've been on my ass all day and I need to get some fresh air."

She giggled, shook her head, and said, "You go right ahead."

"Let's walk down to the boulevard and take a stroll," Atlas declared. I considered it and gave a nod.

"Let me grab my sandals," I said.

"I'll grab my cut," Radar said.

I didn't know what that was but when I came back out of my borrowed room, he stood in the entry way to the house with Atlas, wearing the same rough-looking leather vest covered in similar but not precisely all the same patches on the front.

"Shall we?" he asked, and I nodded, a bit apprehensive now that it clicked what those vests were. I wasn't used to seeing the people that wore them walking around but the motorcycle in the garage... The guys turned around to go out the front door and I got a look at their matching backs.

The Kraken arched above a patch depicting a giant squid dragging a broken ship beneath the waves, the bottom below that read *Ft. Royal, FL* and in a box next to the colorful orange and brown patch with its subtle blue at the bottom was a box that had a big *MC* in it.

Never judge a book by its cover, I thought, not unironically, considering I designed them just for that purpose for a living now.

I was almost as tall as Atlas while Radar was just above my shoulder on my other side. Not for the first time today, it surprised me that he was shorter. I mean, despite his height deficiency, as far as I could tell, he was the tallest of our trio as we walked down the sidewalk back toward the diner. He just had a presence.

"You doing alright?" I snapped my head up from where I'd been watching the sidewalk and looked over. Atlas was ahead of us by a bit and Radar had me fixed with a considering look at my side.

"Hm? Yeah, why?" I asked.

"Just look lost in thought in a big way."

I forced a smile and nodded. "I am," I agreed with a gusty sigh.

"I can't blame you," he said, nodding, his hands thrust into the pockets of his cargo shorts. "Just feel like I should tell you, you're alright... you know?" I blinked in a bit of surprise and reached up to swipe some errant hair from my loose ponytail behind my ear.

"Come again?" I asked.

"I know the shit feels deep, but you're okay. You're safe and you're going to make it back home just fine. I promise you that."

I swallowed, laughed nervously, and nodded. We paced one another silently, following Atlas's right turn onto the busy, touristy boulevard through the center of town.

"Thank you," I murmured a little bit later, the tightness between my shoulders easing, the Gordian knot of anxiety like a fist in the center of my chest finally loosening just a little bit, making it easier to breathe.

"It's no sweat," he said. "I'm serious."

"You know what you need after a shitty day?" Atlas called from ahead of us. I looked up as he paced backward down the busy sidewalk, laughing, slightly mollified as he just sort of expected everyone else to pay attention and to get out of his way and surprisingly? They *did*.

"What's that?" Radar asked and Atlas came to a stop. We paced forward to close the gap between us and Atlas pointed off to our right, his left.

I turned my head and laughed.

We stood outside the do-it-yourself frozen yogurt bar.

5

*R*adar…

"There's something else there," I muttered, and Atlas gave me some side-eye as he licked some frozen yogurt off his spoon.

Justice walked ahead of us on the beach, smiling with a ridiculous amount of delight at the little sandpipers scuttling along the beach, the sky turning all sorts of subtle pastel pinks and yellows as the sun dipped in the west.

"Most definitely. You going to fill me in on the full meal deal or what?" he asked.

"Later," I said.

"Don't want her to know you're digging?" he asked.

"When do we ever let any of them know we're digging?" I asked.

"Fair," he said with a lift of his shoulder.

"It's not like you to take on a project like this," he said, and I nodded.

"I know it. Like, I don't see anything long term and it's not like that… I'm just saying—"

"It's a puzzle," he said, and I nodded.

"Been a while," I agreed.

"Nothing serious since Marisol," he agreed, and I scowled at him. He held up his hands, his spoon sticking out of his mouth.

"I just got done telling you it's not like that, didn't I? I mean, shit. I just met her today."

"What is it about then?"

I took a bite of my own frozen yogurt and rolled it around my mouth as it melted, considering the question.

"She seems like genuinely good people," I said.

"And? Good people get fucked over all the time, bro. Why her?"

I sighed. "Maybe I'm tired of good people getting fucked over without consequences. Maybe if I can do something about it this time, I should."

"Why?"

"I mean, what if it were Lucia, or Mariposa?" I asked, rolling their names with their proper Cuban accent as I always did when I spoke of them.

Atlas sputtered, "Pssht! Don't lie to yourself, bro. That woman is nowhere near your daughters' ages—"

"No, she's not, but it still stands."

"Don't move too fast," he said with a grunt, and I rolled my eyes – apparently I was where Lucia got it from. I told him honestly, "I don't plan on moving on her at all, bro. I mean, what's the point? She lives in Texas, has a life there. My life's here. It's dead before it could even get a chance to begin."

"So, you have thought this through," he said with a wolfish grin, and I pushed him off balance.

"Fucker," I snarled. "In passing, *only*. I mean, look at her. She's gorgeous."

"Oh, trust me," he said. "I've been looking." He eyed her back appreciatively.

I shook my head and said, "I don't think that'd be the best idea given the circumstances."

"Aw, spoilsport," he said with a snicker.

I gave him a sidelong look and reassured he was just yanking my fucking chain, backed off white knighting for the moment.

"I don't get it," he said.

"Me either," I intoned and my best friend and business partner, my club brother and all-around hetero life mate, clicked his tongue as we both stared after the woman walking slowly through the sand, eating her frozen treat ahead of us. She was wholly absorbed in watching the sandpipers with a faint smile and leaning down to look at the tiny shells along the sand.

She was sweetly somber – if I had to describe her demeanor – and there was just something about that. I just wanted to make her smile, and I didn't know where the urge came from. I really didn't. I didn't think I could ever remember a time where I felt similar.

I spent the rest of the walk low-key talking with Atlas over the problem that was the dipshit that'd left her behind and making sure she didn't hear us. She was whelmed and didn't need any more piled on her.

"Right." Atlas sighed and finished off his frozen yogurt. "It's been a long day and I'm gonna fuck off back home. I'll swing by your place on the way and snap pictures of what you've got so far, so drag this out about fifteen minutes or so before heading back."

I nodded.

"Thanks, man."

"Not the kind of shit we want to go down in our town," he said with a one-shouldered shrug. With a final lingering look at Justice, he clasped hands with me and pulled us into each other to tap shoulders.

"Justice!" he called and raised a hand in a wave. She looked up. "It was nice meeting you!" he called. "I'm sure I'll see you around."

She swept some of her hair caught by the wind off the water behind her ear and raised her hand in a wave, calling back, "It was nice meeting you!"

Atlas jogged back up the beach and I wandered down it in her direction and smiled. She smiled back. She was far more relaxed than she'd been all day, the smile an actual genuine one.

"A little better?" I asked and she nodded, holding her empty cardboard yogurt cup down at her side, bracing the spoon against the side with her thumb. I held out my hand for it and she handed it over. I dumped the spoon into my empty cup and wandered over to the line of surf, rinsing the sticky remnants out of hers and straightening, holding it out.

"For your shells," I said, and she smiled and dumped the few she had in her other hand into it, then took it back from me.

"Thanks," she murmured.

"It's no problem," I said, and we continued at a sedate pace for a bit.

"Thanks for giving us the privacy to talk business," I told her.

"Oh, it's no problem," she said brightly. "Just…" she trailed off and I could tell she wanted to ask.

"What do we do?" I supplied.

"Yeah," she uttered shyly, and I smiled and chuckled.

"We're Bail Bondsman – Bounty Hunters," I said.

"Oh. Oh, wow."

"Private investigators when things are slow – which lately that's been less and less."

She lifted a shoulder in a one-sided shrug and said, "I can't imagine people want to face the consequences of their actions, nor would they like to stay in jail if they don't have to," she said, and I barked a short laugh.

"No, that's true. There's no shortage of runners, mostly drug offenses which is just sad."

She nodded and her expression sobered.

"Addiction is ugly," she whispered.

"Yes, yes, it is," I agreed wholeheartedly.

"You knew somebody?" she asked softly. "The way you said that…"

I nodded. "The girls' mother. It got her in the end."

"I'm so sorry," she said.

"You?" I asked curiously.

She rolled her lips together and looked guarded a moment and I thought to myself, *direct hit, I may have just sunk one of her battleships.*

"My ex-husband turned to alcohol to deal with some of the

things… some of the things he saw on deployment. He came back very different from when he left," she said quietly and shuddered as though someone had just walked over her grave and I don't know, maybe I had with the question.

"I'm sorry," I said, and she nodded.

"Me too."

We lapsed into silence, the moment heavy. That heaviness dispelled when she bent to pick up another small shell, rinsing it in the surf before dropping it into her fro-yo container.

"Thank you," she finally murmured. "For everything. I know you don't know me, and that you're taking a risk by inviting me into your home like you have, but I promise, I'm a good person."

I met her gaze and said truthfully, "Somehow I knew that about you. I have a radar for these things. It's how I got my road name."

"Road name?" she asked. "I don't know what that means."

"It means my nickname was given to me. That's how it works in a club. Your name is earned. It's bestowed upon you like sort of an honor."

"Oh, I see," she murmured, so quietly that had I not been fixated on her lips, the words would have been lost to the wind.

She didn't press further or ask any more questions. In fact, she seemed doubly lost in thought over the information she'd already received.

Truthfully, she earned major points with me for not being any sort of judgmental when my cut had come out. I low-key worried she was afraid, and I sincerely hoped not.

Nobody in this town that was from this town meant her any harm… that guy had left already and fuck him. He would get what was coming to him.

She stopped suddenly and looked back up the beach in the direction from which we'd come, and at our footprints dissipating in the sand.

"Getting tired? Ready to turn back?" I asked.

"If you are and you don't mind?" she asked. I shook my head.

"Not at all, you've had a big day," I reminded her gently.

"Oh, I don't know," she said with a nervous laugh turning around with me.

"No, you have. Mental and emotional lifting can be just as heavy as any physical activity," I told her, and she nodded mutely.

"Sage wisdom," she observed.

"I have my moments," I said with a smile and a shrug. It teased another genuine smile from her lips which looked soft as all get out.

"Don't sell yourself short," she said softly, and I smiled and nodded.

"Fair enough," I said. "Don't you do it either."

"Deal," she said, and the smile stayed this time; lighter than air. We moved back up the beach and toward the house.

I got the door for her, as much to be a gentleman as to ease any weirdness about her just opening up my house to waltz in. It was only day one but honestly, she felt right – like she'd been here longer than that. Was that weird? That was weird, wasn't it?

Except it didn't feel weird, which was what was sort of weirding me out... like what the fuck?

"Thank you," she murmured as she passed through the door.

"You're welcome," I said. "And before you say it, for everything. I mean it. Just try to breathe, try to relax, and I know it sucks given what's happened but try to enjoy the rest of your stay here in Ft. Royal. We really are a great little town."

Her light smile intensified, but her eyes... she was tired. I could see it in her eyes.

"I don't hold anything against the town," she said. "You all have been so wonderful to me."

I smiled and nodded. "Good. I'm glad."

"Oh." She paused at the opening to the living room, and I turned my head. Lucia was out like a traffic light on the couch as whatever she'd been watching played on the television.

I sighed and chuckled. "She's too big to pick her up and carry her into her room like I did when she was a kid, but never fails any time I look at either of my girls, grown or not, I still see those gap-toothed smiles from when they were like six."

That's when she let another piece of the puzzle that was her slip when she said, "I never wanted children."

I looked over and cocked my head, inviting her silently to continue.

"Too afraid I would turn out exactly like my parents," she said with an embarrassed shrug.

"Ah, yeah, my parents were great," I said with a sigh. "Hard-working people, direct immigrants from Cuba while my mother was pregnant with me." I shook my head.

"I still turned out nothing but a pain in the ass. Still, I managed, and I don't know how, to turn out two of the finest women despite how much I fucked up." I shrugged and moved into the living room to wake up my youngest kid and send her into bed.

So rough childhood, rough marriage, and now – this, I thought. There was a thread. I wanted to pull it and start unraveling the whole mess but everything in its own time.

"Lucia, baby, wake up. You're done, kid. It's time for bed," I said kindly. When I looked up, as Lucia began to shift fitfully in her sleep, groaning, it was to a curious look from Justice as she turned and disappeared down the hall.

"Come on, baby." I held my hands out for my daughter and helped hoist her to her feet.

"Night, Daddy," she muttered groggily and fell into my arms for a hug. I hugged her tight and thought to myself *I just wish a motherfucker would try something on one of my girls like what'd been pulled on Justice.* I'd have to kill him. No hesitation.

"Night, baby." She went down the hall after Justice and I stood in the middle of my living room, hands on my hips and let out a sigh, my body sagging.

As fucking early as it was, it was probably time for bed for me, too. I had my laptop in there. I could still do a few things before I completely crashed for the night.

6

*J*ustice…

A light rap fell at the open portal of my borrowed bedroom door, and I looked up and over from my laptop screen, my tablet perched in my lap, stylus poised over it. I tilted my head down slightly so I could look at Radar over my glasses perched on the end of my nose. He grinned at me and said, "You got the whole naughty librarian thing going on with the whole bun and the outfit – it's a whole look."

I laughed slightly, and shook my head, pulling my glasses off my face and setting them aside. They were just a pair of simple, black-framed readers but he was right – they did give off librarian vibes and with my hair coiled and pinned at the nape of my neck. I could see the whole librarian thing.

My outfit, however, was probably the one hold out, though. I wore a turquoise cami layered with a white tank over it, with a matching turquoise broomstick skirt, a wide leather belt canted over my hips. I'd sort of developed a sort of southwest hippy chick vibe while living in Texas and it suited my thin frame. The lighter, cooler clothes seemed to suit the Florida weather as well, so that was a bonus.

"What 'cha need?" I asked with a sardonic smile.

"You to take a break," he said.

I set my tablet, glasses, and stylus in a jumble on the small desk beside my open laptop.

"You need held with something?"

He shook his head gently.

"You've been holed up in here for two days now. It's low-key driving me crazy that I've been in the office that long. Come take a ride with me."

"Oh." I straightened and forced myself to my feet, wincing.

"What's the matter?" he asked.

"Back is stiff is all," I answered, pressing my hands to the back of my hips, and leaning back into a stretch.

"All the more reason to get the fuck up out of here for a couple of hours. I'll see you in the garage," he said, tapping the doorjamb a couple of times with his fist. It was light, just a couple of taps, something to do with his hands and no doubt done a thousand times without thinking but I suddenly flashed on a different set of hands, scarred with a myriad of small cuts and splits to the knuckles... some of them created *on me...*

"You can't leave me, Jussy. You just can't. I won't let you. If I can't have you, no one can..."

I pasted on a brave smile and said, "I'll be right out."

I slung my little purse across my chest, tucked my phone into its pocket and grabbed my little denim jacket to protect my shoulders from the sun. When I stepped down into the garage, and turned, shutting the door behind me, I gave a startled jump and screamed a little as his motorcycle fired up.

I turned with a hand pressed to my chest and Radar grinned at me over his shoulder.

"You're alright!" he called, and I swallowed hard.

"When you said a ride, I didn't know you meant..." I waved my hand over the bike, and he laughed.

"Do I need to go change?" I asked and he shook his head.

"We're not going fast, or far," he called. "What you got on is just fine. Come here!"

I went over to him, and he pointed out things I needed to know, handed me a helmet, and told me what I needed to do to be a good passenger.

"You ever ride?" he asked, and I shook my head. His grin grew. "Glad I'm your first and there's a first time for everything. Now, hop on, just like I showed you and mind the pipes!"

I got on the back of his motorcycle, gathering my long skirt as he turned to face forward in case I flashed. I was wearing my cowboy boots, so I wasn't as concerned with burning an ankle or something on the pipes, but still, I was a little breathless with fear. Especially when he put the bike in motion as we pulled out of the garage. I yipped at the sudden motion and held on as he chuckled, the sound drowned out by the thrum of the engine, but I could feel it through his body, the leather of his vest slick beneath my hands.

The wind whipped loose tendrils of my hair against my face, and I reached down to slip my sunglasses from my purse and over my eyes, squinting under the bright sun. Radar took it slow, and I guess it said something that I was comfortable enough to even do this, but he was sort of something else. A soothing presence but at once outgoing. He had an infectious smile and he and Lucia were clearly close.

There was no screaming, no yelling in his house. There were no harsh words, and no berating. It was refreshing, and it also made me sad for how I'd grown up in some ways which had been all those awful things and more.

I'd taken the first opportunity to leave with Rodney as soon as we were able. We got married pretty much right after he joined the Army at eighteen and we'd lasted a good while until I just couldn't take things anymore...

I held on to Radar, secretly pleased with my bravery at even thinking I could do this. Rodney would have a conniption if he saw me now, a thought that honestly made my blood run cold, but Rodney wasn't here. He was in prison and would stay there for a long time and even though I didn't *feel* safe, because who would after all of that? I knew intellectually, I was. It was kind of nice that Radar would remind me of that fact every so often.

I didn't think he had a girlfriend, or was with anybody, but after Rodney, and then Billy pretty much right after as soon as I was willing to try again? I didn't think I should honestly really be trying anymore. Plus, not the best way to meet someone – first impressions and all of that.

Still, he was exceedingly kind over the last several days and this portion of my trip, even though it was through forced extension, was turning out to be more wonderful even than it'd started which was saying something. I mean, the way it'd started had almost been a dream, even if it had ended on sort of a nightmare.

Radar turned us off the boulevard and into the marina's parking lot, parking us with several other bikes and shutting the motorcycle down. He tapped my knee twice, and I assumed that was the signal to get off, so I did – carefully, and went for the chinstrap on my helmet, handing it over to him and wondering why he hadn't worn one.

"Thanks," he said, setting it on the back seat that I had occupied. "You did great. You sure you've never ridden before?"

I shook my head and smiled, sort of glowing from the small praise.

"No, I haven't."

"You're a natural," he declared.

"Thank you," I said. "What are we doing here?" I looked out over the parking lot and down the broad cement steps leading into the sand.

"Club's having a party. They're typical around this time of year – don't really need an excuse. Just barbecue, and brews, a bonfire or two and chill out. Talk, music, throw a frisbee around or surf. Just something to do when we all could stand to get out."

I nodded carefully and sighed. "I could definitely stand to get out," I said. "Thank you for bringing me."

He smiled at me and lightly knocked his shoulder into my arm and said, "Come on, I'll make the introductions."

I followed him to the steps and said, "Wait." He paused as I sat on one and took off my boots and socks.

"Good idea," he said and kicked off his sneakers and stripped off his socks, too. We went down into the warm sand and headed down the beach where there was a knot of people under an easy up canopy that were wearing the same leather vests as Radar.

"Radar!" someone crowed and there was a flash of silver as they chucked a can of beer at him from the cooler. Radar caught it much like a football and cracked it open, holding it out from his body as it foamed and sucking some of the froth off the top.

"Thanks, Lightning!"

"Hey, Papá," Lucia called.

"Hey, baby," he called back. She smiled and went back to talking to another blond woman, older than her but still in her twenties somewhere. She wore a vest that was form fitting that read *Blossom* where the nametag was, although unlike the boy's vests, hers was embroidered directly into the leather in a carefully stitched cursive.

"Ah, hey, Captain," Radar called and a bigger man with long brown hair in a loose braid down his back came over. He rubbed along the neat, trim beard he had and over his mouth as he sauntered over to us, measuring me up from behind his wraparound, orange-lensed sunglasses.

"Justice, this is the club's captain, or president, Cutter. Cutter, this is Justice. She's staying with me and the fam until next week when she can catch her flight back home."

"Nice to meet you, Justice." Cutter's voice was a rich timbre as he held out a big, calloused hand to me. I took it and shook it quickly and weakly.

"Nice to meet you," I said meekly. Lord, he was an imposing figure! So was his second in command, Marlin and the captain's purported best friend and business partner, Pyro. Although Pyro wasn't as physically imposing as he was presence wise… and not like Radar, either. No, in Pyro I saw the familiar mannerisms of unpredictability that bespoke anger issues and maybe even alcoholism.

I made a mental note to avoid being alone with him in any capacity as he went and got himself another beer and cracked it open, the set of his mouth grim and his energy roiling as though he were on a hair trigger. I caught Cutter eyeing him grimly out of the corner of my eye and when Cutter realized I was looking, he turned his attention fully to me and gave me a grim nod... as though to say he saw it, he recognized it, too, and he would somehow keep a lid on it.

Funnily enough, I believed everything that he telegraphed in that one look and when I turned back to Radar and Atlas, who was again chatting a mile a minute – there was a curious look on Radar's face. He gave me a single nod as though to reinforce what the captain's look had communicated.

It took me a while to politely extricate myself from the boisterous throng of bikers and their women, but I managed just so I could catch my breath from it all. It had been a whirlwind of introductions and curiosity on their part, and I was embarrassed to find they all seemed to know my story which *how humiliating.* I was quickly recognizing that I was getting whelmed, and thus I made my polite but swift exit to walk along the shore solo for a bit to catch my breath.

I was an introvert by nature, and too many people all at once when I was in the headspace that I was in could be a detriment to my stress levels and could lead to even further decompensation of my mental state into a deep depression.

Yeah, there had been quite a bit of therapy after what'd happened with Rodney, focusing on coping mechanisms for the PTSD that'd resulted.

"You doing okay?" I jumped and turned to Radar who had somehow crept up on me and strolled beside me. He held out a soda to me; the can crisp and cold, dripping with condensation.

"Thank you," I murmured and opened it. It didn't froth or overflow. I took a healthy swallow, the carbonation burning all the way down.

"I'm alright," I lied.

He snorted and said, "Bullshit." But his accompanying laugh took any of the sting that should have been in it right out.

I smiled and said, "I'm sorry, I just get sort of overwhelmed really easily and with everything that's happened with Billy..." I paused and looked out over the water and sighed. "I'm just not in the best head-space for meeting new people or to make new friends. I just don't feel like anyone should have to deal with my bullshit, you know?"

"Hey." He put a hand to my arm and stopped us in the sand. "It's not bullshit, and it's not a bunch of made-up drama, either. What happened to you was really super shitty and even though it's been a few days? It's not gonna magic be all better – it might never really be better. Being left like that has to be traumatizing as hell, but you're gonna be alright. We'll get you all taken care of."

I smiled and murmured, "Thanks. I mean, I don't know what else to say." I let out a nervous laugh. "And that seems so woefully inadequate, but I mean it, thank you... for giving me a place to stay, for making sure I don't lose my shit and for all the little reminders to keep me from doing so." I pressed my lips together and quit my gushing, blushing faintly and taking another drink of the crisp, citrusy soda.

"You know how you can thank me?" he asked.

"Mm?" I asked taking another mouthful of the drink and rolling it across my tongue before swallowing.

"Just talk to me. What's your story Morning Glory?" he asked with a grin.

"Um, where to start?" I asked back, stepping slowly. He obliged me and we strolled slowly and lightly along the surf.

"How about with how old you are?" he asked.

I laughed slightly and said, "Thirty-one, about to turn thirty-two."

He nodded and thought about that for a bit.

"What about you?" I asked.

"Forty-five, be forty-six in a couple months."

"You don't look forty-five," I said.

He looked me over and said, "Right back at you, thirty-two."

"I said thirty-one *about* to be thirty-two. Don't rush me, now."

He laughed a little and shook his head and said, "I wouldn't dream of it, but I *am* curious about you."

"I mean, you have me living in your daughter's bedroom, so that's only fair," I stammered.

"You told me how you met Billy, and how you got out here, but what about before that?" he asked.

I drew in a deep breath and let it out in a big rush. "That's a long story," I said.

"I got time," he offered, and I nodded.

43

"I was raised in Iowa by my mom and dad. They, uh, they weren't good people. Super judgmental conservative types, very fire and brimstone – but like in all of the *worst* ways, you know?"

"Thankfully, I don't have firsthand knowledge, my parents were great – but I can get a mental picture," he said, and he scraped his generous bottom lip between his teeth.

I nodded slowly and said, "They didn't beat me a whole lot, per se, but I could never do anything right, you know? Forget any sort of affection or love. I was an only child, but it was like they almost couldn't wait to get rid of me. A lot of rejection, you know?"

He nodded but remained silent.

"When I turned eighteen and graduated from high school and said I was going to move out, my mom actually said to me 'good, it's our turn to have a life now.'"

"Holy shit." He stared at me, shocked.

I nodded and winced, saying, "Yeah. So, I did. I got married to my high school sweetheart, who joined the military for a career, and I stayed in his room without him at his parents until he got out of bootcamp and was stationed somewhere that I could move to be with him."

"Okay." He nodded slowly. "You're here now, and I don't see a ring, so I'm guessing that didn't turn out."

I bowed my head and shook it, suddenly feeling scrutinized by his warm brown gaze but it didn't feel judgmental in the slightest. I was surprised to find he was easy to talk to, so of course I immediately had to begin overthinking things and worrying.

"That's a whole different story and not one you probably want to hear," I said with a touch of forced laughter.

"Oh, but I do," he said. "So hit me with it. Good, bad, or ugly, I'm here for it."

I raked my bottom lip between my teeth and took a deep cleansing breath letting it out, *whoosh*, as they say, before taking the plunge.

"Rodney's in prison for trying to kill me," I said and took another quick drink from my can, so I didn't have to say more right away.

"That's…" he looked a little stunned. "That's fucking awful. Jesus Christ." He actually crossed himself and I tried not to smile. Radar

44

didn't strike me as the religious type in the slightest, so I had a sneaky feeling that the whole crossing himself thing was something he picked up from his parents. Maybe even his mamma, but that he didn't realize he even did it.

"Yeah, um, he was deployed a time or two, came back with PTSD and started drinking to manage his symptoms... things got bad. Really bad... and sort of ended with me getting hit a whole lot, and um eventually he um..." I took another deep breath and let it out all shaky. "He stabbed me seven times and I had to play dead. While he was distracted, digging my grave, I managed to get away, ran to a nearby house, and the people there called 9-1-1 for me. I almost died. The trial was really long, really bad, and really ugly, but he wouldn't take a plea – for which I am grateful. He's serving the maximum sentence."

"Well, that last part is good, but it's not lost on me that here it is however long later and you're finally willing to try again and... well... this. Holy fuck."

"Yeah, if I didn't have bad luck, sometimes I think I wouldn't have any luck at all." I laughed, and it sounded forced.

"I'm so sorry, babe," he said and shook his head. "But look at it this way... that shit is all behind you and in the rearview and you just keep driving. Your best life is just ahead of you and truth be told, I've peeked at some of your artwork. It's really good, and you seem to do well for yourself on that front."

"It's a living," I said with a shrug. "Ultimately, I would like to work for myself, but it's hard getting started when you don't have the formal education backing you up, you know?"

"I know that's right. I'm in the same boat... just high school diploma here, and took the long way to get into the business that I'm in. Really wish I could do more PI work and less of the bail shit – but I gotta do what brings in the money and the bail bonds industry is where the surefire money is."

I nodded slowly and asked, "So what about you?" My curiosity was piqued. "What's the Cliff's Notes on how you got here in your life?"

"Ahh, it's a bit of the same and also a bit more involved to be honest," he said. "Graduated from high school, got into the bail bonds thing through a friend of mine's dad who was getting a little long in the tooth to be chasing down young bucks through back alleys and shit. So, he got me and my buddy to do the running and cuffing instead which is how I got started with this whole thing. At the same time, I did what you did and married my high school sweetheart, but she was a wild child and got mixed up in all kinds of drugs and shit while I was putting in the hours. I didn't know, at least not right away. We got pregnant pretty early on. She lost the baby and I think the drugs went from recreational and became a way to cope. You know?"

I nodded. Sounded similar to how Rodney had fallen down the alcoholism rabbit hole. Of course, at the end? I couldn't be sure alcohol was the only thing he was on, but that was neither here nor there. I was genuinely interested in this man, who had taken me in, and his family and how things had come to be.

"She got pregnant again, lost that baby too, and really fell into addiction. Doctors told her she couldn't get pregnant again after that and then lo and behold, she got pregnant with Mariposa out of the blue. She was clean then, and things were going alright. We made it – Mariposa was born, and things were good. Real good. I was working a lot though, and with the new baby – she was stressing. I couldn't be two places at once and she ended up relapsing and that was rough. We got pregnant again after she got clean, but the call of the drugs got to be too much. I ended up losing her back to that shit and then we had Lucia. I had to file for sole custody and got divorced." He stopped, hands buried in the pockets of his cargo shorts and sniffed, staring out over the open water. I could see the guilt weighting his shoulders down.

"I hadn't been in love with my wife in a long time by that point," he confessed. "I was just going through the motions trying to be a stand-up guy, the man of the house, but I was using work as my own drug of choice to cope with a failing marriage and the fact I was honestly not ready to be anyone's dad. I fucked up a lot in the beginning, but eventually realized me and her together we were going down like the fuckin' Titanic, you know? Slow, and eventually the casualties of us together in that relationship? Yeah… my buddy got me into the club at that point and, man, I fuckin' needed it. Especially when he got shot by this guy we were trying to apprehend. He didn't make it."

"Oh, God, I'm so sorry," I murmured.

"My mom and dad stepped up, and were doing most of the work raising my girls. My buddy, he left behind two kids of his own. By then, I wasn't a prospect anymore and the demands on my time? Shit, Cutter was taking over from Mac, and he *understood*, you know? That I was and needed to be a father first. The girls were growing up so damn fast. Then I met Marisol, and everything changed."

I perked up a bit and asked, "How so?"

"Man, that woman was *my rock*. She was my ride or die and she had it *down*. She stepped up and stepped in and made everything better for all of us." He looked wistful and sighed. "Everything was good for like a solid almost ten years and then she got sick. They tried everything, but we lost her right when the girls were turning twelve and fourteen. I was suddenly on my own again and what she taught me?" He shook his head. "I wasn't gonna hide in my work or the club like before. I wasn't gonna be that absentee dad when the girls had just lost their second mom. Their bio mom died several years before from an OD and it was a waste. It was all a big damn messy waste, and I had to be strong for them so I did." He shrugged but there was a clear pain etched in his posture and on his face.

"I'm so sorry," I said, and he nodded.

"Me too, about you," he said and shrugged. "We all have fucked-up shit in our past," he said. "Trick is to not let it define us and who we are now."

"Wise words," I murmured, and he smiled as we started to walk again.

"Hope they help you like they helped me," he said.

I smiled at that. I didn't know what they were doing, honestly, except they *were* making me think.

7

*R*adar...

"You got it bad for her, don't you?" Atlas asked, laughing.

I frowned and looked up from my phone and over at my partner and club brother.

"What you talking about?" I asked.

"Since when have you ever been prone to long walks on the beach?" he asked.

I rolled my eyes. "We were talking, that's all."

"Uh-huh, I haven't seen you talk to a woman that much in *years*, bro."

"Most of the women in the last several years I wasn't interested in talking to," I said, scrolling down my screen.

"You interested in anything else with her other than talking?" he asked.

"Why you asking?" I demanded absently.

"Duh," he said. "If you ain't interested in tapping that, I damn sure am. She's not half bad looking."

"Don't even fuckin' think about it, man," I growled, and he chuckled.

"That's what I thought," he said. "You *do* have a thing for her."

I rolled my eyes and asked, "You watching for our suspect?"

"Yeah, I'm watching," he muttered and turned to face back out the windshield of our decoy van.

"These fucking junkies are almost too easy to bag and tag," he said, sighing.

"They are creatures of habit for all that they can be unpredictable," I agreed coolly. I'd learned firsthand at both sides of that coin and still harbored some major bitterness about it.

We were in Tampa, outside this shithole motel, waiting on our boy to show up for a fix. We'd watched a steady stream of desperate individuals walk up to room 126 and knock on the door, a short exchange and they wandered off. All of them were in various states of walking decay... at the stage of so far gone-ness that most of them would end up OD'ed or dead from suicide before they ever got anywhere near the point of clean.

If we caught our guy, he might end up with a fighting chance of some kind. He was looking at serious time for fraud and burglary charges all in the name of getting that next shot of poison into his collapsing veins.

Sometimes jail straightened them out. Sometimes they got out and immediately went buck wild and OD'ed trying to pump the same amount of shit they'd needed just to sustain in a body that was no longer geared to tolerate the same amount.

It was what'd happened to the girl's mother. She'd been jailed for knowingly passing bad checks and as soon as she'd gotten out after her several months' stint... well, they'd found her on a dirty mattress in this shithole flophouse with rats chewing on her face. How did I know? I'd had to ID her body. It'd been soul crushing, but at the same time not for the reason you'd think. I mean, I knew she was my baby mama, had looked down into that same face, eyes heavy lidded with passion as I'd made her come, as I'd come deep inside her, but it didn't matter anymore. It wasn't the same woman on that slab, cheeks plumper than I'd remembered after putting on weight in the county lockup.

Just as the gaunt visage of her mugshot hadn't been the same woman either… that woman had already died a slow death and had her soul taken by the demon of addiction. The same addiction our daughter Lucia had been born with, but thankfully our baby girl had been otherwise healthy and had pulled through the detox. We'd gotten lucky with her. So very lucky… but still, I worried for my bright, plucky little girl because I knew it was there inside her somewhere – squatting like a fucking toad. The ability to become addicted, and so easily, too.

I worried for her like any father would worry for his daughter except maybe more because I'd lived through the slow deaths of two women I'd loved already, and I don't think I could take it if I lost one of my little girls the same way.

"I think that's our guy," Atlas grated, and he double-checked the dude's mugshot on his phone. I let go my train of earlier thought and focused, looking at the mugshot and up to the guy shuffling stoop shouldered and haggard across the parking area headed in the direction of room 126.

"I think you're right, buddy."

"Better grab him before he scores. You know he's got shit on him it just means that much more paperwork."

"Yeah," I agreed. We got out of the van, leaving the doors open so as not to clue him in we were coming up on him.

Smooth as silk with the practice of a thousand busts and more just like it, Atlas and I ghosted up from behind the guy and seized his arms, coming up alongside either side of him.

"Sorry, Carlos," Atlas declared. "No fix for you tonight."

"Aw, shit! C'mon, man!" He was so skinny, there wasn't putting up any kind of a fight. Not between Atlas and me. We practically picked the guy up, turned around and walked him back to the van, I had a set of cuffs out and around one of his wrists already before we'd even taken two steps.

"I'm sick!" he cried.

"No, you're addicted, there's a difference," I said.

"But it's alright," Atlas declared. "You'll get clean in lockup."

Any sympathy for guys in his predicament had been burned out of us a long time ago. I mean, it was a situation of his own making. And yeah, I know how addiction works and I know it's not a matter of willpower for some people but these fucking guys... the shit they put their families through? No. I had no sympathy. Even with the mother of my children's face, discolored, swollen with bloat, chewed on by rats, strobing across my memory.

I saw her in every one of these types of captures, and it never got any fucking easier.

When the cuff went around his other wrist behind his back he wailed, and we tossed his ass in the back of the van before he drew too much attention. He was crying and screaming back there as we got into the front driver's and passenger seats, and I looked at Atlas and he looked at me.

"I'm getting too old for this shit," I declared, and he nodded.

"Same, bro. Same."

The winds of change were fucking blowing, as the captain liked to say and just like before any storm, the pressure had dropped, and our shoulders were heavy as shit with it.

"Let's get him to county, collect our bounty, and fucking be done with this scumbag," Atlas grated.

"Yeah," I agreed.

I hated the drug-related cases.

I PAUSED outside Mariposa's door when I got home that night. It was late, so late it was early, but I didn't much care about that. The paperwork was done, the money would be coming in, and while it wasn't a huge amount, it all added up. It'd gone quick and slicker than owl shit and that's the important part. We hadn't wasted any time on apprehending Carlos Santiago... I hated the ones that were hard to pin down. All things considered, that'd been easy fucking money.

Still, talking and rehashing my sob story on the beach the day before to Justice had picked at the scabs of some old wounds some and I was feeling some type of way. Not quite nostalgic per se, but something.

I held my breath and twisted the knob carefully to my eldest daughter's room.

Was I being a creepy fuck? Maybe. Probably. I don't know. I just know that after seeing Carlos's gaunt and yellowed appearance, veins all gnarly and tracked with scabs anywhere where he could inject that shit – open sores and shit running with infection. I needed to burn those fucking images out of my brain with something good and peeking in on Justice? There wasn't honestly anything better than her peacefully sleeping face.

I leaned a shoulder against the doorjamb and just drank her in, her glossy dark hair surrounding her sun kissed face, her dark lashes fine crescents against her freckled cheeks. She was beautiful like this. Angelic, really. Stronger than she knew, certainly.

She shifted, her brow furrowing in her sleep, and I frowned, my own brow crushing down as she moaned out, her hands appearing from under the blankets to reach out. As though she scrabbled or clawed at some invisible surface for purchase. She twisted, another soft moan that could be pain or could be something else emanating from her throat.

I went to the bedside and kneeled, reaching out and cupping the side of her face, capturing the hand closest to me to keep her from scratching herself. The nail polish was gone from her long nails, and they looked a bit rough, white patched on them from where it'd been picked off, which was a stupid thing to notice... but I did, and I honestly don't know why it bothered me deep down.

She whimpered, and I stroked her cheek with my thumb.

"Justice," I called gently, keeping my voice low. "Justice, honey, wake up."

She sobbed in her sleep and on the broken exhalation, she inhaled sharply, and her eyes flew open as she shoved herself with her free hand back and away from me, sitting up.

"Easy," I declared, giving her hand that was still in mine a light but firm squeeze. "Easy," I repeated, holding that hand fast as she reflexively tried to pull away. I got to my feet from my kneeling position, turned, and sat on the edge of the bed.

"You were dreaming, I heard you when I came in from the garage." A white lie, sure, but a harmless one… still, it felt oily on my tongue, and I regretted it almost immediately.

"I'm sorry," she murmured thickly, shaking her head to clear the sleep from it.

"It's all good," I whispered and let her hand go, pleasantly surprised when she curled her fingers around it and held on.

"You want to talk about it?" I asked a moment later.

She shook her head, "No one wants to hear it," she muttered, and it sounded so broken, so defeated.

"Try me," I said quietly, and she raised her eyes in the dim diffuse ambient light from other parts of the house and reached over to click on the bedside lamp. Both of us winced and squinted against the sudden brightness.

"Any time I've tried to talk about anything pertaining to my past guys have been all the same… they don't want to hear it," she said.

"Sounds more like insecure little boys than men," I grated, and she smiled slightly.

"Come on, I have the perfect cure for bad dreams," I told her. I got up, tugging on her hand.

She blushed and muttered, "Please don't judge…"

I raised an eyebrow.

She got up too, and I smiled.

She was in a light peach satin tank and short-shorts sleep set that was edged in ivory lace and left nothing to the imagination. It was at once sophisticated, sexy, and looked cool.

"Sorry, can't help it, and the judgment is that's hot…" And it was, I could feel myself starting to grow hard at the press of her nipples against the thin fabric.

She giggled slightly, a half-nervous half-pleased sound as I towed her gently into the hall and in the direction of the kitchen.

"Have a seat," I murmured, and she pulled out one of the stools from under the counter and sat, resting her arms on the counter itself and leaning on them in such a way that her chest was covered.

I went around to the stove and took down a saucepan from the rack over the island, setting it on the stove.

"What are you doing?" she asked.

"Making us up a hot adult beverage that will help us both sleep. You want to talk about it?" I asked again.

"I don't know that talking about it will make anything better," she said softly, and I nodded.

"I get that," I said, pouring milk into the pan and turning on the stove. I got out my fine grater and my block of hot chocolate spiced with cinnamon and began grating it into the milk.

We lapsed into silence, and she leaned way forward on her arms and huffed out a breath. "So alternatively, you're going to just make me hot chocolate?" she asked after a moment and I smiled, stirring the liquid in the pan and waiting on it to heat.

"Seems to me it's the only thing worth doing at the moment. You can lead a horse to water but you can't make him drink and that's okay. In your own time, Justice. There's no pressure here. It's just a pleasure to have the company after tonight."

She looked thoughtful, dropping her eyes to her hands for a moment before looking back up.

"Do *you* want to talk about it?" she asked softly, almost hesitantly.

I stirred the hot chocolate in the making with a wooden spoon and then leaned on the edge of the stove heavily, looking her in her lovely eyes, contemplating her for a moment. Finally, I gave a nod.

"That'd be nice," I said and cleared my throat. "We were picking up a bond jumper for drug and possession charges, burglary, all the things related to hardcore addiction, you know? Had to camp out in the van outside this super shitty super seedy hotel that a dealer was operating out of." I shook my head. "Just stirs up a whole bunch of shit about the girls' bio mom, you know?"

She nodded and looked empathetic.

"Always does," I said.

"What can I do?" she asked.

I smiled and said, "You just did it. You listened. Didn't have to hold it in for a change." I felt my smile grow. "I feel better already."

She gave an echoing ghost of a smile and looked pleased, and I was glad for it.

I got down two mugs and went to the freezer, pulling out the bottle of good dark rum and adding a little to each one. I topped it off with the scalding hot chocolate, the alcohol cooling it off a bit and dropped a spoon into each one.

"Give that a stir," I told her, and she obliged and raised it to her lips. She took a tentative sip and smiled.

"Good?" I asked.

"Very," she answered, licking a fleck of foam off her top lip.

"Good," I answered, and we sat up and sipped our hot chocolate in comfortable silence.

8

*J*ustice...

We talked, softly, about simple things as we sipped our boozy hot chocolate in the quiet, air-conditioned hush of his kitchen. Of art and music, television shows and movies, just staying off the heavy topics for a change. It was nice, calm, and too soon the hot chocolate, heavy with milk and booze started to work its magic. My eyelids grew heavy and my muscles a little more languid.

"Come on," he said and slid off his seat. He held out his hand to me and I took it and got to my own feet.

He led me gently up the hall by my hand and into my borrowed room, pulling back the blankets on the bed.

"Are you tucking me in?" I asked with a slight laugh.

"Indulge me," he said, and I sat down on the edge of the bed. He kneeled and cupped my heels with his hand, lifting my legs and twisting me to settle them on the bed. I giggled and let him do what he wanted and weirdly, I trusted him. Trusted him to this simple act of kindness and to not get fresh or inappropriate with me. He pulled the blankets up to my chin and I wriggled, settling in.

He brushed his lips against my forehead and my eyes closed even as I froze, my breath stilling in my lungs.

"Get some good sleep," he breathed, murmuring against my skin and then he pulled back, straightening, and the door was swinging shut behind him.

I blinked stupidly into the dark and wondered at this lurching, falling, sense of... I don't know... but I liked it.

I WORKED through the morning and into the mid-afternoon the next day until finally, my stomach would not be ignored.

I got up and stretched, went through my things, and found something clean, or at least cleaner and took myself into the bathroom for a shower. I stayed under the hot spray for an inordinate amount of time letting it soothe sore muscles in my neck and back from my poor posture at the too small desk where I'd been working. I was powering through as many commissions as I could in a blind cash grab. The more covers I did, the more money I made, and I could use the boost.

I made really good money, the problem was where I lived was on the expensive side and I was still paying down debt from my marriage; most of it Rodney's but I was too proud to declare bankruptcy. Some months, I just did the bare minimum for survival, other times, when I felt like too much was too far outside my control – like now – I threw myself into it whole heartedly in an effort to regain some semblance of control in another sector of my life, so I didn't feel like I was so completely going to come apart.

Yeah, I know it wasn't the healthiest of coping mechanisms but it did put out some healthy returns, so I guess there was that.

Once out of the shower and dried, I slid my denim cutoffs up my legs, the strings tickling my thighs. I always had an urge to cut them off but resisted until they no longer bothered me. I threw on my racer back bra and my racer back tank and sighed, looking at myself in the mirror. I looked tired, and I felt tired, but it wasn't the type of tired that a nap would fix.

I brushed out and put my hair up and opened the bathroom door to Lucia going by.

"Hey, sorry, did you need in here?" I asked.

"Ah, yeah, but I was just going to use my dad's it's no biggie." She eyed me. "You know there's soap and stuff on the shelf above the washer and dryer in the garage if you need to do laundry." I looked down at my dirty things clutched in my hands and nodded.

"That would be great, actually."

"Help yourself," she said brightly and disappeared into the doorway to her father's room.

I bit my bottom lip and thought about him. The hot chocolate had been nice, but the way he'd tucked me in after? That'd been far nicer.

I couldn't remember a guy treating me so nicely or with such consideration.

Even Billy, who had been nicer and a good lover – better than Rodney anyhow – hadn't been as sweet to me outside of sex.

It was some serious food for thought.

I mean, it was sad to think about but... but what if I had been treated so poorly up to this point that I seriously just couldn't recognize douchebag behavior for what it was? Where was the bar, really? Should I be setting it higher?

If I had to ask myself, then the answer was probably *yes*, but how much higher should it go? I sorted my carry-on out on the bed, making a neat pile of laundry destined for the wash while I thought about it before scooping it all up into my arms and crushing it to me – making my way to the garage and the waiting laundry facilities.

I was bent in front of the front-loading washing machine when hands fell to my hips and a man's voice declared, "Ooo, mama. That is one fine ass," before he thrust against me, bumping my bottom with the front of his body pantomiming a sexual act. I straightened up immediately and whoever it was gave a shout and leaped back.

"Oh, shit! I thought you were Lucia!"

I turned to the boy and raised an eyebrow. He was older than Lucia but not out of range. I mean, she was eighteen going on nineteen and he was in his twenties, for sure.

"Not Lucia," I snapped and tried not to shudder. I mean it wasn't wholly out of the realm of possibility that I could be his mom if I had gotten pregnant very young – which happened a lot in the middle of nowhere, bumfuck Iowa. There wasn't anything else to do...

"I am so sorry!" he exclaimed.

He wasn't a bad looking kid, but my thoughts drifted back to how high that bar should be set and I worried for Lucia. Was he respecting her enough?

"Javier?" Lucia asked from the door leading into the garage.

"Shit, uhhh..."

"It's okay," I said and had to laugh now. Lucia looked amused.

"That'll teach your dumb ass," she said dryly and held out her hand to the boy. He went to her and wrapped his arms around her waist resting his chin between her breasts and looking up at her with pure adoration.

Ah... there it is... I thought to myself, and I had to smile.

"I seriously thought it was you," he said, and I shut the washer door.

"Mm, come inside and I'll teach you the difference," she said seductively, and I sort of froze. Like, I didn't know if I should be here.

"Sorry again," he said to me and had the grace to look embarrassed all over again as Lucia hit the switch for the garage door to come down.

"Mistakes happen," I murmured, and she towed the boy inside and in the direction of her room and I was somewhat mollified.

I mean, her father was home! What?

I started the washer and sighed, leaning against it when the garage door leading into the house popped back open and I jumped giving a yip. Radar looked from me to the closed garage door and asked, "Javier here then?"

"Yeah," I said and nodded slowly. Radar grinned at me.

"What happened?" he asked.

I told him and he burst out laughing and I do mean he laughed until he almost cried.

"Serves him right," he said.

"I'm still a little mind blown that you allow him to be in her room alone like that." Some of my old midwestern accent twanged with the sentence and I tried not to cringe outwardly as much as I was inwardly.

"She's gonna do it anyway," he said with a shrug. "All kids do. I'd rather she does it where I can intervene on her behalf if she needs me to, you know?"

I nodded slowly after thinking about it a minute.

"How very progressive of you," I said soberly and where I had come from it absolutely was.

He eyed me a second and said, "Isn't it just?"

"My dad would have screamed at me for even bringing up such an idea," I said. "Not that I would, because my dad was terrifying when he screamed and I couldn't wait to get out from under it."

"I never understood that," he said. "Screaming at your kids for their natural inclinations just seems counterproductive in the long run and seems like it would make for an unhappy maladjusted teenager."

"That's the thing," I said and intentionally put on my midwestern twang for the next bit. "The Bible says it's unnatural so…"

"Ahhhh, raised by a pair of those fools, that's right." he said. Stuffing his hands in his pockets, rocking back and forth on his heels and nodding in understanding.

I nodded, too.

"Believe me, they were thrilled to get rid of me."

"That's unfortunate," he said, pulling one hand free to hold open the garage door into the house for me to go through. He caught my eye as I went to move past him and said, "I think you're wonderful."

I replayed the exchange the rest of the day and when I went to bed that night it was with those words echoing in the chambers of my heart.

"WHAT THE FUCK? Who the fuck are you!?" the screeching demand for answers came right on the heels of the blinding overhead light flaring to life. My sleep was shattered, and I sat up, shielding my eyes from the glare of the light just as another screamed demand for an answer hit my eardrums. "Answer me, bitch! Who the fuck are you and why are you in my bed?"

"I'm sorry," I stammered. I was trying to untangle myself from the blankets, the young woman I didn't know still yelling at me although the roar of blood in my ears was drowning out her words.

"*Mariposa*!" the thickly accented, masculine snarl put a stop to everything.

Radar stood behind what was presumably his eldest daughter in the bedroom doorway, his arms crossed and a dour look on his face.

"Who the fuck is she?" Mariposa demanded, gesturing in my direction.

Radar ignored his daughter and spoke to me gently. "Justice, come on, honey. Let me get you situated."

"Papá!" Mariposa grated in irritation, and he stopped, his hand coming up and pointing right in her face, muscles tense and coiled in anger. I froze where I stood.

"*No!*" he barked, and he proceeded to rail at her in a rapid-fire Spanish that was so accented with the Cuban flavor of dialect I couldn't even begin to follow in my dazed and still half-asleep state if I wanted to.

He finished in English, barking out, "Now I raised you better than that!"

She came back at him with more of the speedy, heavily accented Cuban as I picked up my laptop and cords stacking my drawing tablet on top.

"This is still my fucking house, girl! Don't you forget it!" he snapped, and his countenance gentled as he turned to me.

"Come on, Justice." He glared daggers at his daughter. "I'll deal with you later."

I stepped around her suitcase grimly, my nerves rattling, jangling the alarm in my skull as I flash backed to my own childhood and teenage years when my mom used to wake me up the same way in the middle of the night screaming about a chore that I'd left unfinished. The urge to clean was a strong one suddenly as panic gripped me. The two events different but smashing together nonetheless in my skull.

"Come on, no, this way," Radar chided and took me gently by the elbow. I jumped as he steered me down the hall away from the living room and toward his room. I let him, unsure what was happening.

"You'll take my room," he said. "I'll take the couch."

"Oh, no," I said and pitched backward on my heels, digging in.

He tugged gently on my elbow and said, "Oh, yes. My house, my rules, remember?" But his voice was kind, good-natured, as though the threat of anger was suddenly gone, spun back up in the clouds just as sudden as it'd touched down.

"Come on, now, let's get you put back to bed."

"But—"

"No buts, Justice. That's not how we treat guests in my house," he said firmly.

"Jussy," I said.

"What?" he asked.

"Call me Jussy. It's like Jessy except with a u instead of an e. Only my parents call me Justice and I really don't want to think about them right now."

Radar paused and turned to me completely, searching my face as I stood there trembling in his hallway – why I didn't know.

"Shit," he muttered. "You triggered by something?"

I swallowed hard and realized, yes, that's just what it was. I breathed deep and even, counting under my breath to get my anxiety under control and simply nodded unhappily.

"It's okay," he said softly and smoothed a hand up and down my arm. "You're okay," he said. "Nothing and no one's going to hurt you here."

I nodded a little too rapidly and he urged me forward again with his voice, saying gently, "Come on, now."

I nodded back a little too rapidly and took a halting step forward. I was shaking pretty good, and I knew it was just reactionary, but it was still disturbing, you know?

I clutched my electronics to my chest like a shield as he led me through the portal of his doorway into the hushed dark of his bedroom.

"There you go, sit down," he murmured, and I sat down on the edge of his bed.

He wrapped his fingers around my tablet and big laptop and tugged gently saying, "Let me..." I relinquished my white-knuckled hold reluctantly and he kneeled at my feet and put everything down in the cubby at the base of the nightstand on this side.

"There you go, it's all right here. You settle in," he urged and lifted my ankles and slid me under the covers atop the bed as he had before. He tucked me in and said, "You just take it easy, now."

"I'm sorry," I whimpered, and he shook his head.

"It's okay. You didn't do anything wrong. You're all good, baby."

He tucked the blankets around me and kissed my forehead and I felt some of my hyper-vigilance diminish momentarily until he moved off.

"Try to get some rest, we'll talk in the morning," he said. "I'll be right back with the rest of your stuff."

"Okay," I said, my voice shaky.

He shut the door, and I bit my lips together and tried not to cry, except I didn't know *why* I wanted to cry. I swallowed past the lump in my throat and waited.

I couldn't hear anything, so there wasn't any yelling. A few minutes later, the door opened quietly, and he rolled my carry-on into the room and up against the wall by the closet door.

"Thanks," I murmured.

"You're welcome," he said, and he slipped back out.

I shook beneath the blankets and closed my eyes, but sleep wasn't coming. Finally, I got up and went to the bathroom. It was neat and orderly in here, but I had the urge to do *something*. The panic rising rather than receding and so I peeked under the bathroom sink.

Jackpot... it had a bucket of cleaning supplies. I pulled on the rubber gloves, heaved a sigh, and got to work distracting myself from all these awful feelings and quite honestly, feeling like I was doing what I was supposed to do after being woken so abruptly.

Like I had told Radar days before, my parents weren't physically abusive, at least not often or not as often as Rodney had become, but they were abusive nonetheless. Expecting perfect grades, perfect obedience, and coming unglued on me for some of the simplest transgressions including a put-off chore I had intended to do the next day.

Everything was on their time and my time was not my own... and so it wasn't unusual to be woken late at night at ten, eleven, or even the wee hours of the morning being screamed at and verbally attacked for not getting something done or not doing something to my mother's satisfaction.

She would scream at me, berate me, and stand over me with her arms crossed while I cried, and did what she wanted to whatever standard she'd chosen and always with the parting shot as she sent me back to my room, *"well if you did it right the first time you wouldn't have to do it like this."*

No, my parents hadn't whooped my ass on the regular, but they'd sure done a bang-up job of murdering my soul until there wasn't a day that went by even now where I didn't think I wasn't some kind of piece of shit.

I wept, and scrubbed, and cleaned, and grew frustrated that I didn't feel any better. Only worse.

God, I was so fucked up but I did my level best to hide it so no one would know... maybe I wasn't doing as good a job as I thought? I mean, that was a thought and right on the heels of that I had to wonder... *is that why Billy had left me behind?*

I just didn't understand... I just didn't understand what was wrong with me and why I was just so universally hated and disliked when I didn't do anything wrong.

9

*R*adar…

I sighed on the other side of my bedroom door, and I can't tell you how much I wanted to go back in there, crawl into bed, and hug myself to Justice's back and console her. She looked wrecked, standing in my hallway clutching her computer and tablet thing to her narrow body like it was a lifeline or some kind of shield. Her whole body racked with shivers that had nothing to do with how high or low the AC was cranked. Her eyes were wide, showing too much white and her lips pressed thin, and she looked like she was about to fly apart any second but she held it together.

I'd gotten her settled as soon as possible, grabbed the rest of her shit, and put it in there with her and now it was time to deal with my wayward fucking eldest daughter who wasn't even supposed to be home – it was only mid-term but not any sort of break.

I went back to her room and shut the door behind me and turned, crossing my arms over my chest and fixing her with a flat look.

"Just what in the Christ was that?" I demanded.

"What? Can't I come home for the weekend?" she demanded, standing up from the edge of her bed.

"Sit your ass down," I said imperiously through gritted teeth. She looked like she swallowed her own tongue as she complied.

She had the bed half stripped already, and I sighed, putting my arms to my sides.

"What happened?" I demanded. "Why are you really here?"

She looked scared, like she was trying to decide…

"Out with it, Mariposa," I demanded, and I tried not to snarl. It wasn't her fault that Justice was sensitive, just like it wasn't Justice's fault she was as sensitive as she was. There were a whole lot of traumas to be unpacked there but right now I was here, my kid in front of me looking scared and I needed to know if she was scared of me.

"Campus police thought it would be a good idea if I came home just for the weekend because there's this guy that's been bothering me," she muttered finally. I raised my eyebrows at her.

"Come again?" I asked.

"Dad, I can handle it," she said, and I ran my tongue across my bottom lip.

"Baby girl, this is one of those things you handle by telling me and the boys – period. End of."

I dropped onto the bed beside her and asked her, "What's he doin'?"

"Nuh-uh," she said. "First, *who was that?*" she demanded, and I looked down my nose at her for a second and conceded.

"Justice was in town with a guy and when they checked out of the hotel across from your sister's work, he said he'd be around with the truck to pick her up and left her here."

"Oh, that's fucked up!" Mariposa said, rubbing the tip of her nose with the back of her hand.

"No shit. Your sister had gotten to know her over the week or two she was here with the dude and when she came into the diner with all of her shit, crying, Lucia asked questions then came and got me."

Mariposa nodded and said, "I'm sorry."

"You ain't gotta tell me that," I said and scoffed. "You gotta tell her in the morning."

"It's just been a lot," Mariposa said with a moan, keeling over and putting her head on my shoulder.

"Take it from the beginning, *mi corazon*. What's happening?"

She sighed and said, "He's just this boy – a freshman, and I don't know he's a little weird. He asked me out and I said 'no' and he just, I don't know – he keeps like *showing up* places and I mean the first few times maybe were a coincidence but like seven, eight times a day? Then I got this..." She opened her phone and showed an email she'd received.

You only have a few more times to give the right answer and the right answer is 'yes.'

It wasn't signed, the email address that it came from was generic... but none of that mattered.

"Come on," I said, towing her to her feet. "Let's get this up on my systems."

She sighed in defeat and said, "Okay, but if you're gonna hurt him you better put the fear of *God* into him, Papá... because if you don't? I'm afraid it's only going to get worse. I think he's crazy."

"You don't get to worry about what I'm going to do," I said, and I gestured for her to step out into the hall.

"Things all good?" Lucia demanded from her bedroom doorway.

"Yeah," Mariposa said glumly.

"Go back to bed," I told her a little more tersely than I intended.

"Tell you in the morning," Mariposa said, and her sister gave her a chin lift and went back into her bedroom shutting the door.

I had my eldest daughter follow me into my den where I dropped into my seat at the controls. I opened the email service she used and ordered her to log in, sliding the keyboard and mouse over for her.

She sighed and did as she was told, logging in so I could retrieve the email.

"What's this kid's name?" I demanded.

"Levi Baumgartner," she said with derision.

"Sounds like an entitled white boy," I said.

"Nailed it," she said, pursing her lips and handing the controls back to me.

"Alright, off you fuck to bed. I'll take it from here," I said.

"I don't think I'm the only girl he's doing this to," she said.

I looked back over my shoulder at her and told her, "He's not your problem anymore." I put as much finality into my voice as I could, but Mariposa knew. She'd grown up in and around the life and I straddled the line – a foot in each world.

I shot a mass text to the club's burners and settled in to do some digging. Church had gone well, and I'd tried getting Justice to come down to The Plank a little later, but she had opted to 'stay in her bubble' as she'd called it and to get more covers done.

There'd be another short Church sometime tomorrow to decide a course of action when it came to this, but for tonight I would do some digging and find out just how deep this dipshit's rabbit hole went. Atlas pinged me back almost immediately online with *let's fucking do this,* and I had to grin. He lived for this kind of cyber bullshit far more than I did but I wasn't no slouch, either.

I sighed. It would be a long night, but there wasn't anything I wouldn't do for one of my girls.

I glanced at the legal pad with *Billy's* info on it and yeah, that was seriously chapping my ass, too.

I shot it over to Atlas, *when we're done with this, I want to dig on the dude that left Justice behind.*

Atlas came back the only way Atlas would, *you got it.*

I nodded slowly and sighed.

She would be leaving in a couple of days, and I wasn't really all that surprised to find that it didn't sit right with me.

I thought about that, long and hard in the background while I went through the motions on Mariposa's problem, shifting into a sort of work-mode on it.

She would be leaving in a couple of days, but that didn't mean that had to be it. I didn't want it to be. I really wanted to stay in touch with her – and I knew how. I had the power. Seemed to me Justice needed a friend and she had one in me. The distance was a problem, but I just needed to stay the course.

Be right back, putting a pot of coffee on, I tapped out to Atlas.

Go, I got this for right now, he shot back.

My kids were his kids, too. My two girls were *all* of the club's girls, meaning they had more aunties and uncles than any two kids could want. I had no illusions about that the club's place in my kid's life and had no problem accepting the club standing up for my girls as much as I did as their father. It was nice to have the help and that they had my back.

With that thought, I pushed to my feet and went to the kitchen. I needed that coffee. It was going to be a long night.

WHEN I GOT up the next morning, it was only after a few hours of shitty sleep, but it was also to the incessant buzzing of my fucking burner across the coffee table I had in here. I sat up on the couch, the leather groaning underneath me – all my shit snapping, crackling, and popping in unsettling ways as I got myself vertical.

I answered the phone with a gruff, "Yeah?"

"You called this meet n' greet, princess. We're waitin' on you." The captain's voice was rough, but that's just how he was.

"Be right there," I groaned, and he grunted in response.

I got up and wiped the sleep out of my eyes dragging my ass out and down the hall toward my room for fresh clothes. The first thing that hit me when I opened my bedroom door was the heavy chemical tang of cleaning products. I frowned and edged into the room so as not to disturb Justice who was sound asleep in my bed and peeked around the corner into my bathroom.

Holy shit, I mouthed silently. I mean, my bathroom was kept clean, I paid a cleaning service pretty handsomely for that, but this was *next-level clean*. Shit sparkled that'd never sparkled before and I low-key wondered if I was paying the fucking service too much.

What the hell? I wondered as I turned to look back over my shoulder. Justice way laying still but her eyes were open, roving up and down my back, a nervousness giving her brow a slight furrow putting a tightness around her eyes.

"You do this?" I asked stupidly, already knowing the answer.

"I'm sorry." She apologized immediately and sat up. I snorted a laugh.

"You're sorry you cleaned my bathroom?" I asked.

"I just had all this pent up…" she held her breath and let it out in an explosion of air. "I needed to do something, and I tend to clean when I'm that." She formed her hands into claws and shook them back and forth like she was strangling something while making the cutest angry frustrated face.

I laughed lightly.

I shook my head. "Did it make you feel better?" I asked.

"Yes and no," she said, sighing tiredly.

"Look, I gotta step out – club business. You mind if I grab a quick shower and some fresh clothes? I can use the other bathroom if you want." I hitched a thumb over my shoulder.

"No, don't be stupid," she said, waving me off. "Use your bathroom. Just pretend I'm not even here."

I nodded and looked at her sitting up on the edge of my bed and it was out before I could stop it, "Yeah, that ain't going to happen."

She averted her gaze and blushed hard, but she didn't do anything else to signal she was uncomfortable. Didn't cross her arms or try to hide under blankets. I smiled. "Sorry, just the more I hang out with you, the more I like you," I confessed.

Her expression blanked a bit and she blurted, "Even with how crazy I am?"

I chuckled. "You have issues, maybe even a lot of issues, but you're not crazy, beautiful and all of the issues you do have? You came by them honestly. You're fine, believe me," I said. "Try to get some more sleep. When I get back, I'm taking you out for a ride. You need to get out of the house."

"Okay," she murmured. "If you're sure."

"I'm more than sure, but the guys are waiting on me so…"

"Right," she said.

I took the fastest shower in the west, er… technically east, and by the time I was out she was out and when she slept and all of the troubles and anxiety were erased from her face, she looked like a fucking angel.

Clutching my towel around my waist I liberated a pair of underwear out of my dresser drawer and ducked into my walk-in closet to pull everything on. I shrugged into my cut, looking back one more time at her before I closed up shop and headed out the garage door, hitting the switch to open things up. I took the bike; I'd fucked off and wasted enough time while the guys cooled their heels waiting on me to help me with my problem.

"There he is," Marlin grated as I came through the front door of The Plank. He raised a mug of coffee to his lips and sucked some down.

"About fucking time," Hope chirped from the arm of Cutter's throne. His hand tightened on her hip, and she chuckled.

"Sorry, house full of estrogen and a long fucking night," I declared, dropping into my seat at the lined-up tables.

"Oh, yeah? What happened?" Lightning asked.

I recounted the tale of Mariposa coming home and how freaked out Jussy got, and the whole damn mess.

"I'm not done mopping it up, either," I said.

"Well, some things are best sorted in the light of day," Cutter declared.

I nodded, chiming, "Exactly."

"First things first, though... to order." He smacked his gavel on the arm of his chair Hope wasn't perched on.

"What's going on with our girl?" Pyro asked.

"I left it to you," Atlas said, holding up his hands.

I filled them all in, including everything Atlas and I had dug up on this kid, including his high school counselor's records where she noted her concerns about his behavior.

"Well, ain't he sweet?" Marlin sucked his teeth.

"Sounds a step down from Ren's ex," Stoker said soberly.

"He's a problem," Cutter agreed.

"I know it's not our usual thing to go all vigilante," I declared.

"No, fuck this guy," Hope declared, and she looked pissed.

"That's my girl." Cutter chuckled and squeezed her hip.

"What'd Mari say about it?" Lightning asked.

"Mari's spooked," I said, using the affectionate shortening of her name the club had gifted on her when she was little. "She told me whatever I do about him, to make it fucking stick that she's sure he's going to get worse or retaliate if I don't."

"She ain't told you everything, bro," Galahad said from down the table.

"I know it," I said.

"He hurt her?" Beast growled.

"He's scared her, that's for damn sure," Atlas declared.

"Hmm, young buck with a taste for older women, huh?" Hope grinned with a savage, bloodthirsty glee. "How about I handle this one?" she asked.

"What you have in mind?" I asked cautiously.

She shrugged. "Head on up there, lurk at a few of his favorite haunts, wait for him to take the bait and get pushy and serve him up," she said.

"Oh, now *that* is guaranteed to piss him off," Atlas said laughing.

"It's also guaranteed to take the heat off Mari and put it on me and if he wants to push it—"

"Game, set, match... I like it," Cutter said rubbing along his jaw. "'Sides, got it on good authority you have your hands full the next couple of days with a certain stray."

I sniffed. "She flies out Monday," I declared.

"That don't mean shit." Marlin chuckled. He looked me right in the eye across the table and said, "One man's trash is another man's treasure," before winking one of his brilliant blue eyes at me.

I smiled. "Yeah."

"So we good?" Cutter asked.

"We good," and "Yeah's" coursed around the table.

"Alright, then." He banged his gavel, meeting over.

"I might be getting a little old for this, but the dim light of a bar and the right makeup, pretty sure I could pull off senior in college," Hope said judiciously.

"Bitch, you ain't age," Pyro said laughing. "You're like a vampire or some shit."

Hope flashed her teeth and hissed and there was laughter.

"I gotta get home and finish cleaning up the emotional mess from last night," I said getting up and stretching. "Hopefully, Jussy's still asleep so I can deal with Mariposa."

"Good luck with that," Atlas declared. "I don't want no part of it."

"Thanks, bro. You've done more than enough," I said, and he got up. We clapped hands and pulled each other in.

"Don't hear from you by tomorrow, I'm gonna assume you were savaged and are lying in a bloody heap on your floor."

"Probably a fair assumption with Mari. She's just like her fuckin' dad," I declared. Laughter followed me out.

When I went through the front door to the house, Mariposa and Lucia were in the kitchen. A glance down the hallway showed my bedroom door still shut tight. I jerked my head in that direction with a questioning look at Lucia and she shook her head. I nodded.

"Gimme a minute with your sister," I said, and Lucia rolled her eyes but nodded and got up, taking her coffee with her.

"Come here and sit down." I dropped onto the stool Lucia had vacated and pulled out one in front of me for my other child.

Mariposa sighed and brought down another mug fixing a cup of coffee. She brought hers and the fresh one over and handed the fresh one to me. I set it aside, and she took a seat drinking out of her cup with both hands, her expressive dark eyes looking over the rim of her mug expectantly and I shook my head.

"Look, I get it," I said gently. "You were comin' home, it was late as fuck after a long-ass fuckin' drive in Florida fuckin' traffic no less, and you're met with the unexpected but that was no way to treat another human being. Especially not a guest in my home." I searched her face and nodded when it fell.

"I know," she said. "And I'm sorry. I forgot myself for a minute with everything going on but, Dad—" I held up a finger and she pressed her lips together and took a second.

"No buts, right... *and* Dad, life in the dorms is kind of fuckin' brutal. I'm not gonna lie. These bitches be fuckin' out of their minds. No home training whatsoever… I guess I just failed to make a full transition and I know – that's my bad and it's not an excuse, but it *is* a reason, and I will totally apologize and do better."

I smiled at her and hooked a hand behind her head and dragged her forehead down to my lips. Both my girls were taller than me. They got it from their bio mom's side of the family.

"Now there's the baby girl I raised, I know, and I love. That's legit all I ask, kid."

"I know," she said and sighed out.

"We cool?" I asked, and she nodded.

"We're cool… I really do feel bad, though."

I nodded. "I'm going to take her out for a ride today. Get some wind therapy and see if I can put some distance between last night and that apology you got coming. You got big plans with your sister today?" I asked.

She nodded.

"K, you two get to it before she wakes up."

"K," she said and sighed. "What about…?"

"Uncle Atlas and Hope are on it, that's all you get," I said. "No more questions."

She nodded and seemed relieved that Atlas was involved. She stopped in the mouth of the hallway and looked back and asked, "Hope?"

"Git!" I said with a wink, and she rolled her eyes and got.

I sighed and sucked down her peace offering of coffee like it was going out of style.

10

*J*ustice...

"Hey." I stirred and sucked in a sharp breath, Radar's thumb gently stroking my cheek. I stretched and shuddered as I did, yawning and struggling to wake up.

"Hey," I murmured, and he chuckled.

"Sleep all day, you won't sleep tonight," he chided gently, and I smiled.

"I'm not exactly on any type of set schedule," I said. "Whether I get a cover done at night or during the day, it makes no difference."

"Touché," he said. "More of it's gorgeous out there, not too hot, perfect for a ride and I promised you one. A real one, this time."

"To the marina and back isn't a real ride?" I asked.

He chuckled and shook his head. "Not even close," he said. "Take a shower, put on some jeans, good shoes, I'll have some coffee ready for you when you come out. How do you take it?" he asked.

"Two creams, two sugars," I murmured.

"You got it, coming right up," he said.

I got up, groaning and went through my carry-on, finding the things he asked for. I was just about to go to the guest bath when he appeared in the hall with a steaming mug of coffee and said, use mine.

I nodded. I mean, I had just cleaned it to within an inch of its life. I knew exactly how clean it was, etc.

I fetched my travel toiletry bag out of my little suitcase and took it into the bathroom with me, closing the door and facing the mirror.

I guess I should be grateful I looked nothing like the sleep-deprived monster I felt. Just a plain, boring, ordinary girl staring back at me from the mirror. I didn't know what Radar saw in me to be so nice. I certainly didn't feel like I deserved it. Still, I wouldn't turn it down. My wounded soul couldn't take much more rejection and heartache and all too soon I would be leaving anyway.

His life was well established here, and I was in Texas. Still in that big and lonely house that my husband and I had shared with the big and ugly mortgage to match, but I was trapped. I mean, I could prob- ably sell it but I didn't know where I would go or if I would have enough and it was daunting, you know?

I started the shower and lifted my satin tank over my head and sighed. My torso was pale. I mean, it never saw the sun… that was for a reason. The latticework of puncture wounds along one side and around to the back were ugly and raised. I'd lost a kidney on one side, and I prayed my other would hold out for the rest of my life.

That had been the worst pain imaginable, and I cringed looking at myself. Billy had been so gentle and understanding when it had come to my scars. Letting me keep a shirt on the first few times we'd had sex, and eventually just sort of kindly ignoring them. He didn't look, or even acknowledge them and that had made me feel somehow better.

I mean, I know I'd told Radar I'd been stabbed but seeing it was something entirely different and I didn't know if I honestly had – Jesus. It's not like he would want me anyway.

"Just two more days, Jussy," I murmured quietly into the shower spray as I stepped in. The rest of today, tomorrow, and then however long it took for me to be dropped off at the airport on Monday.

I showered, finished my coffee in gulps between drying off and pulling on each article of clothing, before finally pulling my hair into a high ponytail.

I looked at myself in the mirror and made a face. I had dark circles under my eyes but if we were going out? Sunglasses would take care of that. I felt tired, but I couldn't say for sure if it was the type of tired that a good, less fitful night of sleep would cure or not.

I went out into the bedroom with the dregs of my coffee in my hand and Radar was gone. I sighed, stopped, and pulled on the low-top Chelsea boots rolling up the ankles of my skinny jeans above them in the latest fashion. I sighed and brushed a hand down the front of my loose, flowy, white tank top and went through my pouch of necklaces and earrings, choosing a long bronze chain with a chunky pendant of a small pocket watch and glass beads.

I was as put together as I could manage, casual, and with a mind toward riding today, I pulled on my cropped jean jacket again and lifted my purse over my head.

I found Radar in his den at his computer. He looked up, and I froze in the doorway, looking behind me at first, then down at what I was wearing.

"What?" I asked, unsure about the look on his face. Like he was surprised or seeing me for the first time or something.

"Nothing," he said. "What?"

I shook my head and blushed faintly, wondering if I had imagined things.

"Sorry," I murmured, and he chuckled, getting up from his seat.

"Nothing to be sorry for," he said and smiled up at me and once again it almost *surprised* me that I was taller. Like... what? His presence was just so... just *so*, you know? He seemed larger than life if that made sense. It made him seem taller than he was. I don't think I'd ever encountered anyone like him in that regard, actually.

"Come on," he said, putting a hand to my back gently. "Let's go for a ride and see what we can see."

"Okay," I agreed softly.

We rode slowly through the center of town, winding our way inland toward the freeway. I held on, the pace quite a bit more thrilling – read terrifying – than the slow roll to and from the marina earlier in the week.

"Hold on, sweetheart!" he hollered back at me, patting my hands around his waist and then we were on the freeway, and I was holding on for what felt like dear life as the pavement rushed beneath us and all notion of safety or that this was a good idea evaporated with the rush of the wind!

I gritted my teeth and swallowed hard, but soon the rhythm of the bike beneath us and Radar's deft handling of the beastly machine soothed me enough that the riot of color and sound that was the inner coastal freeway took over my senses.

I couldn't tell you directionally, if we headed north or south – and I didn't think to check the freeway signs for the direction. Instead, I enjoyed the hot rush of air, and the sun soaking through the back of my jacket. The fear turned to thrill and my death grip on Radar eased as he piloted us through traffic with precision and skill.

We took an exit, and there wasn't much to look at, at first. We wound through what felt like country roads Florida style and I half worried we would see an alligator or something. Like, Billy had taken me to a gator farm tourist attraction thing, but I was wholly unprepared to see or find one of those gargantuan relics out in the wild.

We turned down a long, white, crushed shell drive and I held my breath, missing the sign we passed that was larger than life about where it was that we were going. It was getting to be mid-afternoon, heading on toward evening in the next few hours. Eventually, he stopped in a small parking area to the side of a great big old antebellum home. He had to tap my leg to remind me I had to get down, so capti- vated was I at the beauty of the old place. He shut off the bike and stood up and I looked over.

"Where are we?"

"Sugarland Distillery," he said. "They have great food, a beautiful tasting room, and tours. I thought it would be a nice and low-key after- noon. Get a late lunch, early dinner and take the walking tour; try a few things and head back home. Maybe stop at the beach for a sunset stroll. What do you say?"

"I say it sounds wonderful and relaxing," I said. He smiled.

"Good deal."

He came over to me and winged out his arm. I smiled and slipped my hand through it, and he tucked my arm close, into the side of his body. It felt good. Nice, and normal.

We strolled up the wide front steps of the old home, the wrap-around porch festooned with white rocking chairs and small round tables set low between them.

Overhead on the porch, were old, old-fashioned belt driven ceiling fans that circled lazily, and I could just picture it – Sitting on the veranda with a mint julep under the lazy circle of those fans over-looking the sugarcane fields the sky turning golden and pink with the setting sun over them.

It looked good on the surface, peaceful, nice even... but I couldn't help but feel like the whole 'experience' was nothing but a polished turd when I looked out over the modern fields surrounding the house with their irrigators and far out there the roof of a John Deere barely visible over the cane.

I had to bet the whole house was built by slaves.

I wiped my suddenly sweating palm on my denim clad leg as Radar opened the front doors for me to step through.

Inside, the house had been thoroughly remodeled. The entryway open and wide, an archway leading to a vast dining room full of tables facing out the tall windows on that side of the house, and on the left? The way was opened up to a tasting room, giftshop, and bar.

A hostess dressed all in black stepped around the podium at the restaurant portion of the house and she asked, "Party of two?"

"Yeah, thanks," Radar said, and she nodded politely and we followed her to a secluded table for two at one of the back windows by the kitchen.

"This place is kind of spectacular, but with how old it is, I imagine it has a sordid past," I said.

Radar gave a charmed smile. "You'd be right. It's one of the oldest and most haunted buildings in Florida if you believe in that sort of thing and it has one of the bloodiest histories of any plantation in the state.

"Yeah?" I asked, opening the menu and trying to keep my eyes off of the prices which were steep, but not as bad as I expected.

"Yeah, this place burned like a motherfucker in the 1860s. Slaves rose up and revolted, hung the entire family from the hanging tree on the tour we'll take."

"Oh, my God," I uttered, and he gave a wicked grin.

"They deserved it," he said.

"What happened to the slaves?" I asked worried, and he winked at me.

"I've already said too much. You'll get it on the tour."

I nodded.

We had a sumptuous dinner. All of it farm-to-table and inspired by the people who had once inhabited and worked this land. I let my eyes wander the framed photos on the walls going back through the years, all of them photos of the original house inside and out. Time marched along the dining room walls and I was enthusiastic about this tour we would take.

I love history, and this was like living and breathing a sliver of it.

"Let's have a taste and do a little bit of shopping while we wait for the tour," he suggested, and I nodded. We chatted quietly and he let me wander the shop while he paid for our dinner and a couple of flights of rums which was the distillery's specialty.

"Jussy," he called softly when they were ready, and I turned from the glasses with the Sugarland logo on them and went up to the bar.

To taste the different rums available was an experience, and I felt as though my nose glowed from it. I was glad that we had the tour between us and attempting to ride back to Ft. Royal and it was nice to just be able to relax and sip rums, discuss cocktails and to laugh with Radar and the tasting room's bartender – not sure if there was another name for it.

"Which one you like best?" Radar asked and I bit my bottom lip and considered the rums in front of me, light to dark. Some aged far longer than others and in various types of barrels.

"I really kind of like the Raw, and the Locker," I said. Raw was the lightest rum, raw and fresh from the still, good for mixing cocktails. The Locker was their darkest rum. Thick with molasses and spices, and according to the label on the bottle from the deepest darkest parts of the sea where Davy Jones's locker resided.

"I dig the Locker, too," Radar said with a nod. He eyed me. "You were looking at those glasses over there," he said. "Why don't you go on and pick four. Two for me and two for you to take home."

"Oh, I couldn't—"

"You ain't buyin'." He cut me off before I could protest. "I'd like to remember you and today if you don't mind and I'd like to send you home with a reminder that things weren't all bad down here." He winked at me with a smile, and I bit my bottom lip to contain mine from getting too big.

I nodded, and I went back over to the shelf and called back, "Which style?"

He chose, and I chose the two that I liked best. I ferried them to the counter two at a time. He had a couple bottles set aside too, a bottle of light and a bottle of dark, waiting to go into the bag that the tender was fixing up. He wrapped the glasses carefully and put them into sturdy cardboard boxes with the distillery's logo on them.

"And two for the afternoon tour, correct?" he asked.

"Absolutely," Radar said, handing his card over. I tried not to look at or fret over the total. It wasn't insubstantial.

"You want, I can hold this behind the bar until the tour is through," the man behind the counter, a bald guy with a big salt and pepper mustache said to Radar, and Radar nodded.

"That would be great, man. I would appreciate that."

He held out a strip of a wristband at me and I stepped forward and let him affix the wristband for the tour around my wrist.

"Tour starts in about an hour, fix you a drink for the front porch?" he asked. "It's included with the ticket price of the tour."

"What looks good?" Radar asked with a grin as he handed me the drink menu.

I raised my eyebrows and asked, "You trying to get my liquored up?"

"That obvious?" he asked coolly, and I giggled. I finally settled on a Rum Runner while Radar ordered something called a Cuba Libre, which I had never heard of.

"It's just a rum and coke with lime," the bartender said affably as he set about making our drinks. "Just leave your glasses on one of the tables out front when you're done with 'em," he said, handing our drinks over.

"Sounds good, thanks, man."

The bartender nodded, and we went out into the heat and humidity of the day under the lazily turning ceiling fans on the porch. It was nice after the super chill of the over cranked air conditioning inside. We found a pair of rocking chairs with a table in between them and sat down, overlooking the fields of sugarcane in front of us.

"It looks like bamboo," I said, and Radar sipped his drink and smiled at me.

"Technically it's from the grass family," he said.

"Grass? Really?" I asked.

"Really," he answered.

"How do you know?"

"My dad worked the fields when he came over from Cuba with my mother who was pregnant with me. She worked cleaning hotels."

"Oh," I murmured. "My dad worked the cornfields," I said. "My mom was a bank teller."

"Always nice to find some common ground," he said taking a sip of his drink. I sipped mine, fruity, cool, and delicious.

"Except from what I know from you and Lucia, your parents were great."

"Yeah, that they were," he said.

"Mine, not so much," I replied with a sigh.

"Aw, yeah? How's that, if you don't mind me asking, that is?"

I breathed out and reminded him; another brief overview of my wretched childhood with added detail, glossing over the truly ugly parts as fast as I could and leaning back in my seat, rocking gently and trying not to let the awful feelings creep out from their vault to over-shadow the day.

"Shit, yeah, they sound like real douchebags," he said and shook his head chewing his bottom lip in thought.

"Right? My therapist said that it's not unusual to wind up in a relationship with or even marrying someone similar when you don't have any therapy under your belt or the tools to recognize what you're doing. I guess it was just my luck that instead of marrying someone similar I ended up running and marrying someone who would turn out to be *worse*." I grimaced. I felt so stupid for that... so, so, stupid.

"Your therapist ever say why it is people do that? Seems a bit counterintuitive if you know what I mean."

"She said something about familiarity," I said. "That when something is your normal, something healthy seems both foreign and scary. She also told me not to beat myself up for it too much, that it was extremely common... still, I feel dumb."

"Don't," Radar said, shaking his head. "From everything you've told me, you have no reason to. You couldn't magically look into a crystal ball and see that boy-o couldn't handle his shit."

I opened my mouth to defend Rodney a bit then, which I know sounds crazy, but it wasn't exactly fair to characterize any veteran that way to my mind.

"You don't have to," Radar said, holding up a hand. "I think I know what you're going to say, and I agree with you to an extent."

I looked amused. I was sure.

"Okay, what was I going to say?" I asked.

"Not fair to paint a war vet with that brush," he said, and I laughed slightly.

"Okay, you're right, so why did you?"

"Let's go back a few seconds, what I *should* have said was something more along the lines of, a lot of soldiers come back fucked up by the shit they had to deal with over there. Where they fail to handle their shit, is by not taking the opportunities that I *know* are available to deal with it in a responsible manner. No, instead they hit the bottle and, no offense, take it out on their wives and then expect a pity party afterward."

"That's scarily accurate," I said dryly.

"Oh yeah?" he asked.

I sipped my drink. "Mm-hm, nailed it all the way through the pity party. He tried a temporary insanity defense, the only thing that stopped the jury from believing it is that he took too much time to premeditate the attack."

"Fuck," Radar muttered and shook his head. "I'm so sorry."

"Yeah, me too," I murmured. "It's like between my family and him, I just... I don't know, it's like I don't know how to operate within society anymore. I feel so broken and..." I faltered. "And maybe I am. I mean, just look what happened." I got really quiet then, thinking about Billy, tearing it apart and putting it back together, just so I could tear it apart all over again convinced that it just *had to be* something that I'd done.

"It wasn't you, baby." Radar's voice was soothing and empathetic as it interrupted my thoughts.

I looked over sharply and asked, "How could you know?"

He shook his head and said, "When it comes to thinks like that? That was a conscious decision on his part to leave you behind and it was shitty. There were a million different options he could have picked but when you pick that one? Honey, the professional bounty hunter is telling you – he was running from something."

I looked down at the whitewashed planks of the porch floor and rocked gently, turning what Radar had said over in my mind. Finally I had to concede, he was right.

"You're right," I said with a sigh. "I mean, I can't really come up with anything else that even remotely makes sense."

He nodded solemnly. "Was there anything else? Anything you can remember that supports the theory?" he asked.

"I mean, he took *a lot* of calls for work," I said. "Some he would take with me there, mundane stuff that was a bunch of numbers and switches that didn't make any sort of sense to me. Things about camera placement and fiber optic line..." I shook my head.

"But then there were calls that he would step outside, and he would be gone out of the room for *a while*. Like thirty, forty-five minutes. Sometimes more than an hour, and he would always walk away from me for those calls and would be unhappy if I came too close. I tried to respect his privacy, but those calls always made me some kind of uncomfortable." It sort of felt good to get the confession out. Like I finally set down something heavy.

Radar nodded. "Always trust your gut, honey. Always."

I nodded slowly and took a bigger swallow of my drink.

"Be rude, stay alive?" I asked tentatively and he smiled.

"Exactly, but sounds like there's more to that little catch phrase. Where did you hear it?"

"A women's self defense class I took," I answered. "They meant it in the context of don't let societal niceties gaslight you into putting yourself into a dangerous situation."

"Okay, I follow." he nodded.

"Want an example?" I asked.

"Yes."

"Okay, so," I shifted in my seat, "take for instance, you're one of my girlfriends, and we're at a bar." He laughed, and I shook my head. "No, no, this scenario doesn't work if you're a guy!" I cried and laughed.

"Okay, okay, so I'm your BFF Carmine instead of Camilo – I get it."

I froze.

"Your name is Camilo?" I asked.

His smile grew and he said, "Yeah."

I searched his face, his kind smile, the sparkle in his lovely dark eyes and I nodded carefully. "I like it. It suits you."

"Yeah?" he asked, and he was smiling so hard I thought that it would freeze permanent on his face.

"Yeah."

He chuckled after a moment and said, "You were saying, you and Carmine are living it up at the bar."

"Right, a bar, a party, it doesn't matter. The thing of it is, a guy comes up to me and sets down a drink and says, 'here I got you a drink' and the *polite* thing to do would be to say thank you and take it, right? But that isn't the *safe* thing to do, is it?"

"Right, okay, I follow," he said.

"So, I say, 'no, thank you' and the guy gets huffy and says something about wasting money, his time, or whatever right?"

"So, he's trying to guilt you."

"Right, but what do I honestly have to feel guilty for?" I asked. "I didn't ask for the drink, it might not even be something I like, but it could also contain a shit ton of GHB or some other date rape drug but now, socially, I'm sort of obligated to take it or I'm a bitch, right?"

"Fuck, yeah, okay, I see your predicament," he said.

I nodded. "So, in this case, not knowing this guy, not knowing what is in the drink is it better to be polite or to be rude?"

"Rude, definitely rude, but there's nothing rude about saying 'thanks, but no, thanks.'"

I shook my head. "Not until he makes it so by being all like, *'come on, I'm a nice guy!'* or like I said before, *'come on, don't make me waste my money!'* when in fact, I didn't make him do anything."

"Right, and then I guess he'd be all like, *'not all men are douchebags out to hurt you,'*" Radar said, and I could see the wheels turning in his head.

"Right, and I'll give him that," I said nodding. "But I have a counter question to that argument."

"What's that?" Radar asked.

"How am I supposed to tell *which* men?"

I could see him stop and think about that for a good long second and then he looked up at me with a sort of admiration in his eyes. "And yet back at the diner you decided I was alright."

I smiled and said, "Your daughter loves you and thinks the world of you. If it hadn't been for Lucia, I wouldn't have even considered it."

He smiled then, and it was one of huge pride. I could tell it was pride in his daughter and he even looked a bit emotional for a moment when he reflected on what I said she'd said about him.

"I don't know how I got so lucky, you know?" he asked.

"How's that?" I asked.

He shook his head. "I made a lot of mistakes along the way. I honestly don't deserve my girls to be such the awesome human beings they turned out to be, or for them to love their papa like they do."

"They got all of it from somewhere," I said gently, and he nodded.

"I always thought it was Marisol."

I shook my head. "Maybe some of it, but I feel like a lot of it is blood."

He looked at me then and asked, "If that's so, how do you explain you?"

"Me?" I asked.

"Yeah."

"What about me?"

"Well, from everything you've told me about your parents, they're a couple of miserable fucks – sorry not sorry."

I shook my head. "No, there's nothing to be sorry about. It's true. I'm still dealing with a lot of the damage they inflicted upon me, and I swore I would be different."

He nodded. "Exactly. You are different. Nothing like them… makes me kind of upset you're leaving in two days."

"What? Why?" I asked.

"Because if circumstances were different, I would love to have the chance to shoot my shot." He eyed me and I sat frozen, numb with the shock of his words.

"Me?" I squeaked out skeptically.

"You," he said with a nod.

I sat quietly and stared back out over the fields and confessed without looking, "I wish circumstances had been different, too."

11

*R*adar...

Her soft utterance was a green light as far as I was concerned, but that didn't mean I wasn't going to move carefully where she was concerned. She'd been through a lot, and after watching Marlin with Faith and Charity with Galahad, I knew I needed to tread carefully. I didn't know how shit was supposed to work – her being in Texas and me in Florida, but I had a will and where there was a will there was a way.

Was I crazy? Maybe, probably, but I felt something when it came to Justice. She was something different – a breath of fresh air, cool and sweet, fragrant with flowers and something like fruit.

I wanted to taste her so fuckin' bad but I could hold back. Nothing got accomplished that was worth accomplishing by rushing.

We finished our drinks and talked softly for a few minutes about different directions our lives could have taken in order for us to meet much earlier and under different circumstances. Laughing at some of the ridiculousness, both agreeing it would have still had to have been after I'd had the girls and even after Marisol. I loved that woman, I missed her fiercely, and I wouldn't trade my time with her for the world. I tread carefully around my feelings on that, but Justice picked up on it and she smiled gently, the serenity of an angel on her face and she got it. She understood and let me have it with no sign of jealousy.

She had a grace about her, a soothing and quiet way that was somber on the surface and I liked that. I liked that a lot. There was something just so damn appealing about it.

Probably because my life wasn't anything remotely quiet, or soothing; but then again, I sort of thrived on chaos and dynamic situations.

There was another couple or two that slipped out of the tasting room and a pair that arrived only moments before the tour was set to begin, slipping into the tasting room and giftshop to get their tickets and right back out onto the porch as a young woman, skin smooth and perfect, dark and dusky, stepped onto the porch, her natural hair in glossy tight curls held back by a headband. She was dressed in a pair of tight jeans rolled at the cuff, her black distillery tee shirt tucked in and neat. She smiled at us and called out, "Good afternoon! And welcome to the Sugarland Distillery walking tour! I'm Aneesha Thomas, and my family owns the mansion, the grounds, and the distillery and boy do we have a history and tour for you!"

I slipped an arm around Jussy's waist and gave her hip a gently squeeze and she looked over at me, her look one of surprise at first, then her expression settled into something like pleased before she turned her attention back to the tour guide.

I'd been here before, a while back with the rest of the club, and we'd taken the tour, so I knew what to expect.

It *was* a hell of a story. The history of the house was one thing, but it was the Thomas family's history that made the story fantastic. It seemed that Mrs. Thomas senior, that would be Aneesha's dad's mother, did a bunch of genealogy research up there in Connecticut where they were from. She'd gone way, way, back and had discovered some family roots among the slaves of the Sugarland estates. Some of those ancestors having been part of the uprising and revolt that wiped out the landowners back in the day.

Her son was pretty successful in the distilling industry up in Connecticut and as a favor to his mother, when the Thomas family had come down to Florida on a family vacation, he'd swung by here to take pictures of the place whereupon he'd found that it was for sale and that the house – a historical landmark – was in dire need of proper repairs and the like.

He'd gone home, his wheels turning, went to his partners at the distillery up there and they'd hatched a plan to buy the place and thus Sugarland got its second wind.

There was a certain poetic justice to it. The descendants of the slaves of this place buying it, fixing it, and turning a more than tidy profit with it all these years later.

We went around the house, Aneesha telling the story, before we stopped at the hanging tree off the house's back left corner. It was a great big gnarled old thing draped with Spanish moss that drifted ghostly in the light breeze out here.

From the house's history, we were invited to come back for one of their ghost tours they held every night of October for Halloween, before we were led to the processing barn for the sugar cane.

There we were each handed a piece to suck and chew on and it was a treat watching Jussy's face light up with surprise. Not a whole lot of people got to encounter raw sugar cane, and it was something else.

We were taken through the whole process; from the cane, past the copper kettles and how they worked all the way through to bottling and labeling. Justice took photos at every opportunity. Aneesha made sure we knew we could get a free drink with the cost of admission, hoped that we had a good time, said to come back and visit again, and departed.

"That was fantastic," Justice declared, and I grinned.

"Thought you might like that," I said.

We went back inside to retrieve our bag of purchases and then wandered back out to the bike. The sunset would be spectacular by the time we reached Ft. Royal. I could just feel it... so I got our things stashed in the saddlebags and got us underway headed back home.

I parked at the marina.

Justice sucked in a deep breath and let it out, taking her hands from around me and planting them atop her thighs as she stared out over the water.

"Come on, let's stash some of what you got on – your purse and jacket, shoes and the like, with the bike and take a stroll. Get your toes in the sand."

"That sounds lovely," she said.

We made room and locked everything up tight. She left her purse but kept her phone in her back pocket, and we went down the nearby steps fingers linked.

The sunset was spectacular, the sky a golden color, fading into peach, up into pinks and lavenders, breathtaking, like her, as she stared out over the water and teased some loose hair blowing along one of her cheeks behind her ear.

I snapped a picture, and she took a second to snap out of her reverie to turn my direction.

"Did you just take my picture?"

I grinned. "Sure did. I want to remember you just like this," I said.

She smiled and her cheeks flushed just the prettiest of pinks a near perfect match for the sky.

We strolled hand in hand, quietly talking about this and that and nothing at all really and with every step, she seemed to grow more comfortable, more confident, and I liked that. I wasn't surprised, per se, but I was definitely delighted with this version of Justice. She was sweet, funny, and unsurprisingly, kind. We walked for about an hour and then I realized we were getting a bit far and so I turned us back.

It was pretty close to full dark when we got back to the marina, Jussy with a pocket full of shells. We threw on our boots for the short ride home and I said to her, "Come here," before she could get on the bike behind me.

"What?" she asked smiling, and I lifted myself up and scooted back. I pulled her down onto the bike in front of me, her back to the handlebars, and hands on her ass, pulled her close to where she was sitting in my lap. She yipped and put her hands on my shoulders to steady herself and looked down at me from her superior height brought on by the position we were in curiously.

"I know you head home the day after tomorrow, but I don't want to give you up," I told her. "I want to kiss you. I want to know you, and when you go, I most definitely want to keep in touch," I said. "I just need to know if you want the same."

She stared into my eyes from inches away, searching them out in the gloam of twilight, and I waited patiently, letting her see that I was dead fucking serious.

She cradled my face between her hands and pressed her lips to mine as though she were afraid if she didn't take the leap right then and there, that she never would.

She tasted just as sweet as I thought she would her tongue hot and velvet against my own as it boldly swept over mine. I kissed her back, just as hot, just as fierce, and I cursed myself that I was going to try tonight when I got her home. I was going to make us some drinks, curl on the sofa with her, and watch something and then I was going to take this woman to bed. I wanted it – wanted *her*, so fucking bad and I hoped like hell she would be down with my plan and would let me love her body.

She tore her mouth from mine, gasping, looking to the sky for a moment. I touched the side of her face and brought her forehead to mine and said gently, "Breathe, just breathe. Everything's all good." I sighed and looked up, groaning, "God I want more of that," before I captured her mouth with my own once more.

She whimpered against my lips and scooched forward, writhing against me just a little and I know she felt my boner through my shorts. I half groaned, half growled into her mouth and felt her gasp, and it was a good gasp. Not afraid, no that gasp was most definitely one of desire.

"Well, shit. Look at you go." Justice jumped and tore her mouth from mine once more and I rolled my eyes.

"You fucker," I grated out at Atlas who laughed.

"Where you been all day, man?"

"Sugarland," I said. "And then a sunset walk on the beach. You fuckin' mind?" I gave him a warning look and a wink. "I'm trying to romance this woman right here."

Justice had the back of her hand pressed to her swollen lips and her face turned away from me and my partner.

He jerked his head in her direction and grinned, forcing down a laugh. I glared a warning at him.

"Catch anything?" I asked and Atlas shook his head.

"Naw, but it was good times on the pier," he said, shifting his stance, his pole bouncing, his cooler dangling from his other hand, a bucket at an awkward angle with it.

"Better luck next time," I said mildly, and he nodded. When she realized she wasn't going to be made fun of or some shit, Justice eased her posture and turned to look. Atlas gave her a kind smile and a wink, and her cheeks flamed but she didn't look away.

"Right, I'll let you two lovebirds go back at it," Atlas said, and he wandered away, across the lot to his old pickup he used to go fishing and haul shit if he needed to.

I shook my head, Justice gazing after him and then turning back to me.

"You two have known each other a long time, haven't you?" she asked, and I nodded.

"Yeah, we knew each other before either of us joined the club," I answered. "We both worked for the same bail bonds company but didn't really connect and become friends until after my best buddy died."

"Oh, I'm sorry again… that your friend died…"

I shrugged and though it hurt, the hurt had dulled with time.

"Was a long time ago," I said and sighed.

"Yes, but sometimes things like that no matter how old hit like it was just yesterday," she murmured, and I looked at her.

I bit my lips together and nodded, finally letting them go so I could say: "Let's go back to the house, I'll make us up a couple of drinks and then we can watch a movie or something before going to bed."

She nodded, and I let her get up. "That sounds good, actually," she said, and I smiled.

What sounded good was having her lithe body up against mine on the couch, where I could slide my hands over her and learn her body, wake up those nerves, and low-key excite us both before we retired to the bedroom.

Even if she grew skittish or decided she didn't want to go that far, I would be cool with it. The truth of the matter? Having her at the house made me realize I'd been lonely for a while. Deprived of physical contact, and I probably needed something good just as much as she did.

We pulled into the garage, retrieved our bag of stuff, and let ourselves into the house through the garage's entrance. I paused and waited, watching the garage door to the outside close all the way – ensuring no one slipped in. It was a habit, and a good one to have, especially as an example to my girls.

"Hey, Dad!" both of them chorused in unison from the kitchen when the door shut behind me and Justice. I smiled and jerked my head in that direction.

"Oh, hi…" Mariposa said when she saw her, and she looked guilty. "Can I talk to you?" she asked, and Justice looked to me.

"Me?" she asked.

"Yeah," Mariposa said, and I couldn't help but notice the nervous shift in Jussy's stance.

"Sure," she said, and Mariposa came around the kitchen island and gestured to the living room.

"Where you guys been?" Lucia asked cautiously.

"Went for a ride out to Sugarland's Distillery for lunch and the tour," I said nonchalantly.

"Like on a date?" Lucia asked carefully. She wouldn't look at me, instead stirring what she had going on that was on the stove.

"Would it bother you if I said yes?" I asked curiously.

She looked at me over the steam rising from her pan and wrinkled her nose, grinning. "Are you serious?"

"Answer the question," I said laughing.

"No, you answer the question!" she cried, laughing.

"I asked first!"

She scoffed. "No you didn't, I did! I asked if you went on a date!"

"Yeah." I nodded. "Yeah, I think we did."

She squeed. My eighteen-year-old daughter squeed like she was five and I handed her that giant unicorn I'd won sharpshooting at the fair.

I shook my head and put a finger to my lips in the classic sign for shush. She pressed her lips together but there was no denying the sparkle in her eyes, and I had to wonder if this was somehow by design. If my kid had seen an opportunity, had seized it with both hands, and run giggling like a little lunatic with it up the boulevard.

"Something I should know, Lucia?" I asked coolly.

"Nope," she said.

"Lucia..." I drew out her name and she grinned and shook her head.

Mariposa came back into the kitchen smoothing her hands over her hips and retaking her seat at the counter. I raised an eyebrow and she nodded.

"Might want to take her a drink, Papá. I don't think anyone has really ever apologized to her. I don't think she knows what to do with it. It's... it's weird."

I smiled at my eldest daughter and kissed her forehead.

"Not everyone was brought up like us, *corazón,*" I reminded her.

"I guess not," she said, and she was quiet. I think she had a bit to think about, so I went about fixing four drinks. Yeah, I know Lucia wasn't technically old enough, but I was her father and if she was gonna drink, she was going to do it at home or with the club where she could be safe and get silly, and be unbothered by these little boys parading as men out there.

Jussy's words from earlier came back to me and I asked my girls, "Say you're at a party..." Both of them looked over at me attentive. "A boy you don't know brings you a drink and says 'you look thirsty – I got you this,' what do you do?"

"Pfft! Fuck off!" Mariposa said.

"Uh, say thanks?" Lucia asked.

"Mariposa has it right. I mean, you don't have to tell him fuck off, but you say no."

"Right, okay." Lucia nodded and took the drink I offered her after I set one down for her sister.

"And if he says something about you wasting his time or his money," I said. "Don't you let him guilt you into taking it."

"Be rude, stay alive," Justice murmured from the doorway. "Can I have one of those?" she asked.

"Coming right up," I told her and smiled.

I SMOOTHED my hands over Jussy's back, her head on my chest, her body draped warm over mine as we lay on the couch. She was so relaxed after two drinks. Her breathing evening and deepening as I rubbed her back and massaged her neck up into the back of her hair. I don't even know what was playing anymore. I had stopped paying attention so that I could pay attention to her... she was a feast for the senses, and I couldn't wait to get her nude and writhing beneath me in my bed...

But god*damn* this was comfortable. Just cuddling... I couldn't remember the last time I had cuddled with such a pure woman. It was something I hadn't realized I had missed, but fuck had I missed it.

"Goodnight, Papá," I heard Lucia call, and I craned my neck back over the arm of the couch to look at her.

"Night Mr. G," Javier, her boyfriend waved from behind her.

"Better wrap it the fuck up," I called.

I could hear Lucia roll her eyes when she admonished, "Papá!"

I looked back and caught Javier's grin and wink. I grinned and winked back at him as my daughter towed him toward her room.

Nah, Javier and I were cool. He was a good boy. I liked the kid.

"Did I tell you he accidentally grabbed my ass the other day?" Jussy asked in a murmured almost sing-song voice with her sleepiness.

I laughed. "Yes, and I still maintain; what the fuck? Still, that shit was funny so tell me again if you please?"

She told me the story again, and I busted out laughing. She made a noise of protest at me bouncing her, but I couldn't stop – even when tears collected at the corners of my eyes.

"Oh, God!" I gasped and wheezed. "That is some funny shit!"

"It was," she agreed. "You should have seen the look on his face."

"Oh, man. I needed that," I said and smiled down at her as she looked up at me with sparkling mirth in her eyes and God, she was beautiful.

"Come on," I murmured. "Let's get you into bed."

She nodded tiredly and pushed up off me with a groan.

I got up, shut things down out here, and led her by the hand to the bedroom.

"You mind if I stay with you tonight?" I asked, and she froze and looked at me with such a look of surprise.

"I mean, it's your bedroom…" she said, and I grinned.

"It's your comfort that I'm worried about, babe. Nothing else."

"I… would I be a total slut if I said I would like that?" she asked.

I shook my head.

"No, and I don't know who ever told you that but they couldn't have been more wrong."

She nodded slowly and I said, "You want to change out here or in the bathroom? Do you need me to step out, or am I good? You just tell me what you need."

"Um, just turn around?" she asked.

I nodded and turned around for her, just a little disappointed.

I listened to the rustle of her clothing and the click of buckled and the rasp of zippers and it drove me a little crazy. The whisper of cloth against her skin and suddenly she was like, "It's okay, you can turn around now."

I turned around to see her sitting up in my bed and shit, wasn't that just inviting?

I pulled my shirt over my head, and she blushed, averting her eyes.

"Gonna grab a quick shower," I told her. I didn't want to come to bed with ball stank or something. She nodded, and I went into the bathroom after grabbing a clean pair of boxers out of the drawer.

I showered lightning fast for me, lathering and rinsing in record time before shutting off the water and running a towel over myself so I could pull on my boxers. Out in the room, she was curled on her side beneath the sheet, eyes closed, drowsing lightly. I turned on my bedroom television for just a little ambient noise, sparing a thought for my girls before sliding into the bed beside Jussy.

She immediately cuddled into my side as though she was meant to be there.

I loved that.

I kissed her forehead and asked, "Tired, baby?"

"Mm, mm-hm." She was adorable, taking a moment then admitting she was indeed tired… I couldn't blame her.

Fuck.

I was torn. On the one hand, I just wanted to fuck the hell out of her, on the other, she was just so sweet, too sweet and I could watch her like this forever.

I sighed and cuddled her close.

I mean, maybe in the morning? I didn't want to rush things…

12

*J*ustice...

It was warm, and so comfortable being fetched up against his side, head on his chest, his hand in my hair massaging my neck and the back of my head, his other hand smoothing up and down my arm. I was drowsing lightly the drone of the television in the background soothing, and I know, I know, it was so incredibly selfish of me to soak this up, but it'd been so long... if ever, that I'd felt so cared for and cherished.

Finally, with a contented sigh, he pressed his lips to my forehead and switched out the bedside light.

God, when his warm lips touched my forehead, I just *melted*. My light drowse deepening into sleep. I didn't even notice when he twisted under me to settle himself, drawing me into the circle of his arms more completely. His free hand which had smoothed up and down my arm slipping beneath my satin cami's top and suddenly I froze, eyes flying open and body drawing taut, on high alert as I grabbed his wrist and threw up resistance to his touching my ruined side.

"Shhh, easy, baby. It's okay," he murmured and kissed my forehead again. I felt myself go slightly more lax under that touch of lips and I had to lick my suddenly dry ones and try a couple of times to get my voice out of my tightening throat.

"It's not," I said, voice thick with emotion.

"It *is*," he insisted but he kept his hand from my side, and while he refused to move it back, he didn't force me to do anything. It was my decision, let him touch or pull his wrist away, I could feel the vibration of his waiting all the way to my soul.

I looked up into his dark eyes, the look on his face impassive in the wavering blue light from the television and I didn't see any judgment there… just patience, waiting on me to make my decision.

I released his wrist and his hand felt gentle and warm on my side. I closed my eyes as he smoothed it lightly over my raised scars and when I opened them, he was smiling faintly, his gaze warm.

"Thank you," he murmured. He pressed his lips to mine with an almost reverence. I sucked in a sharp breath and opened to him as he dug his thumb and fingers slightly, massaging my flank. I swallowed hard and he rolled me onto my back, leaning over me protectively as he deepened the kiss as though he couldn't get enough.

Which, fancy that, I couldn't get enough either.

I cradled his face with one hand my other drifting to his ass and pulling myself closer and he groaned in appreciation.

"Mm, keep that up I'm going to do more than just pet you," he purred, and I giggled.

"I think I'd honestly like that," I said, surprising myself a bit. I mean… I had just been with Billy under a week ago and in Radar's arms, he was almost all but forgotten and wasn't that some sort of unseemly?

When he kissed me again, I didn't care if it was unseemly or not. In fact, it felt as though *all* of my cares just fell away under his kiss, his touch, the shelter of his hard compact body.

He slid his hand from my side and dipped it below the waistband of my satin sleep shorts and the lace panties beneath, his fingers questing for and finding my pussy, gently stroking me until a gasp left my throat and a whimper left my lips for his.

He stroked me with his fingers, gently; teasing my pussy lips lightly, splitting them to slick a finger in the gathering wetness there. He tilted his hand to apply a little extra pressure to the top of my sex and my clit and I moaned, bucking my hips against his hand, begging without words for more.

He obliged me, plunging a finger up inside me, rocking his hand firmly against me until I panted, writhing for him and against his hand to get things just right. My body coming alive, my hunger to reach that pinnacle and to take that plunge suddenly *ravenous* as he stoked my desire with his mouth on mine.

I wrapped my arms around him and held to him tightly as though he were an anchor, tethering me to the earth, even as he brought me higher and higher with his hand. I closed my eyes, moaning and whimpering into his mouth – he swallowed each one as though it were a piece of candy or better yet, the sustenance he craved. He perched me on that razor fine edge and kept me there for what felt like forever, my body responding to his touch like it had to no others.

"That's it, baby," he whispered roughly in my ear. "That's my good girl." He captured my earlobe with his teeth, and I cried out, slapping my hands over my mouth as I arched. It felt like my body crashed into him and the bed as though I had fallen from a great height while simultaneously it felt as though I was still falling.

I whimpered and moaned from beneath my hands as he kept playing with my pussy, his touch lightening and slowing by degrees as he let me recover, my legs twitching unbidden whenever his fingers swished over my highly sensitive clit. Finally, he withdrew his hand from my shorts, cradling me with his other arm as he rose at my side to look down at me and suck his fingers clean.

Oh, God...

"There you go," he whispered encouragingly. "That's my girl."

I lay a broken shattered mess on his sheets as he smiled serenely above me, a slight smirk on his generous lips as he ran his free hand over my body and the satin of my sleep set.

He looked down the length of me, and all I could see etched and written in his expression was a softly glowing pride. He looked as though I was a work of art, instead of this ragged, tired, broken woman and I felt suffused with a glimmer of elevated confidence at that look. Like if he saw it, then it must be true, and I sealed that look away in my memory to cherish.

"You're okay," he murmured, stroking my cheek, and thumbing the tear at the corner of my eye away. He raised his thumb to his mouth and sucked it clean and I closed my eyes and turned into him, huddling against his chest as tears of overwhelming gratitude fell and I know, I know… he probably thought I was *so weird!* But I couldn't help it.

I thought Billy had been sweet, and kind, but my time with him had also felt so cold and clinical as compared to this.

Radar, cuddled me close and kissed the top of my head, wrapping me up tightly in his arms.

"Shhh, I've got you," he murmured. "I've got you, babe."

I think I honestly cried myself to sleep in the circle of his arms and yes, I did feel so damn guilty about it but… but I would make it up to him, if he let me.

13

*R*adar...

    I think she was just emotionally exhausted, and even though I was hard to the point of pain, I got it. I really did. I mean, of everything I knew about her I had to ask myself, rather rhetorically, *just how much was one woman supposed to take?*

The answer was apparently, *a lot*, especially where Jussy was concerned – but I had seen it all before. I mean, her situation was bad, but comparing it to the next woman? A woman like Faith... well, it was an apples and oranges comparison.

The two did have one thing in common, though. As broken and fucked up as they liked to think they were, these two women had a common iron core. It made me wish for more time. More time to put them in one another's orbit.

I sighed, and held her close, settling in for some sleep.

God, it felt good to have her like this. Close, secreted away against my chest... and the fact that she trusted me as a refuge from the world that had beat her down so thoroughly? Man, that was something. Made me feel like the biggest man, you know?

I slept like the dead that night, with her tucked against me, and in the morning, I happened to be the one to wake first, or so I thought.

When I looked down at her, she was looking up at me with those wide and beautiful eyes of hers, her expression calculating and holding an edge of sorrow. I smiled down at her, and holding onto her stretched as best I could.

"Morning," I said softly, and she gave a tremulous smile.

"Good morning," she whispered cautiously, and I dipped my head, silently asking permission.

She eagerly met my lips with her own and we kissed slowly, with farm more consideration than the passion we'd done it with before.

"You aren't mad at me?" she asked against my lips. I jerked my head back and searched her face.

"No, why?" I asked.

She winced, her face scrunching and I chuckled. "Because I didn't get any?" I asked softly and she nodded. I shook my head.

"Naw, I'm not mad about that. That's not what you needed," I said.

"You have needs too," she said haltingly in argument.

I nodded and said, "Yeah, but they'll get met on your time not mine and I'm okay with that."

She looked mollified at that.

Man, she'd been with nothing but a lot of self-serving motherfuckers. I rolled and turned her onto her back, my cock stiff as much with arousal as morning wood and if she was down, I was certainly willing to put it to good use... but first, I wanted to make damn sure she was down.

I kissed her and her arms went around me, and I met no resistance when I nudged her knees apart with one of mine.

I pressed myself over the top of her, between her thighs, and rubbed myself against her. She gasped at the feel of me hard through our shorts and I smiled against her lips.

"Here whenever you want it, baby," I whispered against her mouth.

She murmured back, "Please?" and it was so sweetly begging, I had to let out a measured breath. I could have come from that alone, the sound of her sweet voice begging me like that... such a thrill, such a turn on... *fuck*.

She slid a hand down the front of my chest and into the front of my boxers and gripped me, her soft hand firm as she stroked me mid-shaft to tip, putting a bit of a twist to her wrist action and *oh fuck*. I was throbbing, hot, fully engorged and desperate to bury myself inside her soft and fragrant warmth.

"Oh, fuck, Jussy *yes*..." I moaned beside her ear, burying my nose in her silky hair.

"Mm." She made the small lilting noise of attraction and satisfaction at the way she had me wrapped around her little finger if she wanted me to be.

I pushed up and pulled back, a sound of protest escaping her as I pulled myself out of her grasp and her reach to hook fingertips into the waistband of her sleep set and the panties she wore beneath, she bucked her hips obediently without being told and I whisked the garments off her long legs.

God, she looked inviting, and I warred for a second about going down on her – the taste I'd had of her sweet musk off my fingers the night before tantalizing, but not nearly enough. My balls gave a throbbing ache and that answered me.

"Might not be able to last long," I said divesting, myself of my own boxers. "Want me to use a condom?" I left the choice to her. I would love nothing better than to be inside her raw... just something about the thought of it was so primal, like I'd be staking my fuckin' claim on her sweet pussy irrefutably.

"Yes, please," she murmured.

I confess being slightly disappointed, but I wasn't about to argue like a fuckin' tool – no, I went into my bedside drawer and pulled out a round foil packet and tore that son of a bitch open with my teeth.

I rolled it down my length as she watched, a heat in her eyes and I loved it when I woman watched me make myself ready for her like that. Like my cock was the most beautiful thing she'd ever seen and like she just couldn't *wait* to have me.

Not like this, she wouldn't though... she was still too clothed.

She sucked in a sharp breath and her hands went to the hem of her tank to pull it down as I went to lift it. I gave her a sharp but silent look and she froze.

"Not gonna happen unless I get to kiss every inch of you, babe," I told her in an imperious tone. She swallowed hard, staring at me with wide and lovely eyes, the wheels turning, and I so wanted her to be brave for me.

I waited, and just when I thought she would say it wasn't happening, she took her hands away and lifted them shakily over her head, leaning up for me to take the scrap of satin and lace from her. I lifted and swept it up over her head, her long hair trapped momentarily and falling shiny and slick from the material, cascading over my pillows as she lay back.

I exerted my desire for her to understand just who was on top, just who was in charge in the bedroom, and at the last second gave the tank in my hands a deft double twist, trapping her hands and wrists in the material and holding her hands over her head. She gasped, eyes widening with a mix of desire and fear, and I smiled reassuring, letting my eyes drift from her face, over those luscious lips and that perfectly sculpted chin, over the winging collarbones that begged from my lips to her small but perfect tits with their dusky peach nipples.

Her chest rose and fell with deeper, slightly panicked breaths as my gaze repelled down her body, over her flat stomach, her slightly too prominent ribs, and came to the smattering of scars, whiter against her pale skin, slightly puckered and raises, dribbling down her plank to disappear around her back.

"You keep them there," I demanded, letting go of her tank top, and with a slightly strangled noise that almost sounded like she was resisting a sob, she kept her hands where they belonged.

I checked her face, and while her eyes were wide, they weren't wet. They showed a touch too much white for my liking, but I was working on remedying that. Everything in its own time.

I started with her lips, giving her an almost chaste, pure kiss laden with my intentions to make things better. She sucked in a sharp breath, but she kissed me back. I then pecked her chin, then chose a side of the long, graceful column of her neck to press chaste but fiery kisses one after the next, after the next. I kissed out along her shoulder and down her chest, taking a nipple into my mouth. She gasped and writhed beneath me but kept her hands up where I'd ordered them.

I lathed my tongue along the curve of the underside of her breast and she gasped and squirmed so I growled... it had the desired effect as she froze and I worried only slightly that it might be too intense with her fragile state, but I kept on – ignoring the typical route of the center of her being toward her bellybutton, deviating to the side.

Her breath stilled completely as I kissed just above the first raised scar, flicking my tongue out to run gently along the ridged seam of the stab wound even as my damn heart tried to break in the center of my chest, cracking with an almost audible noise at the pain she must have endured, the fear... I didn't know the gory details. Maybe one day she would see fit to tell me, but that wasn't for today, or even right now. Right now, it was time to recognize what a fucking little badass this woman was for surviving such a night full of terrors that most of us would never have to endure outside a movie theater with some bimbo hamming it up on the screen as the corn syrup flowed.

Except what'd flowed from these wounds hadn't been corn syrup. With the state of Jussy beneath my lips and hands, I would have to say she'd bled more than just blood. The scars beneath my lips and light kisses tasted of many things; bitter disappointment, broken trust, fear, anxiety, and the bitter ash of dreams that'd been burned to cinders.

She gave a stuttering gasping breath and her body curled slightly, and I climbed the bed over and around her to kiss her tears away and bring her the light of hope into that dark place, the scars the key hole to opening it up, my acceptance the key to let me in to *shine*.

It'd worked like a charm, but she wasn't meant to live in this dark place. Not at all, and I wouldn't let her.

I kissed her fiercely and she kissed me, orders forgotten as she captured my face between her hands, but that was okay – some things were more important.

I kissed her deeply, the salt of her tears mingling with the sweetness that was purely her as I settled between her thighs and tried to take her somewhere else... at least for a little while.

14

*J*ustice…

He slipped inside me, and I gasped, wrapping my arms and legs around him, twinging around him and clinging to him as though he were my lifeline out of the dark – and who knows? Maybe he was. He certainly felt like it at this point.

He drove into me to the hilt, and I writhed beneath him, working my body in a frantic counter rhythm to his own and it felt so *good*. My whole body tingled from the light line of kisses he'd laid against my skin and the one's he'd placed against my scars? Well, it'd sent a sensation like I'd never known around to my back, up my spine in a wash of tingling effervescence making me feel lighter than air as it took over my entire back, crept up my neck and spread creeping tendrils of feel good along the back of my scalp and around into my face.

It was incredible, and again, I had never felt anything quite like it.

"Oh, fuck!" he groaned, and panted, his voice strained and filled with something I had no name for, but just made me all the wetter for hearing it.

He was on a steady pace for fucking me, a deep, slow rolling thrust that touched off all manner of sparks inside me – touched all of the right places.

I closed my eyes, pleasure flitting along every nerve like lightning bugs throughout a grove on a sultry Texas night and I dared to dream that this wouldn't end, that this wouldn't be our only encounter... that somehow, some way, there would be more.

I let all of that fall away for now, though. Because if this were only to be the once, I was certain I would never find anything like it again, and I needed the memory of it to last me forever. So, with that being said, I did everything in my power to live within this moment wholly and completely; and to that end I let myself take an untethered leap from safety and let myself fall completely into love with the man atop me who treated me so tenderly.

He let himself weight me down into the mattress beneath us, and I had no complaints. It felt safe, not oppressive. I felt claimed but not in a way that reeked of possessive male ego trophy woman bullshit – no, I felt claimed in a way that bespoke this man would fight to the death to protect me. That he would go to the ends of the earth to find me, that he would take me places never seen and never dreamed of in my limited scope of a reality, and I lived for the sensation as much as I lived for any other that he had introduced me to, thus far anyway.

I kissed him, claiming his mouth as much as he claimed the rest of my body with his hands and his thrusting cock inside of me, driving me closer and closer to the fall, both of us floating effortlessly along a warm shining river of slivery light of pure intention and the belief that there would be several more tomorrows in each other arms.

I closed my eyes, breathing in his masculine and slightly spicy scent and with a cry as primal as a wolf calling to the moon, I didn't so much feel as though I came apart, but as though the shattered pieces of me gathered back together.

I was vaguely aware of his sharp cry echoing mine as he lost his even and steady cadence, and we fell over the waterfall in perfect harmony such a complete tangle of limbs, souls, and intentions there was no telling where one of us left off and the other began.

We gave so much of each other to one another, there was nothing left for either of us than languid, beautiful, exhaustion...

∾

I woke with a soft start and opened my eyes. I was lying on my stomach in Radar's bed, which was otherwise empty. I sucked in a sharp breath and pushed myself up.

"Easy!" he said gently from the doorway, coming through in a pair of low-slung basketball shorts, two cups of coffee, one in each hand.

"What time is it?" I asked thickly, my body just deliciously sore from his attentions.

"Late morning, like eleven," he answered.

"Oh, God. I don't normally ever sleep this late," I groaned, twisting around, and sitting up, putting my back against his headboard, clutching the sheet to my chest in case one of his girls traversed the hallway.

I blushed furiously at the thought... I mean, what must Lucia think?

Radar grinned at me and sat down on the edge of the bed as I accepted the mug he offered.

"Worried about what the girls will think?" he asked, and I looked at him, startled.

"How did you know?"

"Your eyes keep darting to the hallway and it's written all over your face," he said.

I rolled my eyes and swallowed down a healthy dose of the caffeine in my cup.

"I never was much of a liar," I admitted. "Could never and can never keep anything off my face." I sighed. "I wonder if that's what made me such a convenient target sometimes, you know, for my mom and dad and later..." I trailed off, and he put a hand on my knee.

"That life's over, baby girl," he said.

I gave him a crooked smile. "Oh, yeah? How's that Mr. Confidence?"

"Haven't quite figured that out yet," he said, much sobered. "But we will."

I bit my lips together and said, "I don't want to get on that plane tomorrow," I confessed. "I especially don't want to do it if I'll never see you again."

"Hey, don't," he said flatly, a hint of warning in his tone that made me meet his eyes which bored into mine. "This isn't a wham, bam, thank you ma'am," he said. "No fucking way would I do that to you. You gotta go home tomorrow, I get that, but this isn't the end, Jussy. This is a new beginning, okay?"

I reached for his hand reflexively and he took it, and the way he looked at me... the emotion radiating from his face... God, it was killing him as much as it was killing me that tomorrow, we would have to let each other go.

"In fact," he said, handing me my phone off the bedside table. "Put my number in now and give me yours." He took up his phone and we traded numbers and addresses, and emails, and all the things to ensure we wouldn't lose each other.

At the end of it, we were laughing a little, and I felt marginally better.

He stopped and looked at me as though committing every detail of this moment to memory before hooking his hand behind my head, smoothing along taut muscles with his thump and pressing his lips to my forehead.

"I've got you, girl... and I have no intention of letting you go until a time you tell me to fuck off; and if ever there is that time, no matter how much it hurts? Off, I fuck. No psycho bullshit," he promised.

I nodded, and I could see the solemn vow in his eyes and etched into every line of his expression and I nodded.

"Thank you," I murmured, and he nodded.

"I don't like to tread the previously trodden path," he said. "And I don't get jealous psycho bullshit."

I pressed my lips together, "He was diagnosed with a myriad of issues in prison," I said with a halfhearted shrug and Radar shook his head.

"Maybe it's a reason, but it's not an excuse," he said.

I nodded. "No, I know…" I trailed off, took a deep breath and let it out. "I know it probably sounds like I'm trying to defend him, but I'm not… really. I guess I'm just trying to rationalize his behavior. Make sense of it, you know? For me."

"There is no defense for the indefensible," Radar said gently, and I nodded.

"No, there's not, and I know that."

"Okay," he said with a crooked smile of his own.

"So," I murmured, taking another swallow of coffee. "It's my last day…"

"Yep."

"What did we want to do?" I asked and he smiled.

"I think I've got just the thing."

I raised my eyebrows at the slightly cryptic response, and he grinned.

"But I'm not gonna tell you, instead, I'm going to see if one of the girls has a bikini you can borrow." He stood up.

"Excuse me?" I asked. "Do what now?"

He chuckled. "Baby, you're hot, and you're mine. I want to show you off."

"Oh, I don't know—"

"Ah!" He cut me off and gave me a stern look and I just suddenly fell silent, swallowing hard.

"You and Hope look to be about the same size, I'll start there," he said.

I stayed silent and brought my eyes back up from my coffee to his eyes and asked, "You really want me to do this for you?"

"Yes, I do," he said with a nod. "You're a survivor, and a badass one at that. So, let's show the world just how badass you are."

Me? A badass? I thought. *Not hardly…*

Although his confidence in me did inspire a confidence in me… so I guess there was that.

15

*R*adar...

"Yeah?" I answered Atlas's call as I padded into the kitchen. Thankfully, the vibrating phone hadn't disturbed Jussy, and I was able to slip out of bed unnoticed. I figured I could take my partner's call and make me and my girl some coffee.

My girl... it was still so shiny and new, and held that excitement that came with the new... but not only did I like the sound of it, it also felt *right*.

"So," my partner said. "I was finally able to take a breather from some of the other shit we've got cookin' and look into your girl."

"I didn't ask you to look into my girl," I said, my tone and mood instantly tempestuous. "I asked you to track the dirtbag she rolled into town with."

"Whoa, things got serious last night, huh?" he asked, laughing a little at my expense.

"Yeah," I said in such a way that would brook no argument. "Yeah, things are serious," I told him.

"Okay, man. Ease up. You know the drill – sometimes the victimology is just as important as the suspect themselves."

"Yeah, whatever, what did you learn?" I growled.

"This is one exceptionally deep rabbit hole, bro. Like, I can't even."

"Start at the beginning," I told him, tucking the phone between my ear and my shoulder.

"Well, first off, I cracked the seal on her big court case with her ex," he said grimly.

"Records were sealed?" I asked.

"On a kind he was still active duty when the shit went down, and he went full psycho – and I do mean he went full fucking psycho."

"She hasn't said much about it," I said. "Just the quick and dirty."

"Well, the long version is some horrifying shit," he said. "Like *48hours Mystery* bad. I wouldn't be surprised if she gets contacted by a pack of exploitative jackals posing as journalists over this shit."

"Fuck," I muttered. "Gimme the short version," I said. "I don't know how long she'll stay asleep for, I'm out in the kitchen making coffee as it is."

"Okay, well, this wasn't a one-and-done he beat her and stabbed her and dumped her in a Texas killing field type grave – no, he lost his shit, beat her to unconsciousness, she woke up with him on top of her raping the shit out of her, and this went on for *days*, bro. Like he kept her captive in their house for two… three *days*. She kept her cool the whole time and when she finally suggested he let her go? He epically lost it and stabbed the shit out of her, wrapped her in their shower curtain, and took her out and buried her. She came to, clawed her way out of her own shallow grave, and staggered something like six miles to a main road where she flagged down a cop who called an ambulance for her. This is straight up, *Last House on the Left*, horror movie shit, I'm telling you. She's a fucking incredible badass. I'm a little jealous, if I do say so myself."

I stood there stunned, bile rising in the back of my throat. Shit, she'd played things down for me…

"He did all that to her?" I asked, numb.

"Yeah," Atlas said, and he didn't sound happy about it – far from it. He sounded just about as pissed as I would feel once the shock wore off.

"What prison is he in?" I demanded.

He rattled it off. "Cool, okay, I need to talk to the captain about that one," I said. I mean, I couldn't get to him inside like that, but we might know some motherfuckers who could and I was thinking I would be willing to owe no end of fucking favors to make that shit happen. You know? That walking shit stain didn't need to be breathing any of the same air of this planet as my girl.

"Yeah, well, the plot thickens my dude."

"What do you mean?" I asked.

"There's more, a lot more."

"Fuck," I muttered.

"Hey, Papá." Mariposa's voice was soft behind me, and I jumped.

"Shit, ah, hey buddy... gonna have to fill me in a little later if that's alright," I said.

"Sure thing, no problem. You coming to the beach with the rest of the crew today?" he asked.

"Yeah, I'll see you there," I said.

"Good deal – see you then." He ended the call.

"Everything alright?" Mariposa asked, sliding up onto one of the kitchen stools.

"Yeah, baby. Just Uncle Atlas about work is all."

"Ah, is there coffee?" she asked hopefully.

"Coming right up, baby."

I got my hands to work, finishing up and getting the coffee maker going, but how I couldn't tell you. My mind was going a mile a minute, the hamster wheel turning the cogs and gears in my brain going at warp fucking speed trying to digest everything that Atlas had told me. I had a gut feeling, but I wanted to see what he had to say first, before jumping to conclusions.

All the while, no matter how many revolutions that hamster wheel took, it kept sticking on one awful thought... *Jesus Fuck the things Jussy had been through...* and then this, on top of it all.

I tried my best to shake it off. This was going to be my last day with her for who knew how long, and I wanted to make it count.

But first, coffee...

〜

"Hey." I watched Hope, Faith, and Charity sort of mob my new girl-friend and take her into the captain's house to find her a suit to wear. The girls were all smiles and laughter, easy going postures and just an all-around brightness, which was slowly working its magic on my girl's stiff posture and rictus fake smile for politeness' sake despite her discomfort.

I turned to Atlas and Cutter, who were grouped with me in the drive. "What's going on, brother?" Cutter asked.

"You didn't get a chance to fill him in?" I asked Atlas.

Atlas shook his head, and we filled the captain in. Cutter got a hard look in his eyes.

"What prison you say this scumbag was in?" he asked.

Atlas rattled it off and Cutter just met my eyes, gave me a single nod, and turned around and went in the house, pulling his phone out of the inside pocket of his cut.

"Well, that's one down," Atlas declared, and he turned back to look at me.

"Who's to go?" I asked.

"Right, so I tracked both names you gave me and you were right, 'Billy' was an alias he was using to play your girl."

"So, who is the motherfucker really?"

"Well, Travis Morrison *is* his real name, and he *does* work for the kind of company that Jussy described, but he gave her a fake name there, too."

"Okay." I nodded. "Gimme the rundown."

"Travis Morrison, no criminal record, works as a transient contractor for *Communications Direct*, a company that lays fiberoptic line and gets infrastructure set up for internet service. No wife, no kids, no girlfriend, no permanent residence that I can tell. Uses his sister's address out there in Texas near Jussy. About two hours from her – but here's where it gets interesting," he said.

"Ah, yeah?" I crossed my arms and waited him out and it didn't take long.

"Morrison is a vet, served with Jussy's ex."

I pushed out my cheek with my tongue and nodded. "Okay. You got a current location on his ass?" I asked.

"Indeed, I fuckin' do," he said, and I nodded slowly.

"Alright. As soon as I put Jussy's ass on a plane home—"

"You don't even have to say it, bro. There's a reckoning a coming and Karma thy name is the Kraken MC."

I nodded and held out a hand and Atlas clapped his into it and pulled his shoulder into mine.

"How's that thing with Mariposa?" I asked and Atlas grinned savagely.

"Hope and I are supposed to get started on that tomorrow, too – but I think Hope has it handled and maybe I can tag Lightning or one of the other boys in," he said. "I'm your ride or die hetero life mate, buddy. I'm not letting you hare off alone on this thing. Anything I'm skipping right along beside you singin' *somebody's gonna get it*, with a fuckin' baseball bat."

I nodded. "Can the business take the hit?" I asked.

He made a nonchalant face and gave a one-shouldered shrug.

"Travis ain't going anywhere for at least a week, and wherever he *does* go, I can find him. We can tie up some loose ends here with the business, or we can go straight for him. Either way it's only going to take a few days out and back," he said. "Doesn't matter the order of operations, man. It's all up to you."

I nodded slowly and pasted a smile on my face that made Atlas turn around.

Faith stepped out onto the front steps and waved at us to come on.

"She good?" I asked.

"A nervous wreck, but beautiful. She's going to be fine with a little encouragement," Faith confided in us. We found her just inside the back door and in a beautiful royal purple bikini with a wrap she had tied in a high waisted fashion that was in blues, greens, and purples that matched the bikini to perfection.

Atlas let out a low whistle.

"I am impressed," he called out and I followed him up with, "You took the words right out of my mouth!"

Jussy blushed and Hope and Charity stood by grinning.

"Damn, baby, you are fine," I murmured and pulled her up against me. She leaned into me and I put my hand to her chin, bringing her to me for a kiss. She pulled back, cheeks flaming.

"We setting up out back?" I asked.

"Yeah, the usual spot the other side of the marina is fuckin' packed with tourists," Cutter said from the other side of the open slider, holding his phone to his ear but down and away from his mouth like he was on hold. I gave a nod.

"Better for us anyway," I said.

"Why's that?" Jussy asked.

"This section of the beach is private," Atlas answered her. "For the private residences along this stretch."

"We just hang over there because over there we can have fires, but we can move that way, later," Hope declared with a shrug.

I shot a text off to my two daughters that we were hanging at the captain's house and that if they were looking for me to come down this way.

"Alright," I said, arm around my girl. "Let's find you some sunscreen and a cold drink, shall we?"

She smiled at me bravely and nodded. "Let's," she agreed softly.

A WHILE LATER, and after a game of ultimate frisbee with the rest of the boys, I went to collect Jussy from the knot of girls on their beach loungers, laughing and talking.

"Come take a swim with me," I asked, kneeling beside her lounger. She met my eyes and a flash of fear chased by want went through hers.

I held out my hand and with perfect trust, she took it and I helped her to her feet.

"Have fun, you two," Hope called after us and I waved over my shoulder.

"What if someone says something?" Jussy asked nervously as we trudged through the sand toward the water.

"Then I whoop their fucking ass," I answered dryly, and she jerked back in surprise and looked at me.

"You're serious!" she said, voice soft with wonder.

"As a fuckin' heart attack," I said.

"You... you would do that for me?" she asked.

"In a fuckin' heartbeat," I said without hesitation, putting my arms around her.

"You wouldn't be scared?"

"Of what?" I asked.

"Getting hurt or..."

I shook my head. "Been in plenty of fights and will probably get in plenty more. It's part of my job, honestly."

She blinked and thought about it. "I guess I've never thought of it that way."

I smiled. "It's okay. We're still learning about each other."

She smiled and nodded, and I tugged at the knot at her hip.

"Time to lose this, the water is just over there," I murmured. She looked at the few people bobbing in the surf and over her shoulder at a few more nearby.

"Hey," I said softly, and she turned back and looked at me. "Fuck 'em. Any of 'em. Only person on this beach that matters what they think is you." I poked her lightly in the chest with a fingertip and she swallowed hard and stood a little straighter. With a nod, she fumbled at the knot of the wrap at her hip, her hands shaking, and you know what? So, what if she was doing it for me more than she was doing it for herself – which I could totally tell? The woman couldn't keep any thought she had off her face or out of her eyes.

It was endearing to me, but I knew it'd been weaponized on her most of her life. It said something that she somehow managed to stay soft despite it.

I loved her for that.

It hit like a serious shock to my system as she let the wrap flutter to the sand and reached for my hand. I took it, keeping my eyes on hers and smiled, my heart stuttering in my chest.

"What? What's wrong?" she asked, and I felt my smile grow. I shook my head.

"Absolutely nothing, beautiful." I kicked off my flip-flops and she shrugged her feet out of hers.

"Hey, Lightning!" I called up the beach. He turned and gave me a chin lift. "You mind?" I asked, picking up my cut off my bare chest.

"No, man! I got you!" He came jogging over and took it from me and met Jussy's eyes and gave her a nod. "Looking good, Jussy," he said, and he trotted back up the beach to put my cut where it was safe.

"What was that about?" she asked.

I turned back to her from where I watched Lightning's retreating back and asked, "What?"

"The whole having him take your vest," she said.

I chuckled.

"First, it's a cut, not a vest… and it's my colors. You don't let your colors hit the ground and you guard that shit with your life," I said, leading her to the water's edge.

"I don't understand," she said, jumping slightly as the water rushed over her feet.

"What?" I asked, grinning.

"It's so warm!" she cried, laughing. "As warm as bathwater!"

I laughed and drew her in with me until we bobbed in the surf, my arms around her, hugging her back to my front. She felt good against me.

"No, I meant what don't you understand?"

"About the vest, I mean the cut, why are those things important?"

I smiled and told her all about it. About club life, well, as much as I could divulge about it anyway. She was quiet, asked a few questions, and then was silent again to the point I had to turn her in my arms to face me. I smiled at the thoughtful look in her eyes and on her face.

"You make it sound so—"

"So what?"

"I mean, *normal*," she said, and she shook her head in confusion.

"Like, everything you just described is how it's *supposed* to work, but doesn't you know? The whole supporting each other and the like. That's what we're supposed to do for one another and you're right," she huffed out a breath. "A lot of society's rules *are* stupid... I can understand that, too. I mean, I don't know how many times I tried to reach out for help and there was just *'nothing can be done!'* or *'call us when he actually does something'* when we were separated, and he was stalking me... It was all so very frustrating."

I nodded. "I get that. The whole law enforcement being reactionary versus proactive. Like the victim has fewer rights than a perp," I said. "I have a foot in each world, and I gotta say the further along the road called life I get? I want out of the citizen world altogether. It's a sham. A farce."

"*Yes,*" she agreed emphatically. "It's always 'do as I say and not as I do,' you know? People, especially the ones in any position of power saying one thing and doing something completely different and I'm so sick of it! Sick of feeling and being unsafe just by virtue of I'm a woman and I know so many that were even blamed for their own assaults from a lot of the groups and support groups after and... I'm just so tired."

I kissed her shoulder and shook my head. "You shouldn't have to live that way," I said and as long as I was around? I would ensure she didn't have to.

I mean, freedom my fucking ass... so many in the citizen world thought they were free and didn't even recognize the boot on their neck. It was disgusting.

"Even though he's in prison, I learned very quickly there is no such thing as Justice," she said soberly.

Talk about a knife to the fucking heart.

"It's not that way anymore," I told her, and she scoffed. The sound was a bitter one.

"There were so many times they could have kept him locked up after hitting me and they still let him go early because of overcrowding. Then he did this..." her hand drifted beneath the water to her side.

"He'll rot," I said. "And then he'll burn in hell for it."

She shook her head. "I don't believe that," she said sadly, and I knew she was afraid he'd be released; but she didn't know. She couldn't know what I had in store. That was part of this life – at least for our club. We didn't bring our women and children into shit. That's the way it was for the SHMC, too. That's why we got along so well. It wasn't that way for every club out there but that was their fuckin' malfunction. We minded our own fuckin' business unless it directly affected us or ours.

Justice was mine now, I knew it, and the guys definitely knew it by default seeing as I was enlisting them to take up for me and her.

It was a lot at once for me; her, the thing with Mariposa, but that's always how this shit came down. We all had our turns... hell, Pyro was seriously on the rocks with his woman. Had been for a while and he was spiraling hard. Hiding his feelings under a haze of booze and weed.

I liked his girl well enough, but shit had turned toxic in a big way and we all could see it. She didn't want to have fuck all to do with the club and I didn't know how he'd honestly lasted this long with her but hey, they'd worked... right up until they didn't – and I had a feeling the big crash was coming soon, and we'd be on deck for his series of disasters, just like he'd been there for all of ours.

Sometimes you just had to let a brother, or sister, go through it.

Justice and I let the surf suck our woes out to sea to drown, bobbing in the surf, laughing and smiling, enjoying cuddling in the warm water beneath the bright Florida sunshine.

We changed subjects toward plans on how to stay in touch, how we could make the long-distance thing work for the near future, but I already knew – as soon as I could tie up her loose ends and mine, I would make a push to get her moved this way.

I know it was fast, but I also knew from experience – *when you know, you know*.

16

*J*ustice...

Radar helped me wind the wrap around my waist, ensuring my scars were covered at the back where I couldn't see them, and I tied things in a knot to secure them. We wandered back up the beach, to the back of Cutter's house where Pyro and Lightning were manning the grill and we had lunch.

It was nice, everyone very accepting, the women of the club sweet, kind, and outgoing and they were really wonderful and supportive – making certain I was feeling comfortable at every turn.

It was a fun filled day, but toward afternoon, Radar took my hand and with a meaningful look declared we were out. Making excuses that I had final packing to do, and we had to be up super early in the morning.

While he wasn't wrong about the early morning part I had never and would never fully unpack to need to *re*pack. I kept everything in my small suitcase, opening it up and putting everything away and the like, back and forth as I went. It kept me from losing anything for one, and two, I always felt afraid, and I always wanted to keep everything at the ready should I have to run.

Which was silly, really, when you thought about it – but it made me feel better and neither Billy, nor Radar, honestly seemed to notice so it wasn't harming anyone or anything... except maybe me, but what did that honestly matter in the long run?

We went back to his place, and he led me from the garage to his bedroom with a gentle hand.

We showered together, his hands slicking over my skin, soapy and with gentle pressure, washing the salt of the gulf and the sunscreen from my skin, standing close and whispering in my ear about how he was going to taste me. It sent shivers of anticipation down my spine, and I was eager to find out just what he had in store for me.

He led me to the bedroom after drying me thoroughly and laid me down on the bed, climbing up after me and settling between my legs, low, kissing and nuzzling along my inner thigh. I pressed knuckles to my lips and gripped the sheet below me with the other, breath stilling in my lungs as I watched him with breathless anticipation.

Desire swirled through me, every kiss, every touch of his lips injecting it into my veins like a drug. One that I couldn't get enough of; instantly addicted was I to his touch.

I didn't know how I would make it through being separated from him, or how we would manage, but I wanted to try – so badly did I want to try, because Radar was *safe*. He was so solid and warm, so caring and steadfast, and everything about him was so... so... unflappable and – *oh, my God.*

His tongue touched me in the most intimate of places and I felt myself falling back to the soft cloud of his bed, my back arching as he teased my pussy lips with his tongue and brought all the blood rushing from my head to my cunt.

I felt my fingers tangle in the sheet at my hip as my other hand tangled in the dark, slightly coarse crop of his hair pulling his mouth against me harder as he sucked at my clit.

My voice spilled from my lips in an inarticulate cry that rang back at me from the ceiling as I writhed against his mouth, panting, losing myself to the sensations he wrought between my thighs.

He plunged his tongue inside me and suckled me, tasting me, and making satisfied noises as if I were ambrosia of the gods, and I felt so *elevated* in that moment. So wickedly powerful that I could bring such a solid and unwavering man to his proverbial knees before me to pleasure me so thoroughly.

I bit my bottom lip, and both loved and hated how my moans sounded like I was whining, begging for just that little bit more, and oh how he did *not* disappoint!

He slipped a finger inside of me and I felt my body spasm, sending a pleasant shock wave through my system as he thrust it lazily in and out of me, feeling around inside of me as though learning his new territory.

My hips jerked, and a frisson of some new and intense sensation went through me, causing my nipples to tighten and tingle, and a warmth to flood me in a way that I'd never experienced before. He chuckled darkly from between my legs, and I gasped at the sound. So primal, so predatory, so... utterly delicious in a way that called to me to indulge in so much more of it.

I gasped and he pressed a hand just above my pubic bone and swiped with his finger inside once more and *holy shit!* I struggled and he denied me, his hand and arm atop me pressing me and that spot down, his mouth latching over my clit and his finger inside of me edging me with such a fierce intensity that I felt as though I'd just been swept away in a hurricane.

I cried out and struggled anew, the sensations so strong, too strong, coming on so very fast it frightened me when with a slight hum against my clit it was as if the entire world went supernova, flash bulbs going off at the edges of my vision, my body shaking and spasming uncontrollably as a warm fluid sensation, as though the entirety of my insides had suddenly melted and gushed forth out of my pussy took me by force and I could do nothing... nothing but lie there quivering and shaking at his mercy, gasping and voice high and frightened, full of shock asked him – "What was that?"

He chuckled and slipped his finger out of me, chuckling and rising like some leviathan out of the deep, wiping his chin with his hand as he looked imperiously down at me.

"That was the best orgasm of your life, I would reckon," he said. "Hasn't anyone ever made you squirt before?"

I blinked up at him stunned and stupid.

"Do what now?"

He smirked down at me and collapsed over me, looking me deep in the eyes.

"First time for everything, I guess," he whispered huskily, and I dragged his mouth to mine.

No more talking. I just wanted him inside of me.

He leaned over me, and I raised one leg over his hip as he reached for the nightstand drawer. He rubbed himself against me, teasing, tantalizing, and I moaned into his kiss as he finally fished a condom out of the drawer.

He kneeled up, unbothered by the mess of the sheets we'd made and made himself ready to take me. God that was so hot, watching him. I reached for him when he came back to me, and when he slid inside of me, I arched into him dying to feel as much of him as I could over and inside me.

He glided through my wetness, my want of him, need of him, coating the insides of my thighs as he kissed me fiercely, driving up into me, my fingernails digging into his shoulders as I held onto him through every desperate and possessive thrust...

You would think that would frighten me; the possessive part, but it didn't. There was nothing malignant about this, unlike with my husband. No, this was something pure. A light that I so desperately needed to chase back all of the shadows and dark behind me and holy Christ did Radar make me *shine*.

I cried out, trembling finely in his arms and he smiled so beautifully down at me and encouraged me.

"That's it, baby. That's my good girl. Come for me. Yeah, just like that..."

His voice low and intense in my ear made my body tighten, coil with anticipation and as I tightened, *he* moaned in such satisfaction. A few more strokes, his body riding mine, and that shine he put on me burst like the sun over the horizon and turned me into a firebrand of lust and exquisite sensation.

I came for him, just like he wanted, just like he asked, and there was no doubt in my mind that it was more than enough to satisfy him as he came right along with me.

~

WE LAY TOGETHER, after changing the sheets; me cuddled into his side, his arms around me as he played with my hair and absently kissed me on the top of my head from time to time. I closed my eyes and sighed, cuddling closer to him, feeling the grains of sand trickling through the hourglass as the time for my departure grew nearer and nearer with every second ticking by.

"What's wrong?" he asked me, smoothing his hand over my back. I opened my eyes and rolled them up to look at him and found him peering down at me with a heat and intensity that warmed me to my toes.

"Just... just promise me that this isn't the end," I murmured. "Don't let me get on that plane tomorrow thinking this is the beginning only to find out it was something dead before it even started. I... I couldn't take it. I can't take anymore heartache."

"Oh, baby... no. No, no, no," he pressed a hand to the back of my head and massaged it, his other hand going to the top of mine where it rested against his chest, clutching it to him tightly. He kissed my forehead once, twice, and said, "I'm not letting you go for long. I promise you that."

I wanted so badly, so deeply, to believe him. He was the first person I had ever met where I felt as though my jagged pieces fit.

"I'll make any oath you want me to make," he murmured, and he held me as though he would never let me go and I never wanted him to.

Less than a week and I am already in so deep, I thought to myself, and I had no clue what to do with it.

THE DRIVE to the airport was a quiet one. We rode in silence in his big white Cadillac SUV, my carry-on and laptop bag in the back, our hands clasped between us as he piloted us through traffic that was nothing short of absolutely *insane*.

We were heading for the small satellite airport a couple of hours north that the cut-rate airline flew out of. It was the one near St. Petersburg outside Tampa.

"I want you to text me as soon as you get through security," he said as signs for the airport started to show up.

"Okay," I said faintly, my heart in my throat.

"And right before you board the flight."

"Okay."

"And as soon as you're seated on the plane."

I started to smile. "Okay."

"And the very second you land," he said smiling.

I couldn't help but giggle as I said, "Okay."

"I'm going to miss you," he said, and he raised the back of my hand to my lips as he watched the road.

I fought back tears, my voice starting to crack as I said, "I'm going to miss you, too."

"Hey, none of that, baby. You're a strong woman. This ain't nothing compared to everything you've been through. You've got this, okay?" He shook my hand back and forth a bit and I nodded without looking not trusting myself.

"I've got this," I repeated, as much to somehow convince myself it was true.

I tried not to break when he stopped at the curb to drop me off. He gave my hand a reassuring squeeze, and with a lingering look opened his door to get out. I opened mine and met him around back of the SUV to get my bags. He opened his arms before he opened the hatch, and I gritted my teeth as my eyes misted and I practically dove into them.

We held onto each other tightly, and everything suddenly just felt so surreal. Like none of it was really happening.

He leaned back and palmed the side of my face gently but firmly and made sure my eyes met his when he said, "I'll see you soon, baby. I promise. Not gonna leave you."

I nodded, mute, not trusting my voice and he kissed me fiercely before stepping back too soon and letting me go to open the back of the Escalade. He pulled down my carry-on and extended the handle then held out my laptop bag for me to duck into the strap and settle it onto my shoulder.

He kissed me again and it was so bittersweet.

"Go on, now," he grated. "Before I change my mind."

I nodded and still didn't trust myself to speak, instead turning and walking for the doors and disappearing into the sterile so-serous hush that all of our airports had become.

17

*R*adar...

"I think I cried the whole flight home," she said with a rueful little laugh, and I put the cigar back in my mouth and laughed a little too.

I was sitting on my back patio, a stiff breeze blowing through my back yard, a fire going in my firepit.

I had a glass of the fucking good stuff on the arm of my chair to drown my sorrows in. Though our connection was good, the line clear, I swore I could feel every fucking mile between us and motherfucker if that didn't *kill*.

"So, what are you going to do now that I'm out of your hair?" she asked slyly but her attempt at self-deprecating humor fell flat.

"First of all," I said. "You were never any trouble and always a delight. Second of all, I'm going to work my ass off in an effort to fill the void of you not being here and to earn the money to come out there as soon as possible to be with you for as long as possible – rinse and repeat until we figure out where this is going and what we want to do."

She sighed on the other end of the line, and it held relief and something else.

"What was that big sigh for?" I asked smiling.

"It sounds like a solid plan," she said. "For me, too."

"Yeah?" I asked quietly as the back slider off my living room opened behind me.

"Yeah," she murmured.

Atlas dropped into the seat next to mine, picked up the bottle and raised it in silent cheers before pouring some in the glass I had set out for him.

"Speaking of work," I said, blowing out a plume of smoke. "Atlas just got here. I'm going to have to call or text you later, babe."

"That's okay," she said. "I should do laundry and catch up on some neglected chores. Get a shower and all of that."

"You got a few extra hours thanks to the time difference," I said.

"Just a few more hours of missing you," she said, and I could hear the smile in her voice. Probably a forced one, because I could hear her sadness, too.

"Get at 'cha as soon as I can, I promise."

"Okay, tell Atlas I said 'hi.'"

"I will. Kisses."

"Bye," she said on a giggle, and I hung up.

"Yo," Atlas said. "She make it home alright?"

"She did," I said, nodding.

"You alright?" he asked soberly, but not for long. He took a healthy sip of the alcohol in his glass, and I shook my head.

"Not remotely. I want her back, so let's make that happen. First thing's first—"

"Mariposa is gonna be fine, she head back yet?"

I nodded. "Yesterday, and I'd like to expedite that if we can."

He nodded. "Hope and I would have been on it, but it took me a minute to track his card and to figure out where he likes to hang at other than around Mariposa. I gave her some pepper spray and told her to use that shit like Binaca on that happy motherfucker if he got too mouthy. Tell anyone he put a hand on her hoo-ha or whatever."

"Little bastard better keep his hands off my daughter's vag." I glowered.

"Right, we got a few regular bounties to accomplish this week, then we can head up there on Friday night to spring a trap with the most viewers. Make this shit go viral or whatever," he said.

I nodded.

"Sounds good and after that?"

"Gotta pay the bills, my brother. A couple more bounties, then we can focus on Billy boy and finding out what the fuck. Maybe give him some comeuppance."

"You have no idea how eager I am to make that happen," I said and puffed on my cigar. He pulled one from the box I had sitting out and clipped it.

"Oh, I do. Believe me, I do… You beat me to her. If you hadn't gone there, I damn sure would have tried. She's beautiful and you know I love me a damsel in distress."

"I thought disposable little darlings were more your speed," I commented dryly.

Atlas sighed. "I don't know, bro. Maybe I'm getting old or some shit – but settling down is looking better and better the more I watch the lot of you getting to it."

"Jealous?" I asked.

"Fuck yes. I just hope we can score you and her a happily ever after," he said. "She looks and sounds like she's more than earned it."

I nodded.

"Truer words have never been spoken, man." I held out my glass and he clicked it against his and we both took a sip staring into the flames.

"Who's up first?" I asked and he sighed.

"Getting right to it, huh?" he asked.

"Play time is over, buddy. Who's first on our list of scumbags that need reeled in?"

"Time to go fishing for bad guys," he said and pulled out a set of file folders from the briefcase he'd brought out here with him and set beside his chair.

I took them and flipped open the top one.

"Aggravated assault," I intoned. "Sounds like a rush."

～

WE'D HAD a good week catching bad guys, but all good things must come to an end. Really though, we'd caught our three we'd intended to get, two in one night, and found ourselves freed up to go after a couple more – so we did.

The nice part about it? Having Justice to call up at the end of the day or night to talk about it. She was remarkably smart – asking all the right questions, figuring shit out, and to her credit – even making a suggestion or two that had Atlas and I wondering why the fuck we'd never thought of that. Her suggestions brought in one guy that much quicker for us and earned her a hefty amount of respect and street cred from not only Atlas and me, but the rest of the club when Atlas bragged about it.

She would only sigh when I asked about her day and would say it was boring... and honestly, it sounded like it was. Just cleaning an already clean house or more covers. Still, when she talked about some of her covers and sent them to me to look at, they were always amazing and much more full of life and intrigue than she gave herself credit for.

Still with every wistful goodbye, I heard her longing.

We texted non-stop when I could, and it was like there was this hole in my fucking soul that only she could fill. Which is why I was impatient as hell to get this kid who was bugging my kid put back in his fuckin' place.

I was in the bar that Atlas had said he liked to frequent most. Mariposa was under strict instruction to stay her ass in her fucking dorm tonight which she had declared as lame, saying she could just hit a different bar or a club with her friends. I told her no dice, I didn't want this kid sidetracked with stalking her and coming at her.

Hope looked at least fifteen years younger with her makeup job in the dim light of the bar and she sidled up looking gorgeous and giggly to the kid who checked out her ass first thing.

Atlas was in the crowded throng out there somewhere and we both had our phones out and at the ready to catch this from a couple of different angles.

If this shitbird behaved, he wouldn't have anything to worry about but predictably, when did any of these entitled little fuckwits stay in their lane?

I started filming their interaction just in time. Hope rearing back and looking like he'd said something crazy or wildly inappropriate to her. He grinned and laughed whatever it was off and tried again. I could hear her say strongly, "Dude, I'm just not interested!" He pushed again, only this time he put his hand on her waist.

"Dude! Don't fucking touch me!" she snarled. I thought for a second that some kid was gonna get in the way trying to white knight for her but Hope said, "I got it! He ain't shit!"

The guy trying to rescue ranger her sweet ass put up his hands and walked away, and the guy turned back to her and said something I couldn't catch.

She popped off with something likewise lost to the bar crowd and she turned to walk away. He grabbed her wrist and lightning fast Hope had his ass on the ground in a joint lock begging for mercy.

The bouncers showed up then and showed dude's ass out once Hope explained what was up and her white knight vouched for her.

I cut footage and spotted Atlas in the crowd. He nodded.

We waited a while, and I slipped out to find Cutter who was outside in an alley across the street. I took the long way around and when I stopped next to him, he sucked in a breath.

"Man, these citizens," he muttered. "They need to control their fuck trophies. If they did a better job of it, there would be a lot fewer fuckers like this one." He thrust his chin out where this yahoo waited about half a block up likewise tucked in watching the door to the bar with nothing but spite and malice sitting on his face like a Halloween mask.

"This motherfucker's fixin' to get his ass kicked," I said, and I was trying not to laugh.

"Shit, think we should just let Hope handle it?" he asked.

"Nah, he's been giving my kid grief, I want a piece of his ass."

"Wouldn't give him anything to trace back to little Mari," Cutter said, and I looked up at him like *no fucking shit.*

Atlas left the bar first and walked right past the dude, paying him no mind before ducking into an alley halfway down the block past him to, what looked like, take a piss.

Hope came out a few minutes later, the white knight still shooting his shot. She laughed and shook her head, and the guy took the hint with hands raised and a sheepish grin and maybe a few smooth words that had Hope laughing before she turned up the sidewalk to head right past our boy, looking at Cutter's text to head that way.

We left our alley and started pacing her just behind paying her no mind, trying to make it look like we were having our own conversation. Our target ghosted down the way and into the alley to lie in wait and Hope let herself be pulled in. Atlas got into the alley first and we came up short at his back. The kid was holding something, and Hope had her hands up a wicked gleam in her eyes.

Dumb shit had the mouth of the alley and the three of us at his back and didn't even fucking realize it.

"He's got a knife," she said calmly, voice tinged with amusement.

He whirled on us, and I reached out and gave shit a twist. He dropped the knife; Hope standing back while we dropped him. Atlas watched out for us at the mouth of the alley, paying attention to the street while Cutter and I beat the fucking brakes off this piece of wet lettuce.

"Should have stayed a fuckin' stain in your daddy's gym sock, you arrogant piece of shit," Hope said, putting one of her heels against his hip and pushing him over onto his back.

"You're lucky, you won't choke to death on your own blood," Cutter grated. "Bet there are a lot of ladies out there that wouldn't mind if you did."

I resisted the urge to spit on him. Why leave DNA if he did fuckin' die?

We left, and whatever would be would be. Personally, I hoped he fuckin' died. His survival left a good chance he'd just be a Rodney for some poor other Justice out there.

The thought almost had me turning around to put a cap in his fuckin' ass.

~

"HE'S IN ICU. Nobody's crying about it. His jaw could be wired shut for six months," Mariposa said, and she was doing a good job of sounding sad about it on the phone but I knew my kid, and if you listened between the words, you could totally hear her fucking smile.

"Aw, geeze baby, that's too bad. I'm sorry to hear that," I told her and tried to sound like a sympathetic dad to anyone that might be listening. Paranoia before anything else. It kept your ass outta jail and off the radar for people like… well… *me*.

"Anyway, that's what's going on up here. The big news of the day so-to-speak. Lucia says you're going out of town on a bounty?"

"Yep, Atlas and I are packing up now."

"Taking the bike or the Escalade?" she asked.

"Taking the bikes, no sense in taking the Escalade. We'll just take him to a local lockup and let the courts extradite this one."

"That means that whatever he's done is bad – you can't bullshit me. I've been around you too long. Just be careful, okay?" she asked.

"As a virgin on her wedding night, scouts honor," I said.

"Ew, gross," she muttered.

I chuckled.

"Talk to you later, baby."

"Later, Dad."

We hung up. I sighed and looked over my pack and nodded, ticking everything off in my head again.

Honestly, I couldn't wait to get on the road.

18

*J*ustice...

I sighed and straightened up trying to stretch my back, palming the back of my neck and wishing Radar were here to knead sore muscles.

As though merely thinking of him conjured him out of thin air, my music cut, my phone lit up, and his face crossed the screen.

"I was just thinking about you," I said, smiling.

"Aw, yeah?" he asked.

"Yeah," I murmured softly.

"What were you thinking about?" His voice held an edge of teasing.

I giggled, shaking my head, and told him the truth.

"Actually, I was just thinking that I wish you were here to rub my back."

"Aw, again?" he asked.

"Yeah," I said, and I didn't bother to hide the fact that I was bummed in my voice.

"Mm," he murmured. "I wish I was there to take care of it."

I changed the subject and said, "Me, too." I asked, "Where are you now, anyway?"

"Somewhere in bumfuck Alabama," he said, and it sounded like he stretched.

"Any closer to finding your guy?" she asked.

"Not yet, we need to keep heading north by northwest."

"That Justice?" I heard Atlas in the background.

"Yeah." Radar's voice dimmed as he held the phone away from his mouth.

"Hi, Jussy!" I heard called out in the background.

I smiled and said, "Hi Atlas."

"She says 'hi,'" Radar told him.

"So where is this target?" I asked. "I don't remember you saying."

"Somewhere up near Denver, Colorado."

"Oh, my God! You have to ride *that far?*" I asked. "Why didn't you fly?"

"Nah, cheap as fuck in gas on the bikes and saves a lot of hassle keeping our guns with airport security and all," he said.

"Oh, right. I didn't think of that," I said.

He laughed lightly and said, "You think of plenty. You don't have to think of everything – that's our job."

"Hmm," I hummed and smiled. "I guess I should just be happy you're just a little bit closer."

"I know I am," he said. "But still, so close yet so far away."

I nodded, realized he couldn't see it, and said, "Yeah."

"Don't sound like that," he said softly, his voice slightly chiding but still full of understanding.

"Like what?" I asked.

"Like all is lost," he said. "Because, baby, you've only just been found."

I chuckled. "It's only been a week and it feels like a year, ah God, how am I supposed to do this?" I asked.

"One step, one day at a time," he said, and I nodded.

"Yeah. Makes sense.

"It's getting late," he said, and I nodded.

"Not as late as where you are," I told him.

"Right, which is how I know it's getting late there…"

"You telling me to go to bed?" I asked.

"Yeah," he answered. "You sound tired, babe and I need you to take care of yourself. No burning the candle at both ends for you anymore."

"I could say the same about you," I said.

"I know." He sighed. "I know, and I'm trying. I promise."

"I know you are."

"Get some sleep, baby."

"I will, I promise. You do the same."

"Okay."

"Okay, goodnight."

"G'night."

I ended the call and sighed.

My house didn't feel like a home. It hadn't since the nights of terror... it felt hollow, and broken, and as I looked around, I realized – I couldn't stand it here, but I was trapped by debt and my credit score sucked, so here I would stay until I could fix it.

I turned back to my laptop screen and let my eyes rove my work in progress.

"I can sleep when I'm dead," I said to the empty air and picked up my stylus with a sigh. "Maybe I should get a plant or something... so I can talk to it instead of myself. Of course, which actually makes you crazier?" I wondered aloud. "Talking to yourself or an inanimate object? I guess at least the plant is *alive* which helps."

I snorted.

"Who am I kidding? There's no real help for someone like me..." Of course as soon as I said it my heart called me a liar. My thoughts, once again, turned to Radar.

God, I missed him...

19

*R*adar...

"How's she doing?" Atlas asked a couple of days later, handing me a hot dog from a stand. We had eyes on Billy boy's truck, as we'd taken to calling him. Where the fuck he got the name Billy Curtis in the first place we didn't know, but who fucking cared.

"I don't know," I said. "She sounds alright, but it's kind of a false brightness."

"Mm, well, we're on the home stretch for finding out what the absolute goddamned fuck," he said.

"Yeah." I nodded.

"Could swing through Texas on the way home."

"San Antonio ain't exactly in the pan handle," I said.

"No, but since when has that ever fuckin' stopped us before?" he asked.

"Good point," I muttered.

"We're gonna be at this a while," he said, sitting back and sighing.

"Yup." I nodded.

"I fuckin' hate stakeouts," he griped.

"We do more PI work and less bond work, you know it's gonna be more staking shit out, not less, right?"

"Ruin my fuckin' fun, why don't you?" he muttered and wiped his mouth with his napkin. I laughed under my breath.

We waited, and waited, and waited some more, and finally at around five-thirty our boy showed up, dropping his tailgate on his fancy truck to stow some shit in the back.

"Looks like somebody has had a bad fuckin' day," Atlas muttered.

"Yeah, well it's about to get worse," I said, firing up the bike. He followed suit and as Billy boy backed out of his space, we followed him.

We knew where he was staying. We were booked in the same motel under false names. We watched him go into his room and went into ours. He didn't know us from Adam but we had his fuckin' number.

We watched him from behind the gauzy curtain to our room which was on the first floor with a good view of his on the second. He liked to leave his door open and paced from the railing into his room while he talked on the phone.

Whatever was being said, he didn't seem to like it. Not one bit – too fuckin' bad.

He had his dinner delivered, stayed up late watching television and finally, his room's light went out. The blue glow from around the curtain going out about a half hour later.

"On the home stretch," Atlas muttered and we waited some fucking more.

"We're good," he said, looping the close circuit security feed.

"Let's roll," I muttered, and we ducked out. Stockings in hand, to head to dude's room. We left our colors in our room and wore gear we could strip out of in a hurry and dive into our own rented beds looking nothing like the two punks about to get in this dude's room to have some words.

We put the stocking masks over our faces and Atlas slid the key card jimmy rig whatever the fuck it was he had on him into the lock and pressed some buttons on the keypad, the light flicked green, the lock disengaged, and we ghosted into the room.

"The fuck!" dude cried and we were on him. Atlas buried a shoulder into dude's solar plexus diving onto him in a tackle onto the bed and I had the garrote around his fuckin' neck before he could do shit.

He tried to flop like a landed fish but wasn't having much success under Atlas's weight.

"You got two seconds to come clean and tell us why you ditched that woman in Florida," I grated.

"Shit, don't kill me!" The guy wheezed. "I told Rodney I couldn't do it! She was nothing like he said she was, man!"

Atlas and I exchanged a look.

"What about her husband?" I demanded, tightening the noose.

I let him breathe just enough to get it out.

"He asked me! He asked me, man! Had this whole story about how she framed him up – wanted me to fuck a confession out of her and fuckin' do her man but I couldn't fuckin' do it! She wasn't like that at all! Rodney – he's fuckin' crazy! I don't understand it. He was a stand-up normal well-adjusted guy when we served together!"

"This is how this is gonna happen," Atlas grated. "You gonna take this ass whoopin' and then you're gonna stay far the fuck away from Rodney's ex-wife."

"He's already got a group of guys, man. It's too late, I left her there to protect her!"

Oh, shit...

We finished interrogating the motherfucker. Atlas put the fuckin' hurt on the guy and we finished him with a blackjack crack to the skull that was lights fuckin' out.

Wordlessly, we left just as stealthily as we came, got our asses back to our room and fuckin' scrambled looking shit up and calling back home.

"To what do I owe this pleasure?" Ruthless, the president of the Voodoo Bastards out of New Orleans answered the next morning.

"Hey, yeah, Ruth – it's Atlas and Radar," I said.

"Well, hell boys. How do?"

"Actually, I'm calling for a big ass favor," I said.

"How's that?"

I explained the situation. About how he and his crew were the closest to my girl and I would mightily appreciate it if he could send a couple of his crew to watch her and her house while I got on the road.

He listened patiently and was silent for a few heartbeats. I thought I'd lost the connection.

"Ruth?" I asked.

"Yeah, hold on, I'm dispatchin' a couple of my boys right now. Text me her address," he said.

"Thank you, Atlas and I are getting on the road right now."

"Alright then, they'll see you there. Y'all ride safe now, y'hear?"

"I owe you Ruth, big time."

"Seems we do a lot of that owing each other back and forth, and it's no worries! It all comes out in the wash."

"I surely do appreciate this," I said. "You have no idea."

"Just to be clear, man. Is this a club favor or a personal one? And by that, I mean does Cutter know you're a callin' me?"

"It's a personal one, but you know how we operate and Cutter *does* know I'm callin' you. He's the one that actually suggested it."

"Right, then. I do believe we as a club could use some hospitality come this spring break, if you know what I mean."

I grinned, "We'll gladly roll out the red carpet for you guys anytime."

"Well, thank you kindly. You best be hittin' the road now," he said.

"Copy that, thanks again, Ruth."

"Ah huh, bye bye now." He hung up and Atlas and I exchanged a look.

"We just got off hella easy," he said, and I rolled my eyes.

"You know how rowdy Ruth and his boys get, we're gonna be making shit up to the town after that weekend for a month or better."

"They may get rowdy but the last time they came through to hang they kept it to the tourists."

"True, fair enough."

Still, I'd make sure my girls were clear of the town or in Kraken tees the whole damn time to make sure the boys of the Bastards kept their hands to themselves.

"How long are we looking at?" I asked, looking over Atlas' shoulder at the screen.

"Like sixteen hours."

"Fuck, that's a case of monkey butt waiting to happen," I said and slung my pack up on my shoulder.

"Uh-huh, ain't nothing for it. Gonna call her now?"

"No, let her sleep," I answered. "At least one of us should be rested, you know?"

"That I surely do," he answered.

We hit the road.

20

*J*ustice...

A knock fell at my door and I clicked through screens on my computer and brought up my doorbell camera.

Two men stood on my front step, motorcycles gleaming in the background at the end of my drive at the curb, but neither one of them were Radar. In fact, I had no idea who either of these men were. All I knew was they were terrifying to look at, really. One of them was bald, his head and neck heavily tattooed, his face clean of ink except for little tattoos I couldn't make out at the corner of each eye. Even his hands were heavily tatted where they peeked out of the sleeves of his heavy biker jacket.

The other man who stood behind him to one side, facing out onto my street was narrow and shifty looking. The back of his jacket showed a skull in a big purple top hat, it's one green eye magnified by a monocle, a cigar clutched between its teeth. *Voodoo Bastards* was emblazoned above the skull in what Radar had called a top rocker, while down below it proclaimed them as being from New Orleans... but what were they doing here?

"Can I help you?" I asked through the system.

"Justice?"

My mouth suddenly felt dry.

"Can I help you?" I repeated, not wishing to confirm or deny who it was they were speaking to. I held my phone in my hand prepared to call the police.

"My name's La Croix and this here is Collier, we was sent down here by your man Radar out there with the Kraken MC."

"Just one moment."

I immediately called Radar, but his phone just rang and rang and went to voicemail.

"How can I know?" I said through the speaker then cursed myself for giving away the fact that yes, they were indeed talking to Justice.

"Okay, Cher," the big tattooed man La Croix said. "You do what you gotta do to git a hold of him. We'll wait right out here until you feel safe enough to open the door."

I blinked and got up from my seat and taking a deep breath and letting it out slowly went to the door and opened it.

He looked down at me and smiled kindly, his eyes unnerving, terrifying, the whites black with ink the brown dark enough to make them almost solid all the way across.

"You get ahold of him?" he asked and I shook my head.

"Why are you here?" I asked.

"Best if we come inside to tell you that, ma'am," Collier said with a polite nod. I bit my lips together and stood aside, heart racing, hands shaking.

"What made you open the door?" La Croix asked as he came inside.

"It's one-hundred-and-four degrees out there and you're all in black leather…" I said.

"Kind of yah," Collier said. "But we woulda waited."

"What's going on?" I asked. "Why are you here?"

My phone buzzed in my hands and it was Radar.

"Answer 'im, let 'im explain," La Croix said.

I answered the phone.

"Hey baby." It was Radar who sounded breathless. "I heard you call, but we were on the Interstate. Had to pull off. Are the boys from the Voodoo Bastards there?" he asked.

"Yes, but… why? What is going on?" I asked. "You're all scaring me."

"I know, I'm sorry, but you're safe that's all that matters and I am on my way there. Just eight or nine more hours to go. Can you hand the phone to one of the boys?" I handed the phone to La Croix.

"He wants to talk to you," I said faintly and La Croix took the phone.

He took some steps away and Collier, who was much younger and very handsome in comparison to La Croix's heavily tattooed… well, badassery.

"Surprised he's talked this much." Collier smiled at me. "Not like 'im."

"Oh," I murmured. "I'm sorry, I'm forgetting my manners… can I offer you something to drink? I asked.

"Nah, we're all good, but you might want to make a cup of tea or pour a glass of wine or somethin' for yourself. You look rattled, Cher."

I chewed my bottom lip and looked at La Croix who had his back turned, shoulders hunched as he listened to Radar on the phone. He was in my living room while Collier and I had ended up in the dining room. He pulled out a chair for me and I took the seat, my knees turning to jelly.

"Why did he send you here?" I asked, speaking of Radar.

La Croix ended the call on my phone and turned around coming back over, tapping the back of my phone against his fingers.

"It's good you're sitting down," he said and sighed. "I've got some bad news…"

I listened to what he had to say, my tongue gone numb, my hands clutched in my lap, stunned – just stunned.

"I…" I felt my jaw working, that funny taste flooding my mouth as my stomach roiled. "I think I'm gonna be sick," I confessed and both men stood clear as I bolted to my feet and into the bathroom just off of the kitchen down here. I slammed the door behind me and collapsed in a heap on the floor in front of the toilet and heaved up bile. When I was empty, the weeping began and I didn't think it would stop.

I didn't think any of this would stop…

I ENDED up in my bedroom, the two men from New Orleans sweet despite their outward appearance.

Collier had rapped on the door after I had calmed down and I had twisted the knob letting him in. He'd sighed and said, "C'mon, Chere, let's get you to lay down for a minute." He'd pushed the button on the top of the toilet to flush the mess and had reached down to help me to my feet.

"Sit her down here, my man," La Croix ordered when we'd emerged and Collier brought me back to my seat at the dining room table off the kitchen. I sank into it, shaking and he put a cold wet cloth to the back of my neck. "Grab me some wet paper towels and get the lady a glass of water," he ordered and Collier moved to comply.

"Where did you find this?" I asked, stammering.

"Checked the house to make sure we were alone, scored it in your bathroom upstairs," he said and I nodded, just… numb.

Collier came back with a glass of water and I took it.

"Sip slowly, don' want to make yerself sick again."

"Thank you," I said and I shook my head. "I don't understand why you're being so nice to me." They exchanged a look.

"Radar asked us to look after his ol' lady." La Croix lifted one shoulder in a shrug as though that should honestly explain everything.

He tipped up my chin and ran the damp paper towel over my cheeks and eyes, wiping away tears.

"Here, blow." He pinched my nose and with a shaky laugh I complied.

"You must have kids," I said, and he shook his head but didn't elaborate.

"We aren't going anywhere until your man gets here," Collier said.

"Don't feel like you need to entertain us, but can we pull the bikes into the garage?"

I got up and went over to the garage door and clicked on the light. Both the men at my back looked over my head and I shrugged.

"This was Rodney's domain… feel free if you can find room."

Collier gave a low whistle at the two classic muscle cars in the garage and the piles of boxes filling the rest.

"Saw a side gate," La Croix rumbled. "That lead to the back yard?"

I looked up at him and nodded.

"Well, alright then," Collier said brightly.

I didn't know what to say, so I said nothing.

21

*R*adar...

"Dude, how is she?" I asked, coming in the back slider with my gear. We'd texted ahead of time, rolled through the neighborhood, didn't see any kind of surveillance, and when we'd come back around? La Croix had the side gate open to Jussy's back yard. We'd carefully hopped the curb and rolled through the gate and parked in her back yard which needed to be mowed, the grass yellowed from lack of being watered.

"Sent her upstairs a while ago," Collier said. "To have a lie down and rest. She took it bad, man."

"Yeah, I figured. You guys good?" I asked.

"Yeah, man. Go see your woman."

I gave a nod and was surprised when Atlas was right on my heels. I stopped in the hallway up stairs and looked at him, raising an eyebrow and he lifted a shoulder in a shrug and said, "What? I'm worried about her, too."

I nodded and said, "I don't know if she's like that, man; and I don't know if sex is the way to go here right now."

He smiled and shook his head.

"Not here for that, as beautiful as she is – just here for moral support."

I nodded, feeling it'd just needed to be said. We'd high fived over many a girl acting like a pair of finger cuffs for our dicks but yeah, now was definitely not the time for that. A cuddle pile might be just what the doctor ordered, though.

I opened doors until I came to hers and found her curled in a miserable ball on her side in the middle of her bed.

She looked haggard, her eyes closed, her face drawn even in sleep. Dark circles etched under her eyes and a paleness to her that her fresh Florida tan just sort of floated on top of like an oil slick on the water.

I kneeled down, and touched the side of her face, moving some of her glossy dark hair behind her ear and she flinched, shuddering as she drew in a long breath and her eyes opened. She looked at me, and blinked several times as though she was waiting for the illusion to disappear and I smiled at her. Sad for her. Wanting nothing more than to make this shit stop and for her to be safe and have the opportunity to learn to be happy again. To heal.

"Oh," she murmured and crumbled into tears, reaching for me. I got up on the bed with her and clutched her close, as she put her face into my chest and just fucking wept with relief.

Atlas went around the bed to the other side and sandwiched her between us; cuddling up to her back and holding her close. He looked over her shoulder at me and I could see the heat in his strange eyes – not of desire, hell no, but for vengeance. He wanted to make some motherfuckers hurt as bad as I did... and we would. Maybe not by our own hand but it would be done.

I held her tight and we lay there huddled in a pile of exhaustion, mental and emotional on her part, probably more than a little mental and physical on mine and Atlas's part. I don't know who dropped into unconsciousness first but when I woke up in the king-sized bed, it was still with a firm grasp around my sleeping woman and my buddy looking over me at the door. I turned my head, La Croix in the doorway.

"Yer President's been trying to reach you," he said, and I frowned slightly and went to edge out from Jussy's grasp.

She moaned in her sleep and held onto me tighter.

"I got it," Atlas said softly and untangled himself from us and edged off of the bed. He went around and followed La Croix out and it was just me and Justice.

"Hey," I murmured, pressing a kiss to her forehead. She shuddered slightly in my grasp and stretched, sucking in a deep breath and yawning.

"Hey," she murmured, cuddling close and refusing to open her eyes. I chuckled and breathed her in and she sighed out reluctantly and asked, "What time is it?"

"Who fuckin' knows?" I asked. "Don't much care right now." I held her just that little bit tighter.

"I want to be mad that you went after him, but… but I'm not," she said and she sounded a little forlorn and definitely conflicted. I smiled above her head and shifted so I was more on my back. She laid her head on my chest.

"You're a good person," I said. "I understand it. Good people don't want to hurt other people – I mean, I don't but by the same token, I understand that sometimes that's what it takes and I don't feel bad for that motherfucker. Not in the slightest, and you shouldn't either."

"I don't," she said and she sounded cold which put a smile on my face. I kissed her hair and breathed out.

"Good," I told her.

I would be lying if I said I wasn't low-key worried about how she would fit into club life, but I think she'd reached the point of no return… law enforcement hadn't done shit for her leading up to the big break and her subsequent attack that'd nearly killed her. The justice system had clearly fuckin' let her down both before and after the fact and what did you do when that happened?

If you were me, it never got to that point because I, and people like me, handled shit our damn self… but for citizens like Jussy? Who didn't see beyond the narrow margins they'd been written into; educated in, indoctrinated through, what was there?

Nothing but big, bad, scary men like her husband with no account-ability. People like her, they'd been taught to fear men like me just as much – to trust in the authorities which they knew was laughable but *fuck*, where did you go? Where did you turn? If she took matters into her own hands and killed the motherfucker herself, she'd have the book thrown at her no matter the heinous shit he'd done to her.

She was bound by chains of silence and rules made for rich white men – or in her case, just a white man and it was bullshit. It was always bullshit, but the rules weren't written for us, it was written to keep the old, rich, white men that had always been in power in that power. Nothing more and nothing less, and it was in conformity they kept the yoke on the masses to keep on keeping on to earn them that money and allow them to live high on the hog while they kept the rest of us fighting for scraps from their table.

The American dream was broken, the American dream was a lie, and it was good people, genuine people, like my girl who suffered for it... but she had a pack now and we were unabashed wolves in this land of fucking sheep. Fierce and hungry, and ready to rend flesh as much to eat as in defense of one of our own and as sure as I was laying here, Justice in my arms, I had claimed this woman as my own even after so short a time. That made her *one of us,* and when you knew, you knew, and I knew that this was meant to be.

That meant there were some motherfuckers out here that needed to answer for their shit and I would make them answer.

I had power too, and my power was a far more dangerous variety. My power lay in that I just didn't give a fuck about the rules.

Atlas came back in the room and Justice jumped in my arms. I held her tighter and looked over.

"What's up?" I asked.

"Some of the local chapter of the SHMC are gonna roll up," Atlas declared. "Cutter put in the call and the local boys requested a meet."

I nodded. "Fair," I said.

"Ah yup."

Atlas focused on Justice and smiled warmly. "How you doin' baby?" he asked her.

"I don't know," she answered honestly.

"Give us a bit," I said, and Atlas lifted his chin, went back out, and shut the door behind him.

Justice pushed off of me and sat up, sweeping her hair over her shoulder and running it through her hands. She wore this bohemian style white eyelet lace baby doll dress and with her slightly mussed hair and sleep wrinkled face with its faint lines from where she'd been pressed against my jacket and cut she looked adorable if stressed. I sat up too and put my back against her headboard.

"You ain't got anything to worry about, baby," I said softly. "I'm going to handle it."

She shook her head and looked grim, putting her face into her hands and shaking her head, "You shouldn't *have* to take care of it," she said. "But I'm grateful. I just don't know what else to do…"

"You don't have to do anything except chill and let me handle it from here on out. You're tired, you've done everything you can. It's our turn now."

"It's all so overwhelming," she said, shuddering.

"I know, come here." She came to me and hugged into my side and I sighed.

"I want to tell you everything we're doing," I said. "But I can't."

"Why not?" she asked somberly.

"For your protection as much as ours," I said frankly.

"I think I understand," she said, and I believed it. She was sharp.

"Not to put too fine a point on it, I can't tell you as much for your protection as for ours," I said. "You can't tell the cops what you don't know, and likewise you can't be charged for something you had no knowledge of or any hand in."

She nodded carefully and asked, "Are you going to kill him somehow?" I gave her a very direct look and remained silent and she nodded and tears brimming on her lower lashes she nodded and said, "Thank you."

"None of that now," I said pulling her into me and sighing, intentionally ignoring what she'd said.

"I hate it here," she confessed. "This house and what he did to me here… but I don't know how to get out from under it – I have no place to go."

"The fuck you don't," I said as she sobbed silently against me.

"You're going to sell it. Come to Florida far the fuck away from this shithole. I'll put you up, you can make a down payment on something out there, or if we work out, you can keep your money and stay with me as long as you like. Just hang onto it, you know? Have it if you ever feel like you need to go. An exit strategy or an escape plan. Doesn't bother me," I said.

She looked at me stunned. "You've known me all of *three weeks!*" she cried and I nodded.

"I know it," I said. "But I didn't get this road name for nothing. I got a radar for these things and baby; you light it up like the northern sky. All beauty and grace and when you know, *you know* and I know this is the right move… and just like that day in my daughter's diner *I know*." I shrugged. "I just know; and just like that day, it was your decision then and it's your decision now. You just say the word and you don't have to say anything right now – but when you're ready, and I'll be here."

"Hell, I'm going to be here for a minute to see this through. Now that Atlas and I are awake, we'll let the boys from NOLA get some rest if they want it and figure our shit out. You just do whatever it is you need to do to stay comfortable, baby." I touched the side of her face and stroked her soft skin with my thumb in a firm graze. "You ain't gotta do it all by yourself anymore. I'm here to help."

I pressed a kiss to her forehead and she crumbled against me, only think time I think it was with relief. I had a sense for these things.

WHEN I WENT DOWNSTAIRS, leaving my woman in a hot bath to try and sooth aching muscles and to think some things through for herself I found the boys down in the living room.

"Hey, thanks for riding to the rescue guys," I said, addressing La Croix and Collier first.

"Our pleasure, man..." Collier said while La Croix's creepy tattooed eyeballs were glued to the empty stairs I'd just come down.

"She's doing better, thank you for taking care of her," I said, and he nodded.

"So, what's the full meal deal you don't mind us askin'," Collier said.

I told them, all the details as I had them, from what Jussy had said, to what Atlas had dug up out of the court records, to what that fuckin' ass bag in Colorado had told us. We sat around Justice's living room on her leather couches that were clearly not in her taste but his, and La Croix looked more agitated, not less.

"His sister's husband killed her a while back," Collier said. "He don't like these situations."

"I'm sorry to hear that, man."

He nodded at me but didn't say much.

"You fellas can take it from here?" Collier asked.

I nodded.

"I do believe we can, but don't think we're rushing you outta here. By no means," I said. "I feel heavy handed enough but—"

"But she was drowning and the amount of people in the water to rescue her is a little overwhelming, I get that, but it's the best thing for her," Collier said with a nod.

La Croix grunted his agreement.

I nodded. "Still feel like I'm running a little roughshod here."

"I feel you, bro... but this ain't exactly anything Jussy can handle at this point. It's out of her hands."

"I gave her some choices. Some things to think about," I said.

"Oh yeah?" Atlas looked at me curiously and I spilled. He looked impressed, and really thought about it, then nodded.

"Some reasonable choices," he said.

"Feels too good to be true to someone like her, I'm sure o dat," Collier said with a wink.

I nodded and La Croix growled slightly and huffed out a breath.

"When and where the SHMC wanna see my ass?" I asked Atlas.

"Tomorrow, around eleven and I got the address," he said. "Best not be thinking you're going alone."

I shook my head.

"No, I wouldn't dream of it."

"I'll stay," La Croix grumbled. We all turned eyes in his direction. "You go on and do what needs doin', I'll stay with her so she's not alone."

"I sure appreciate that, man."

He nodded.

"Well, fellas, it's late. You all looked pretty cozy up there so why don't you go on and get back to it?" Collier asked. "La Croix and I can find our way around down here."

I nodded and Atlas stood and we went for the stairs.

"You sure I ain't gonna be a third wheel this time?" he asked, and I shrugged.

"We can ask," I said. "But if it's just sleep, I don't see the problem."

22

*J*ustice...

Radar came back into the bathroom just as I was
thinking about getting out of the tub. I was sitting in the
gently steaming water hugging my knees thinking about how no man
had *ever* drawn me a bath or taken care of me like these rough-looking
outsiders when his light tap fell at the bathroom door.

"Oh, uh, come in!" I called fairly certain it was him and knowing
full well there wasn't anything about me that he hadn't seen before...
and I do mean anything.

"Hey," he said softly, closing the door behind him and coming
over. His jacket had disappeared, as had his chaps, and it was just his
leather vest over a white tee with faded and soft looking jeans. I missed
his long shorts he'd preferred in Florida. Long pants just looked
somehow wrong on him.

"Hey," I said softly, and he kneeled down by the tub and then
finally took a seat on the floor.

"How you doing?" he asked.

I nodded and said, "Better, I think. Feeling a little stronger."

He eyed me and nodded slowly.

"I have to go out in several hours and handle some business," he said to me. "You going to be alright with La Croix and Collier staying with you until I can get back?"

I nodded and said, "For as scary as he looks, La Croix is a nice guy."

Radar smiled at me like he thought I was adorable.

"Yeah, he's pretty okay," he agreed.

He traced a tendril of loose hair behind my ear and his eyes wandered over me with a certain amount of reverence and I closed my eyes. That look frightened me to a degree. Partially because things *were* still so new, and partially because if anything happened... I didn't know if I could live without seeing it again.

"With La Croix and Collier in the house, space is kind of limited," he said. "You mind if Atlas crashes with us? Like before?"

I swallowed hard and rubbed my lips together. "Can I tell you something without you taking it the wrong way or getting mad?" I asked quietly.

"You can tell me anything," he said and I nodded.

"I wouldn't mind," I said. "It was actually kind of nice."

He smiled big and laughed a little, "Liked that did you?" he asked, and I nodded without looking at him.

He hooked a hand behind my neck and kneeled half brought me to him half came to me over the lip of the tub to kiss my temple.

"Glad you liked it," he murmured. "You want to explore that more, you just let me know. No judgment here."

I looked up at him as he got up and I knew my eyes were wide.

"What's that supposed to mean?" I asked and he looked down at me like I shouldn't play stupid. I felt color creep into my face and cleared my throat which was suddenly tight with embarrassment.

"I'll go tell him it's all good then be right back to get you out of that bath. Don't move."

I nodded mutely, a shiver going down my spine that had nothing to do with any cold or chill – quite the opposite in fact.

When Radar returned, it was without his vest – er, cut and he'd ditched his tee shirt, boots, and presumably socks. I blinked in silent wonder at him traversing the bathroom in just those old jeans and worn leather belt slung low on his hips. Any thought or care I'd had the moment before I saw him flying from my head as though a bird through a cage door left open. He gave me this dark little half smile and of course it was written all over my face. I must have turned as red as a tomato. He kneeled back down and whispered, "Let me get your back, then get you out of there and wrapped up."

I nodded, and turned my head to watch him, laying it atop my knees. He took the damp washcloth from the edge of the tub from when I'd washed my face and dipped it in the water before my feet, giving it a swirl and raising it out. He didn't bother to wring it, just rinsed my back with warm water before reaching for my body wash.

It felt nice to be cared for, and yet I still felt sort of frozen inside, surprised and sort of sitting in surreal disbelief that it was even happening… I mean things like this didn't happen to someone like me.

He washed my back gently and slowly, all the while murmuring about how beautiful I was and how I had such beautiful skin and it was sweet and so… soothing. I closed my eyes and jumped slightly when he touched my jaw lightly with his thumb.

"Sorry," he whispered low and intense and he brought his lips to mine, kneeling above me like that and kissing my so thoroughly I almost forgot to breathe.

"That's my good girl," he whispered against my mouth and I don't know why or what it was about it but those words in that voice… it was soothing to the soul.

He cuddled me to him as much as the side of the tub between us would allow and kissed me so sweetly, kneeling up, head bowed over mine and it felt like… it felt like a powerful exchange. Like he took some of my fears and handed me some of his strength and I know that sounds so silly but it was true.

He finished, almost letting me cool down from the fire of his kiss by massaging the back of my head, hand buried in my hair as he gazed deeply into my eyes from mere inches away.

I think when he saw I was somehow calmer, that's when he decided I was good to get out.

"Good girl," he murmured one more time, and then he let me go and said, "Wait right here." He pulled the plug on the tub and grabbed one of the bath sheets out of the free-standing cupboards I had in here. Reclaimed pieces of furniture from yard sales and garage sales… this one happened to be an old China hutch, the doors removed, the chips and scratches and the holes left behind from the hinges filled; the surface sanded and repainted in off-white farmhouse chic.

The shelves Rodney had built to replace the missing ones, sturdy; now held neatly folded towels, washcloths, and bath sheets. Radar plucked one of those large bath sheets off of one of those shelves and let it unfurl, holding his hand down to me to help me up.

I climbed carefully to my feet and he wrapped me up, rubbing me down briskly through the towel, paying attention to the spots he had discovered as ticklish what felt like a lifetime ago in Florida until he forced a giggle out of me.

He smiled at the sound and I could already feel the pall of stress and negative emotions begin to lift from my spirits.

"Doesn't matter what happens from here on out," he whispered. "I've got you, and I've got your back until you don't want or need me around anymore."

I felt the smile fade from my lips as I put fingertips to his to hush him.

"I don't want to make any silly promises," I told him. "Like I'll love you forever or whatever… because who knows where things will go. We have no way of knowing… but I *do* know that right now I am so grateful for you and I really do hope things last."

He smiled at me and held me close, putting his hand to the side of my neck and drawing my forehead to his, rocking me slowly with a twist of his waist back and forth minutely as we stood in the circle of each other's arms and just soaked in the moment until an involuntary shiver from the air conditioning against my damp skin made him jerk back slightly and he said, "Let's get you bundled under the covers."

He stood behind me and walked me into my room. Atlas was already on the side of the bed he'd claimed the night before. He lay on his side, back to the room, facing the window and Radar lifted the blankets.

"Oh, let me put something on," I murmured quietly so as not to wake Atlas.

"If that's what makes you comfortable, honey but I sure don't mind," Atlas declared and I looked to Radar who chuckled and said, "Up to you, baby."

I stared at him for several heartbeats.

"Sometime tonight, though. The draft is starting to get to me," Atlas said a moment later and I took a deep breath, dropped the towel and scrambled between the sheets as I was. Radar dropped the blankets and tucked them around me before going for his belt. He stripped nude as well and then got in behind me, switching out the bedside lamp and plunging us into darkness. He settled and raised an arm so that I could go to him.

I cuddled into his side, Atlas remaining where he was unmoving and I closed my eyes. I was still tired, but sleep was elusive for the time being.

"You good, baby?" Radar asked, kissing my hair when I fidgeted for the umpteenth time.

"Yeah, sorry... I just... slept and only just got up and while I'm tired my mind is going, you know?"

"You know and orgasm might help that," Atlas declared from behind me and I froze and looked up to Radar who laughed and said, "He's not wrong, but nothing needs to happen if you don't want it to."

I was speechless.

"I..."

"We've shared before, sweetheart," Atlas said. "Partners in all things, right my man?"

I felt my cheeks flame. "Yeah, something like that," Radar declared. "But not tonight or maybe even ever. We mean it, babes. All in your own time. You tell us what, when. You're in control now."

I settled quietly and didn't say another word. The wheels in my head were turning, thinking myself into a rut until finally sleep claimed me.

~

WHEN I WOKE AGAIN, it was to sunlight trying to push its way past the blinds and the sensation of a light teasing touch *there*.

I jumped, kicking out and my legs were trapped, and spread wide with strong arms around my thighs, Radar looking up at me from between them.

I gasped and he asked, "Are you alright?"

I looked this way and that and he shook his head. "Just you and me, babe."

I swallowed hard and not trusting my voice, I nodded and he gave me a nod back before licking me from opening to clit.

I stifled a gasp and let my head fall back to the pillows.

He lapped at me gently and made this sort of animalistic growling sound that made my legs turn to jelly and my pussy quiver and clench just before he slid a finger inside.

"Oh, *God!*" I pressed a hand over my mouth, the other winding in the sheets at my hips.

He wound me up so beautifully, so patiently and so gently.

"I'm going to make you come so hard you aren't going to know what happened then I'm going to fuck you so sweetly you'll think you've died and gone to heaven," he promised and I gasped.

That was all the warning I was going to get apparently, because he pressed down between the hollows of my pelvis and quested upward with the pad of his finger and his lips closed over my clit all at once. I cried out and arched beneath him my hand leaving my mouth to tangle in his hair as my hips thrust, pressing myself against his tongue – silently begging for all of that and more.

He catapulted me into the stars faster than I could comprehend this time until all I could do was howl with pleasure, body going as taut as a bowstring and quivering with the twang of the release as he shot me heavenward. I hung in that perfect moment where the seconds slowed, stretching to five times their length before I crashed back to earth and the safety of his arms.

I lay there, panting, nerveless, electrical impulses still running their circuit throughout my body while he slowly and lovingly climbed my body with a self-satisfied smirk painting his full lips.

He slipped inside me and I gasped, my arms twining around him as though I were a flowering vine and he, my sun.

"So beautiful," he murmured, stroking my hair back from my face, rolling his hips forward, his cock gliding through my wetness, stirring me to life, a subtle blush of pleasure radiating out from my core.

So slow, so gentle, so sweet, he made love to me on the bed I used to share with my husband and I got a sort of malicious vindication out of that.

As though I was taking something back that I hadn't even recognized had been stolen from me.

"Hmm," he hummed out in a mixture of pride and pleasure himself and closed his eyes, his head turning as he rolled his hips, his lips quirking, smiling subtly as though my body made a music a pleasing sound that only he could hear.

I clung to him, shivering with desire and let him slowly pull me from the exquisite agony he'd wrought with his mouth until I felt like less of a beautiful disaster beneath him and more a cohesive, lovely being.

I gazed into his eyes from inches away and felt such a wellspring of emotion within me, each tumbling in a kaleidoscope of color and brightness on the inside of my skull that I couldn't tell where one left off and another began. The jagged pieces of what I'd been still free falling, like raindrops from the sky, refracting light but if you looked hard enough through the downpour, you could see… you could still see a glimpse of what lay beyond and I wanted that.

I wanted what lay beyond this nightmare I'd been living in with such a *fire*… and here Radar was, a light in the darkness, offering me a way. Offering to guide me home.

I wrapped my legs around him, the way we moved pure poetry, and I let him show me through touch, through breath, through guiding hand that *yes,* there was a future for me and *no,* it didn't always have to involve pain.

∽

WE SHOWERED TOGETHER, and he stripped the sheets from the bed so I could wash them. Then he went through all of my things, looking through what hung in my closet and selected a dress.

"I get back, we're donating all his shit to Good Will. I'll have Collier take the truck in the driveway—"

"That's Rodney's truck, my car is the Kia," I said.

Radar just looked at me, an eyebrow raised and I fell silent.

"As far as I'm concerned, all the shit in this house is yours and where he's at, what's he going to do with it?" he demanded.

I shrugged and clutched my towel around me. "I don't know, his brother was supposed to come from Iowa to deal with it but he hasn't."

Radar gave a nod.

"We'll figure it out," he said and selected a long tank dress, white with orange hombre creeping up the skirt into yellow and I smiled and nodded.

"Good girl," he murmured and came to me, kissing me soundly and pressing the material into my hands.

"Get dressed and meet us downstairs?" He phrased it as a gentle question and I nodded.

"Okay," he murmured, and he padded out of my bedroom, towel slung low on his hips and I took a deep shuddering breath, throwing the dress on over my head and sighing it out in a measured even exhale.

I gathered the sheets from the bed, bundling them up and taking them with me stopping in the laundry room to get them started. I heard the low rumble of La Croix's voice and then Radar's. I couldn't make out what they were saying, but to my surprise… I wasn't concerned.

I bit my lips together as I turned the dial and pressed the final button to start the wash and then stepped out and into the short hall to the kitchen.

"Mornin' Chere," Collier greeted and then said, "Hope you don't mind me and La Croix here takin' the liberty and makin' the coffee."

I shook my head. "No, not at all. Is there any left?"

"Yeah," Atlas said and pulled down a mug while Radar told him, "Two creams, two sugars."

I almost shivered at the determination in Radar's eyes as he watched me and I went over to him, hugging him. He hugged me back and asked, "What was that for?"

"I needed it," I murmured, and he nodded, his smile softening the hard look he'd worn.

"Here you go, babe," Atlas said, and I jumped slightly and turned. He held out my coffee. I took it and drank.

"Thank you," I said after the first big swallow.

"Welcome."

"So, um, what's the plan?" I asked all of them nervously.

"First up, I'm fucking off in that badass truck to find some boxes," Collier said and twirled Rodney's key fob on its ring around his index finger.

"We've got some people to meet," Radar said. "So, you stay here with La Croix, and we'll get to it."

"Alright," I murmured, nodding and he came to me, hands on my waist, and kissed me soundly.

I hated watching the trio of them walk out of my house. I watched Radar and Atlas pause at their bikes parked in my back yard and exchange some words with Collier who opened up the side gate and went out.

A moment later I jumped as the bikes started up and in a faint echo, I heard my ex-husband's truck start in the driveway.

I sighed and turned to La Croix, who fixed me with a surprisingly tranquil, yet extremely unnerving stare with his blacked-out eyes.

"Breakfast?" I asked meekly and he just gave a nod. I forced a bit of a smile and sighed.

"Let's see what I have," I murmured.

23

*R*adar...

 We made the meetup first. Pulling in at the burger joint, which was a pretty busy parking lot – I had to say.

"Shit, this ain't good," Atlas muttered when we shut off the bikes.

"Too many fuckin' citizens," I agreed.

"Think we been set up?" he asked.

"I don't know," I said. "Doesn't feel like it. Maybe they're just checking us out?"

Atlas nodded judiciously.

"Paranoid types," he mused. "Plausible. I don't know how these big multi-national crews work. That ain't our jam – but I was under the impression when the national charter president told your local chapter's ass to jump, they're supposed to ask 'how high?' you know?"

"Fucked if I know," I said with a shrug. "Feels a tad disrespectful, otherwise."

"Well, I don't know about you, but I'm hungry…" he said, and I nodded.

"All I've had this morning was a half a cup a coffee and Justice," I said, and Atlas laughed.

"I'll get us some food," he said and jogged over to get in line.

The place was one of those old-school burger drive-in joints where you parked, waited in line and got your shit at the window and went back to your car. To be honest, it reminded me of the concession stand at the old-school drive-in movie theaters. I hadn't been to one of those joints since I was a kid back in the '80s. I wondered if they even still existed outside the spartan dying pockets of Americana...

Like Fairs. There wasn't any sort of old-school pop-up fairs anymore either. I mean, there were – but not in Florida or around Ft. Royal, anyway. Why when Universal, and the House of Mouse were right up the Interstate?

My trip down memory lane for nostalgia's sake was interrupted by the roar of pipes. I scanned the roadway and spotted the trio of black and red bikes with dudes similarly kitted out like me and Atlas piloting them to the corner of the lot our bikes occupied.

Atlas walked my way with a couple burgers in one hand and a couple drinks in the other and when he reached me handed me over my food while the dudes from the San Antonio chapter of the Sacred Hearts backed their bikes in.

I took a bite of the burger while I leaned my butt on my bike as the trio dismounted theirs. My eyebrows went up in surprise. Shit was fuckin' good, no wonder it was crowded.

"Good shit, huh?" the tallest of the three asked. He was an older guy by the liberal silver in his beard. He took off his mirrored aviators and crow's feet fanned out from the corners of his eyes as he smiled. He was ruggedly tan – likely a full time rider – and I was pretty sure I'd seen him before at a Lake Run – but I couldn't be sure and didn't want to presume.

"Real fuckin' good," I agreed, guarded. His smile grew and he reached out a hand.

"Name's Dominion. Boys call me Dom for short. You Atlas or Radar?" he asked. I wiped my hand on my jeans before shaking his.

"Radar," I declared and I gave a respectful nod.

Dominion was the President of the San Antonio chapter. Interesting that he'd come himself.

"This here is Raptor, and that's Washout," he said, jerking his head back over first his right and left shoulders.

Raptor was a taller, but no less compactly built dude like me while Washout was a little leaner but still pretty muscled.

"Nice to meet you guys," I said, giving each a nod of respect. "Like I said, I'm Radar and this here is my partner Atlas."

Both of them gave a chin lift in almost unison and I tried not to snort and laugh.

"So, the big dawgs called me up and said y'all needed a buco big bucks kind of favor," Dominion declared and I was immediately on guard but didn't do *anything* to show it.

"I wanted to come take your measure before we did anything on a kind you're asking my boys inside to potentially pile on a fuck ton of time to a pair of already long sentences." He sniffed. "I take care of my own before anything... so what's the deal? From the horse's mouth if you like." He sat down on his bike and I looked around.

"Ain't nobody here paying our talk any mind," Washout said and I nodded slowly.

"I have a woman," I said. "And her piece of shit ex-husband tried to kill her."

Dominion raised an eyebrow. "I'm going to need more than that."

I chewed another bite of burger and said, "This is a long story. You sure you don't want a drink?" I asked.

He looked thoughtful a minute and said, "Washout."

"Coke?" Washout asked.

"If you please."

Washout nodded and went and got in line. Atlas passed him twenty bucks as he went to go past him.

"On us," Atlas declared.

"Thank you kindly," Dominion said and like me, leaned on his bike.

I took it from the top, the full meal deal as it were – sparing no bit of grit and no ugly detail. He pursed his lips and nodded along, listening carefully, making the odd noise to indicate he was following, that he was still listening, and that he was digesting everything a bite at a time.

His face gave nothing away and finally he said, "Seems to me you might like to make a visit to Huntsville with us and make a few decisions before this justice gets served."

I cocked my head. "What decisions are those?" I asked not precisely following.

Raptor grinned and said, "Whether you just want this motherfucker to fall down some stairs and die, or whether you want him to go through hell first."

"What kind of hell?" Atlas asked, his wolfish grin matching Raptor's.

"Same kind of hell he put your lady through," Washout declared, pushing a pebble across the blacktop of the parking lot with the toe of his boot.

"How far is Huntsville from here and when are visiting hours?" I asked.

"About three hours and tomorrow as a matter of fact," Dom said, his eyes sparkling cold in the punishing heat of the day.

"Stellar, tonight plus three hours should be plenty of time for you to make up your mind," Atlas said.

"Excellent! Meet back here at six a.m., I'll have Raptor, Washout, and one of my other fellas take you on down."

I nodded and held out my hand, Dom clasped forearms with me and I gave a shrewd nod. "I thank you kindly for opening my mind up to the sheer number of possibilities I said."

He nodded and said, "After what you told me, we're more than happy to help, partner."

I grinned and soon after, we parted ways.

Atlas looked over and said, "Back to the house?"

I nodded.

"You know, I'd sure like to see the Alamo while we're here. Think your lady would be up for getting out of the house?" Atlas asked.

I smiled and nodded. "Wonder if Collier and LaCroix have any interest," I said.

"Only one way to fucking find out." Atlas fired up his bike and I followed suit. It was a short ride back to my woman's house and I was grateful for that. I didn't want to be without her for long if I could help it.

When we made it back, we jumped the curb and pulled into her back yard just as Collier was finishing up backing her wasband's truck into the driveway.

"Hey, that didn't take long," Collier called in greeting as we came out around front, closing up the gate in the fence to the back.

We didn't want to leave the bikes out front for anybody to fuck with and with the garage full, this had been the next best thing. That, and if anybody were thinking about pulling some shit – we wanted some element of surprise.

"Yeah, we gotta go back out tomorrow for this – last ride sort of a thing," Atlas told him. "We were wondering if y'all had any interest in doing a little sightseeing while you were here. Thinking about taking a trip out to the Alamo here in town get Radar's little woman out of the house."

Collier looked thoughtful. "Let's see what La Croix thinks. I know I'd like to see it. I've always wanted to see shit like that, the OK corral, all that old-school cowboy shit." He grinned and if I had to bet, he'd played the Marshall or the Sheriff or whatever to a bunch of cowboys. It was a cute thought. It sure as fuck beat all the princess bullshit I'd had to put up with when it'd come to my girls. Not that I'd honestly minded it too much. The tea parties had been fun, but fuck if being Prince Charming hadn't fucked with my head a little.

Being an adult playing kid's games had its moments, you know?

Inside, we found La Croix on the couch watching some fuckin' soap opera on television. while Jussy was perched on her desk chair, working some digital magic on her computer screen with that drawing tablet of hers. I honestly didn't know how she did it. I barely had the hand-eye coordination to play GTA on the console.

"Hey," she said with a false brightness, worry causing a tightening around her mouth and eyes.

"Hey," I said with brightness and went to her, bending to kiss her.

"How… how did things go?" she asked, and I smiled and shook my head. She nodded and I caressed her beautiful cheek, her skin smooth under the rough pad of my thumb.

Atlas disappeared, likely to take a piss or something, and Collier was bent over the back of the couch pitching the whole idea of sightseeing to La Croix who had those creepy tattooed eyes of his turned in mine and Jussy's direction. It was some kind of fucking crazy, the dudes who tattooed their sclera. Even fucking crazier they did it in prison with fucking pen ink or whatever other shit they could source. I didn't know La Croix's story on the sclera tats – he hadn't had them a few years back when I'd last seen him. Back when we'd rescued Faith. I'd missed him when the Voodoo Bastards had come to Ft. Royal for spring break last year and I'd missed out going to NOLA for some fun the year before that. Atlas and I both had… bounties that'd needed to be done took precedent. One because he was a *chi-mo* piece of shit. The other because *damn* – that was a lot of money.

"Atlas wants to see the Alamo," I told my girl in a hushed tone. "Seems to me, you could stand to get out of the house… wanna play tour guide for us and take us?" I asked.

She smiled up at me faintly and raised her eyebrows.

"You do know that it's like *smack* in the middle of downtown San Antonio, right?"

"No shit?" I asked.

"Mm-hm, not kidding. I almost couldn't believe it myself when I saw it the first time. It's also tiny."

"Yeah?"

"Yep, but if you guys want to go, I'd be happy to take you – still you want to see something we should take the Mission Road."

"We can do that, too."

She shook her head. "Maybe tomorrow or the next day, but it's getting on toward the afternoon and by the time we got out of the Alamo, the Missions would be closing. Besides, the Alamo is right there on the Riverwalk, might as well get dinner along it – make the most of the crazy amount for parking."

I nodded slowly and said, "Sounds good. Want to do me a favor and dress to ride while we help Collier get these boxes in here?"

She bit her lips together and nodded.

"You know, I sort of pictured doing these sorts of things just you and me," she murmured for my ears only and she sounded disappointed. I chuckled and kissed her softly, letting it intensify slowly until I had managed to kiss her breathless.

"Plenty of time for that later," I said, dropping my voice into a lower register. "That's a promise."

She shuddered against my palm which was at the side of her throat as my thumb caressed her pulse point. I smiled, and I know it held an edge of wickedness, but she was so sweet in her natural submissiveness and fuck that was a turn on.

"Go on," I ordered gently, letting my voice be a velvet caress against her ear as I whispered into it. "Dress to ride," I reminded her before releasing her and standing.

She nodded mutely and got up, going for the stairs and looking back as though trying to figure something out. I smiled and watched her go, Atlas coming out of the little water closet down here.

"She game?" he asked, looking after her.

"She's game," I said and looked back to Collier and La Croix.

"Big guy's game, too. Looks like we all in," Collier said.

"Good deal," I answered.

JUSTICE WASN'T KIDDING when she said the Alamo was *smack dab* in the middle of downtown. Likewise, she wasn't kidding when she said it was small. I think the four of us dudes had our minds fucking blown by it just a little. We took pictures at the monument, bought our tickets, and went around all the living history exhibits around the outside before making our way in.

I took as many pictures as I could of Justice despite her protests and held her tight for every selfie. Atlas had her in stitches with his photo bombing and we had quite a few shots on my phone with my bro hugging her tight and even the both of us kissing each of her cheeks while she laughed, eyes scrunched, smile wide and worth a thousand bucks.

Fuck, I was enjoying the fall as I plummeted deeply in love with her.

24

*J*ustice...

We went through the giftshop and I wanted to remember today so badly, I bought myself a little miniature of the Alamo to sit on my desk. Except when I went to pay for it, Radar wouldn't hear of it, telling me to put my money away as he bought a tee shirt and a book for himself and a tank top for each of his girls.

Likewise, Atlas, Collier, and La Croix made purchases of their own and then it was to the Riverwalk.

The afternoon had drug on toward an early evening as the summer waned into fall; and it was already growing dark. The majority of us; Collier, La Croix, and myself, were starving and Collier made some noises about some good Tex Mex; I happened to know of a bar up ahead but only by virtue of its reputation for good Tex Mex and cold beer. How did I know? It was all my ex-husband could enthusiastically talk about after going to it with a bunch of his Army buddies one Friday night with broken promises that he would just *have to take me* at the first opportunity, which of course never came.

"Would you like to be inside or out on the patio?" the hostess asked and a silence fell on us and when I looked up, four sets of eyes were on me.

"Oh! Um… um… patio?" I squeaked.

"Sure thing! Right this way." The bubbly hostess plucked five menus and led us through the bar that was crowded, dark, and blaring country rock music and back out into the heat and the bright sun.

The tables out here were shaded by square umbrellas. Each one a solid color in red, orange, yellow, or blue and canted on their poles to face and block the worst of the direct sun. We were seated at a table next to the railing, the patio overlooking the Riverwalk and the river below.

It wasn't too bad in the shade, near the water like this. A stiff breeze blew carrying the faint whiff of chlorine from some of the nearby decorative fountains, and the smells from the bar's kitchen.

We started with drinks, the boys getting beers and myself? I got something off the cocktail menu that was on happy hour special that was both fruity and girly sounding which is exactly how I liked my drinks.

"What do you think?" Atlas said after lowering his beer bottle from his lips. "Get after that garage and packing some of that shit up when we get back to the house?"

"We might can do that." Collier nodded in agreement.

Radar squeezed the top of my thigh under the table and I glanced at him and smiled.

"You guys don't have to do that," I said, taking a deep breath and letting it out slowly. "I suppose I should try his brother Thomas one more time." I shook my head. "I know he's busy, but it's been over a year."

"Fuck him," La Croix rumbled.

"I'm inclined to agree, babe. If Tommy boy ain't brought his ass down to sort his brother's shit by now, it's yours."

"No, I know, I mean I don't know the legality of any of it," I said, shaking my head.

Atlas barked a laugh and I blinked.

"What's in his last will?" Collier inquired coolly.

"I – I don't know. I mean, I don't know if he changed it or anything. I mean, I don't honestly know what to do about any of it. I've just been trying to survive paycheck to paycheck, you know?"

"Yeah, well those days are fast approaching an end," Radar said with certainty. "That is," he backtracked, "if you've thought any about my offer."

I looked to him and searched his eyes and finally, I nodded.

"I hate it here," I said. "I don't really feel like I can start my life over while I'm stuck in that house, you know?"

"Wait, you're still living in the house where it happened?" Collier asked. He gave a low whistle. "You got a big brass pair, don't 'cha, darlin'?"

I blinked, "I mean, not really," I said. "Where else was I supposed to go?"

"What do you mean?" Atlas asked.

"I mean, I have no rental history. Everything was always in Rodney's name… my name is on the house, sure, but half of it is still his and I didn't know anything about the whole process of buying the house it was just 'get me these documents' and 'sign those documents' he handled everything for the most part. I was just in charge of packing and unpacking. Choosing furniture and making sure my money was being automatically deposited into our bank account for bills and such. He kept track of every purchase and told me how much I was allowed to spend where."

"Jesus, control freak much?" Radar muttered.

I nodded.

"He said he didn't want me to screw it up."

"What a fucking cock goblin," Collier muttered, and I snorted.

"Well, if he wasn't before prison he sure as fuck is now," Atlas declared, and I know it was awful of me but I had to laugh. I just had to. Radar raised his bottle and everyone else raised theirs and me my glass and we sort of toasted that one.

"Y'all going out there tomorrow?" Collier asked, and Radar and Atlas exchanged a look.

"Wait, are you?" I asked, looking from one to the other of them.

Both of them sort of clammed up and Collier said, "My apologies, gentlemen," before he turned to me and said, "I spoke out of turn."

"That's not for you to know, baby," Radar said gently and massaged the top of my thigh.

The problem was, that I wanted to know... I wanted to know very badly but looking at the men from the other club sitting opposite me, Radar, and Atlas I decided that discretion was the better part of valor and muttered complacently, "I understand."

Radar hooked a hand behind my head and pulled my temple to his lips and kissed me firmly muttering, *"Good girl,"* in my ear and *damnit*, why did that have such an effect on me?

I felt my breath catch as I was suffused with a tingly warm glow that made me feel like I was on cloud nine and the *calm* that settled over me. The sense of safety and appreciation, the *wonder* that flitted through my system... there wasn't anything like it. It was as though pleasing him had become my new favorite thing and it was quickly turning into an addiction. As in I was willing to do just about anything to make him utter those two little words to me.

I mean, they seemed to have more of an effect, more of a weight, a promise, a solemn fucking vow to them than any of the times Rodney or anyone else uttered the words '*I love you*' at me.

It was strange, it was foreign, and it drove me so *crazy*. Like I wanted to pick it apart and see why it ticked, but I certainly didn't want to in front of such a big audience and I was so... so... suddenly frustrated at having to share my time with Atlas.

I mean, I just wanted it to be *us* as in me and him and nobody else. Not his daughters, which I know was selfish and rude, and not Atlas or any other member of his club or the Voodoo Bastards.

I looked over at him and met his eyes and he smiled, pressing with his thumb and fingers to either side of my spine, massaging my neck until tingles swept up my scalp and I sighed, letting go of some of the tension in my posture.

"You good?" Atlas asked me.

I nodded faintly.

"That just feels so good," I answered.

"Yeah, she's all kinds of tight," Radar said with a wink which immediately made me blush a furious pink which made the four men at the table burst into laughter.

"You're the worst," I grumbled which just made them laugh harder until I couldn't fight off the smile it infected me with.

"You're so wonderful," Radar said, and I glowed from that praise as the waitress returned to take our order.

≈

"YOU, OKAY?" Radar slipped up behind me in my kitchen and put a hand to my lower back, a gentle and supportive touch. I loved how he stepped into my, how he made it so the query was just for my ears and how the tension just drained out of me momentarily giving me a bit of relief from the knotting along my spine.

"I'm okay," I whispered, shaking the aluminum foil skillet thing over the burner. I was making popcorn, the rest of the boys in the living room, as we were all settling in to watch the movie *The Alamo* on whatever streaming service, we could bring it up on and rent it from on my big living room smart television.

"You sure?" he asked and he gave me a look like he didn't believe me. I smiled and nodded.

"I'm sure," I murmured. "I'm just not used to being around this many people for this amount of time. I like my solitude and wish it was just me and you."

He smiled then and asked me, "Don't I count as people, too?"

I looked at him and felt my lips twitch as I fought not to smile and said, "No. You don't count as 'people.' You're something different. I don't know how to explain it."

He touched the side of my face and ran his thumb back and forth over my cheek.

"I think I get it," he said, nodding. "And I promise. I promise to get you some alone time just me and you and soon."

I nodded.

"Guess Collier and La Croix are staying another night?" I asked.

He nodded.

"Just want to make sure you're covered until the rest of my club can get here."

I blinked.

"Uh, do what now?" I asked.

"Yo! How's it coming?" Atlas called from the living room and I rolled my eyes.

"It's not like microwave popcorn!" I called back. "It's not done in three minutes!"

"Should have just let me get the popcorn in the bag," he groused.

"You flavorless heathen!" I cried. "Popcorn always tastes better from the stove!"

"There's no difference that I can tell." Collier sided with Atlas and I looked at Radar.

"You see? Exhausting," I said and rolled my eyes.

He laughed and called back into the living room. "Motherfuckers! My woman's from corn country! She ought to know!"

The pan gave its first pop and I jumped with excitement and called out, "Ooo! Here it goes, won't be long now."

Radar winked at me and I felt lighter than air.

"Where's our fresh beer?" Atlas called and Radar called back, "Alright, alright! Hold your fuckin' horses."

I smiled, over abundance of peopling and drained reserves aside – I was enjoying this and everyone's company immensely.

Some of those reserves came back as we all settled in and started the movie. Radar had me fetched up against him and Atlas pulled my legs up into his lap and settled in with us. La Croix was on Atlas's other side and Collier took up the recliner. I turned into a puddle of goo when Atlas began to rub my feet and Atlas the back of my head and neck.

If I were a cat I would purr, but pretty quickly it would become all I could do just to stay awake. The relaxation was real and I felt every inch the spoiled princess.

The movie was engrossing, I mean, I'd lived here for a number of years and I'd even been to the Alamo a few times now. Once with my parents, once with Rodney's parents, and now with the men surrounding me in my living room. I mean, I knew the story, the history, and how it ended but the movie? I don't know what it was about movies and films. Maybe it was the actors, maybe it was the stirring music that moved my soul but this one? This movie got me right in the feels.

I wept, La Croix reaching in front of him to the box of tissues on the coffee table and passing them wordlessly over Atlas to me. I laughed the sound breaking on a bubbling little sob and pulled some.

"Sorry, I'm ridiculous, I know," I said, and the guys chuckled but made no comment.

"Okay, Beautiful," Atlas said as the credits began to roll. He patted my ankles twice and I shifted my feet off of him so he could get up.

"Yo, bud. You going up?" Radar asked.

"Uh, yeah. We got an early ride tomorrow," he seemed to remind Radar.

"That we do, wanna do me a solid?"

"What's that?"

"Get a bath started for me and my woman. We'll be up in a sec but she needs some alone time and both of us need to relax some for sleep."

"Sure, bro. No problem."

I looked from Atlas to Radar and back to Atlas dumbfounded and like I was some spectator at a tennis match.

"Thank you, my man," Radar declared.

"You guys good for one more night?" he asked La Croix and Collier.

"Fuck yeah, man. We do need to fuck off by tomorrow or early the day after tomorrow, though. Sick leave from the day jobs gonna run out."

"What the fuck do you guys even do?" Radar asked. "I don't think I ever asked you."

"If I told you, I'd have to kill you," La Croix rumbled and Collier laughed.

"We work the docks, ain't nothin' glamorous about it."

I stared at La Croix... mystified. He was always so serious and only ever really talked to me. Getting by with as few words as possible with even Collier who he'd come with so they had to be, I don't know if *friends* was quite the right word but *something*... I mean, I don't think it completely ended with them just being a part of the same club, that that was as far as things went.

Truthfully, the big, scary, tattooed man was a conundrum but by the same token he was very sweet. I didn't think that he was always that way, though. I mean his default was scary for a reason...

"Come on, baby," Radar murmured and his voice soothed the soul.

I was a bit of a turtle on her back at this angle and La Croix reached out a tattooed hand. I grasped it and leveraged myself up into more of a sitting position.

"Thanks," I murmured and he gave me a nod but let go my hand quickly.

Radar helped me to my feet and towed me gently upstairs with a light grasp on my fingertips.

I could hear the rush of bathwater as we entered the bedroom. Atlas was sitting up in bed already, scanning his phone and scrolling.

"Thanks man," Radar said again, and Atlas looked up and smiled at us both.

"You try to relax," he ordered me mock-sternly and I laughed a little. He was growing on me. In the beginning he was a sort of strong personality and his interest a little... intense. To the point that it'd tripped a few wires in my brain and made me want to shy away more – not less. But he'd sort of evened out and the more time I spent around him I realized he was just a bit of an acquired taste at least where I was concerned but it was a taste that I was quite growing to enjoy. The possibilities whispering seductively in the back of my mind.

One of the things I'd liked about this house when Rodney had chosen it for its big and well laid out garage was the bathtub up here. One of those big triangular soaking tubs easily big enough to fit two or three people.

Of course, I rarely got to use it. Any time I did Rodney would immediately start freaking out about the water bill and I learned fast not to argue with him about it. He would just suddenly *explode* with anger and hit the wall or a door and I'd jump and be so afraid that I would be next until... until I didn't have to worry about it becoming a reality when it did. Then I had a whole new host of things to worry about. Like if my husband who would cry and proclaim that he loved me, would kill me the next time he lost his temper.

Eventually, I didn't have to worry about that becoming a reality either, because it did.

God, I was just lucky to be alive.

"Hey." I shuddered as though coming awake and tore my eyes from the filling tub to fix on Radar's worried face.

"I'm sorry what?" I asked.

"I asked if you had anything you liked to put in it, like Epsom salts or baking soda."

"Oh! Yeah, under the sink." I felt myself color. "I'm so sorry."

"Don't be," he murmured. "And don't think you owe me any sort of explanation, either. You don't."

I bit my bottom lip and said, "Okay, thank you."

He shook his head and said, "Get undressed, and get in the bath, baby."

I nodded and he got under the sink and started looking through containers.

"Oh!" I got into the tub, my tenderized feet loving the warmth of the water which was just perfect. Neither too hot nor too cold. "Has he done this before for you?" I asked, laughing slightly.

"What? No, not for a woman, but he helped me with the girls from time to time when they were little."

"That would explain why he's a pro," I said with a smile and Radar grinned. He came back and dumped a liberal amount of baking soda and Epsom salts into the bat and I swished the water around with my feet to help dissolve them.

I found my corner of the tub that I was always most comfortable in, with the jets that hit near enough that trouble spot along my spine but didn't quite reach it enough to be entirely satisfying and watched Radar disrobe. God, he was hot.

He got in with me and came close, and I moved, obliging him my corner so that I could settle back in the curve of his arms.

"How you doing baby?" he asked softly once we'd settled.

"I'm alright," I answered quietly.

"Don't lie to me," he said gently and I looked up at him from where I had scooted down to lounge against his chest. He had me fixed with an intense gaze that bored into me and I swallowed hard, my throat tightening with a fear response and he shook his head.

"Hey, none of that now. You have absolutely no reason to ever be afraid of me," he said, smoothing hands over my arms and massaging my shoulders. I turned my head forward and closed my eyes.

"I'm sorry," I murmured.

"No, I should be the one that's sorry. I said that without thinking but the point still stands you don't ever have to lie to me or tell me what you think I want to hear versus the truth. Nothing about these last few days have been any kind of normal or anything short of terrifying for you, really."

"It's like I was just starting to get my life organized on this tray and someone has come in, grabbed it, and tossed everything in the air and I am waiting to see what else is going to hit the ground and break," I rushed out. "I feel like I'm here but at the same time I feel like I'm a million miles away and I'm scared but I'm not, and I'm grateful but afraid and it's all so contradictory and confusing and I know I am disassociating to a degree because my therapist told me I have a habit of doing that and that there was nothing wrong with me for it happening but I hate it and I just want far away from here but at the same time… and this is nothing against you at all, please, believe me – I'm almost scared I am trading one cage for another, if that makes sense?"

I rushed the words out, afraid to speak them to the air but trying to break the cycle so-to-speak and believe Radar at his word. That he indeed meant what he said…

He was quiet for a long time and I looked up at him and he was looking down at me, thoughtfully, the wheels in his head visibly turning just behind his eyes. He crooked a smile and said, "That was a lot to take in, I'm thinking... I just want what's best for you. For you to feel safe, you know that right?"

I nodded and he kissed my temple, hands sliding down my arms to curve over the backs of mine, his fingers taking up the spaces between my own.

"I've made offers," he said finally after a long ensuing silence. "But I've failed in that I've not asked what you want. I'm sorry for that."

I bowed my head and nodded, suddenly overwhelmed with an unnamed emotion and I wasn't quite sure why at first.

"It matters, you know," he said, dragging one of my hands up out of the water. "What you want." He put a kiss against my fingertips.

"I want to move away from here but I don't know how," I said.

"We can figure that out, together," he suggested. "I've got help a plenty that's only a phone call away."

I nodded, "I already said yes," I reminded him and he chuckled.

"I know, but this is also a real big thing. You're allowed to change your mind."

I shook my head, "I don't want to," I said. "I want away from here and a chance to really start my life. I can't even say I would be starting over," I said with a harsh sigh. "Feels like I never really started it in the first place. Like I've been in limbo all this time."

"Well, I think we both aim to change that," he said. "Not just you, but me and my life circumstances too. I mean, what's the point of living a life as great as mine without having someone to share it with?" he asked with a chuckle.

I had to smile then and cuddled back into him more thoroughly when I agreed, "You do have a pretty fantastic life."

"It was pretty great before," he said and kissed my temple. "Now it's fantastic."

I chuckled myself, and felt like I was more grounded, just a little more centered from the little talk. Plans were both made and being made and I just needed to be patient. The men surrounding me right now had more than proven that I was safe. I just needed to believe in them and myself.

~

"BRING IT ON UP HERE, BABY," Atlas said, setting his phone aside when I finally exited the bathroom. Radar was right behind me and I crawled up onto the bed still wrapped in my towel. "Lay on your stomach," he ordered and I blinked, and blurted out, "Why?"

"Because I'm not done with you yet, that's why," he said with a wink.

I laid on my stomach in the middle of the bed and he whisked my towel away, grabbing a bottle of lotion of the nightstand on his side and getting out from under the covers. He straddled the backs of my thighs and I flushed a bright red, realizing that he was nude.

"Relax, baby," Radar declared and I felt some of the tension ease.

The cap on the lotion tube clacked and cold hit my back between my shoulder blades.

"Cold!" I cried, pushing myself up, but then Atlas's hands landed on my back and pressed and I flattened out for him groaning.

Oh, that felt so good...

He sucked in a breath over me through his teeth and said, "Damn, girl. How do you live like this?"

"Like what?" I asked, melting beneath his touch.

"So tight and all full of knots!"

I shrugged slightly and said, "I don't know?"

Radar got into bed beside us and dropped the blankets over his lap and I flushed realizing that all three of us were nude and likely to stay that way and I just was *not* raised that way!

Except... except looking back on how I *was* raised... huh. The realization started my gears to turning as I groaned in a sort of sublime bliss as Atlas worked the soreness from my upper back, pinching and making circles to either side of the back of my neck.

"Oh, God," I said faintly and Radar took my hand in his and laid them in his lap. He started to work at massaging my writing and drawing hand and if my eyes weren't already closed, I could swear they'd like to roll into the back of my head.

I very nearly plummeted into relaxation, and its kissing cousin sleep caressed my face.

"There you go," Atlas crooned and it was as though I'd been given permission.

"Rest, baby," Radar murmured. "We've got you."

It was the last thing I coherently remembered, even though I do remember the light drone of their low voices as they talked to one another over the rhythmic press and sweeping motions of Atlas's hands against my back. Warm and sweet, firm but gentle…

I felt so utterly spoiled and blissfully let it happen. Who was I to argue?

25

*R*adar…

"She is *out*," I murmured with a chuckle and Atlas smiled. He'd always been the better of the both of us when it came to rubbing a woman down. He just knew the spots and had the patience. Me, not so much. I mean, I would give it a solid go if asked, but my buddy just had the *magic hands*. He also had about as big a raging hard-on as I did at the moment.

"You have no idea how much I want to shove a couple pillows under her hips so I could just slide right in," he said with a grunt.

"You have no idea how much I would like to watch that," I confessed. I loved it. Watching my woman be pleasured by my best friend. There was just something so fucking erotic about that. Any other guy I don't think it'd do it for me but I could trust Atlas. That he wouldn't go behind my back. We weren't like that. The thought of anyone else fucking my woman made me more than a little jealous. Hell, the thought of Atlas fucking my woman without me in the room made me something a little more than jealous but again, I didn't have to worry about that. Me and Atlas had discussed the rules about shared dalliances years ago. The only reason he was so hard up now was because he'd been going through quite the dry spell.

He sighed breaking into my thoughts and asked, "You ever think she might?"

"What? Be down?" I asked.

"Yeah."

I shrugged and told him the truth.

"I don't know, but I do know we've probably been just a little heavy handed," I said.

"She say something?" he asked.

"Doesn't have to, just look at her face when you hit on her – you can read her like a book. She's not exactly comfortable with the idea but the curiosity is there."

"Hmm, her damn confidence needs some work," he said.

I nodded. "For sure."

"Fuck, man. I'm so hard up even your ass is starting to look good," he said and I laughed. We were both straight, we knew that about each other – there was no curiosity there although there was that one time the chick that we were fucking asked us to kiss each other and for her satisfaction we'd obliged her. Afterward, we'd discussed it and both agreed – we were never fuckin' doing that again!

We were the type we'd usually try anything twice but that one we both were sure we could leave at once and once only.

"You get freaky with her yet?" he asked and I knew what he meant. He knew I had a thing for control and tying women to the bed.

I shook my head and told the truth, "With her history I want her to feel safer than she's ever been before bringing that up. I don't want to step on a landmine or trip some trigger," I said.

He nodded and pressed thumbs at the base of her spine and smoothed his hands up her long torso digging gently, working her lean muscles loose and just watching his hands glide over her lotion slicked skin was something sensual and fucking hot.

Jussy hummed out in bliss and I chuckled.

"You listening to us, baby?" I asked her but she didn't respond.

"Nah," Atlas declared. "I think she's out like you said. For real."

"Well, good." I kept absently working her hand and her wrist the delicate bones of her wrist lightly popping and crackling at the joint as

I worked the muscles loose. I flexed her wrist back and forth and nodded as it sort of glided at the joint easier than when I'd started.

"See, you're learning," Atlas teased.

"Should learn a thing or two watching you do this shit often enough," I said and he chuckled.

"She's loosening up," he said.

"Good, I want her putty in our hands tonight. She needs a strong good sleep and some deep relaxation.

"I hear that. I think you and I could both use the same," he said and I chuckled.

I watched her face as Atlas worked out every single knot in her back which was made much easier for him once she quit her guarding posture as she fell into sleep. After, I got up with him to slip the covers out from under her and to cover her up. We got back into bed to either side of her, turned out the bedside lamps and settled down to sleep ourselves.

I don't know about him, but I crashed hard, Justice's arm over me, the contact welcome.

I DROPPED into the seat on the other side of the glass and took up the phone. The white boy glaring at me on the other side like he was hard, or some shit picked up his and demanded, "Who're you?"

"I'm the guy that's making your ex-wife the happiest she's ever been." I said it with a slow, malicious spreading of my lips into probably the coldest smile I'd ever put on my face.

Dude was just about what I'd expected. Your all-American, light-haired blue-eyed washed-up high school football star. He stared at me all cold and I laughed a little.

"Look at you tryin' to be all hard," I said. "We gonna find out just how soft and gooey that center of yours is."

He scowled at me.

"Gonna be a little tough for you there, big guy," he said with a derisive sniff. "Me being in here and you out there and all."

I felt my smile grow both in size and level of nastiness. I leaned back and caught one of Dom's boy's eyes several windows up talking to his fella on the inside and without giving too much away he gave me a sidelong glance and an imperceptible chin lift.

"Oh, we'll see about that," I said. "As for Justice, she's gonna get some and your little Army school butt buddies? They try they're gonna have another think coming. You get me? You might want to call them off."

"Ain't gonna fuckin' happen," he said with venom and I winked at him.

"Your funeral, man. Theirs too if you don't. I *will* defend her."

"You tell that bitch she's gonna pay. Those boys are gonna make what I did to her look like amateur hour."

"Uh-huh," I said. "Yeah, right. Have a nice life, you fuckin' loser. What's left of it. You're gonna know first hand how she felt soon enough and the boys gonna do it to you? They're gonna enjoy every minute of putting your rape-o ass on notice."

I hung up the phone piece with a wink and got up. He punched the other side of the glass and one of the CO's barked at him. Of course I couldn't hear shit – but that was by design. As for if I was worried about them coming at me after this fuckwit died? Because he *was* gonna die. How fast or how slow all depended on him – I wasn't worried about getting got. I used a fake ass ID to get past the guards.

Romero Corazon had a clean record and was about to be dust in the fuckin' wind as soon as we were out of here. A personal touch on Data's part. I owed that fucker several beers for not having to watch what I said to this human embodiment of the herpes virus.

I left, and outside I went to Atlas and our bikes in the far reaches of the parking lot. He shifted on his booted feet. "I just want to get the fuck out of here and back into our colors," he said and I nodded. We'd gone slick-backed up to the prison. No identifying colors for either us or the SHMC boys. We weren't about leaving bread-crumbs.

"Me fuckin' either. You call my girl?" I asked.

"Yeah, she's doing okay. A little butt hurt she woke up without us there this morning," he said and he looked well pleased.

"What's that look for?" I asked.

"She said 'you guys' plural," he said and I rolled my eyes.

"You do know eventually you're gonna get to hit it," I said. "Just on her time when she's comfortable."

"Dude, I know!" he said. "Jesus Fuck, why you all acting like I'm brand fuckin' new to this arrangement."

I shook my head and smiled, "Not you, bro... me. Everything about Jussy is new for me. When you know, you know."

"Shit, fuck me, man. You only ever say that shit when it's *super* serious."

I nodded.

"She's not some passing flight of fancy, man. This isn't some project for me that I get her back on her feet or whatever, get bored, and move the fuck on. That ain't me. That's *never* been me."

"I know that, I just ain't never seen you move this fast and I've never had you get territorial with *me* over any female before except..."

I nodded. "My last ol' lady," I affirmed.

"I'm thinkin' I love the feel of your woman's soft skin and I don't mind rubbing her down, but for the first time, I feel like getting my dick involved is like, overstepping or gonna be counterproductive to our relationship and partnership in some way and I gotta say while I find that *weird*, it's not a *bad* weird."

I searched his face and nodded carefully.

"I appreciate that, man."

"Doesn't mean I'm going to quit flirting like a son of a bitch with her, though. And she *is* nice to snuggle with."

I grinned and laughed.

"The first is your favorite pastime and would be like denying you air or water so no – you flirt all you like. The second?" I sighed and nodded to myself more than anything, "Snuggle and cuddle away. I think she needs it from a lot more than just you and me. Make up for all that time she was touch starved when she was a kid and by that asshole in there."

I jerked a thumb in the direction of the prison.

"Fuck yeah," he said. "New parameters accepted, my dude." He held out a hand and I clapped mine in it and we bumped shoulders.

"You guys are fuckin' way too weird for me," Raptor declared from where he was sitting on his bike.

We both grinned at him.

Our friendship was tight. Pretty fuckin' unique and as wide open as they got. Let's hear it for being well-adjusted dudes. The rest of the male half of the species was missing out as far as we were concerned.

Still, I felt better for having had the talk with Atlas... because he was right. While there had been no jealousy watching him ease my lady into sleep, I *had* felt the prickling energy of jealousy at the thought of him sticking his dick inside her which was something I had not been prepared for. Maybe because she was such an anxiety muffin over the idea? I don't know. Still, even this talk felt kind of wrong.

Atlas caught my eye and gave me a chin lift.

"Talk to her when we get back," he said, picking up what I was putting down with my troubled look.

I nodded.

That was it. I may be naturally a sort of Dom-type but she'd been worked over so hard and was so sweetly fragile in her submissiveness that it felt wrong not hearing what she wanted. I couldn't take my instincts with her totally for granted like I'd been able to in the past with other women.

Shit.

It dawned on me that I'd been going about things all wrong in some regards with Justice and I owed her an apology. That I could be a big part of her stress – maybe bigger than even she realized. It was some food for thought on the ride back.

I checked my phone when I got back to her place before getting off my bike and had a slew of text messages from the boys back home. Since Justice had given me the go-ahead to get her out of here, since she was trusting me to be as good as my word on setting her up on the path to independence should she so chose to go that route, I'd contacted the boys to mobilize and get here to help me and Atlas bring my girl home.

There were a lot of questions, and a lot of congrats; some of which should have felt premature but since our talk outside the prison I felt things were fairly cemented into place so long as Jussy was really on board and wanted to stay with me.

Shit yeah, I was having some insecurity and some doubts now of my own.

The majority of which were dispelled with the smile that lit up her face when she laid eyes on me coming through the back slider.

"Hi!" she called, getting up from where she was curled on the floor in some leggings and, I think, one of my tees to wrap her arms around me and kiss me soundly.

"Hi," I said, smiling. "What're you doing?"

"Packing some things," she declared. "Things I want to keep."

"Good deal," I said. "Where's La Croix?"

"Dump run, we loaded some of that asshole's shit in the back of his truck to take somewhere. If a Good Will won't take it, it'll go to the garbage pit."

"Fuckin' awesome," I said and smiled big. "You guys have been busy."

I looked around at all the boxes and wrapping paper and shit.

"The idea of freedom is really growing on me," she said and the thoughts she was having slightly dulled her sparkle.

"Speaking of, you got a minute?" I asked.

"Yeah," she said, her smile growing with the way I looked at her.

"Y'all take five find some food or whatever," I said and led my girl to the stairs.

She followed my curiously, hanging back and dragging on my hand a bit in silent apprehension. When I closed the bedroom door behind us I turned and immediately told her, "It's nothing bad, I promise. I just owe you a big damn apology," I said.

"Apology? For what?" she asked, sinking down onto the edge of the bed.

"Atlas and I being a pair of randy fuckin' horn dogs making you uncomfortable," I said and cocked my head and raised my eyebrow when she was about to deny it.

She closed her mouth and smiled a little, cocking her head and finally she took a deep breath and let it out and told me the truth.

"I like Atlas well enough; the massage was lovely and I wasn't wholly uncomfortable with that but... but I just wasn't raised that way and with how awful and controlling Rodney was always accusing me of cheating and... well... it's sort of a programming and ingrained and while I like him, I don't really want to sleep with him and I'm sorry!" she rushed out and then closed her mouth and bit her lips together looking at me expectantly.

I smiled and shook my head in wonder and then nodded. "See, I thought so and that's why I owe you a big apology." I sat down next to her and we talked it out. I told her everything Atlas and I talked about in the parking lot of the prison then apologized some more that we'd even had those types of talks without her.

She drank it all in and looked thoughtful for a long time and finally said, "Is this what a healthier dynamic is like?"

I nodded slowly. "This is definitely what open communication is like," I said.

She nodded and said finally, "I'd like more of this, please."

I smiled and reached out and touched the side of her face and she tucked it closer against my hand. Yeah, she was touch starved and I would gladly spend all the time in the world that I could making her realize what a treasure she was.

"Come here," I murmured and she leaned in and kissed me. I kissed her back, but greedy fucker that I am, I wanted and needed more so I pulled her practically into my lap.

She came willingly and whispered against my mouth, "Thank you."

"For what?" I asked, slipping a hand beneath her tank top to touch her skin.

"For paying attention, for figuring out what I need sometimes before even I do, for *everything*," she said.

"I'm by no means perfect," I whispered against her lips. "But I try."

She grasped my face between her hands and deepened the kiss and there wasn't any way I was going to deny her. I pulled her down over the top of me and laid back, letting her at me. She hitched her long skirt up and straddled my waist and we made out for a while until my cock throbbed in my shorts and I could feel her heat even through the thick material of them.

"I'm going to rip those panties off and then you're going to sit on my face," I warned her in a growl, sliding my hands up her thighs under the light, fluttery skirt she wore. Moving them up along the smooth silky skin of her legs, giving her every opportunity to tell me to stop and protest but all she did was moan and give me this breathy little sigh of want.

"Is there something wrong with me that I want that?" she asked and I chuckled.

"No," I said, fisting the material of her cotton panties. I jerked on it, up, bringing the material tight against her pussy and she gasped, dry humping me. I got my other hand involved, so that I could tear them between my hands rather than against her body. I wanted to keep her hot and bothered, I didn't want to potentially hurt her.

There were a lot of reasons why she could be turned on by the edge of violence I preferred when it came to sex, but if I were a betting man, it turned her on so much because she knew without a doubt that she was safe with me – and she was. I would push her, but never so far outside her comfort zone that it would be harmful.

Never.

And I would never let it happen on my watch, either.

It took a few times to tear the fabric, the cotton stubborn and the angle a bit awkward.

I pulled the ruin of her panties out from under her skirt and said, "Take off your top, I want to see those perfect tits."

She smiled and slipped her tank off over her head, and I was pleased that she'd forgone a bra.

"This too." I indicated her skirt and she pulled it up and off over her, too.

"God, you're so fucking beautiful." I smoothed my hands over her skin, rubbing her all over, drinking her in with my eyes as well as by sense of touch. I breathed in deep and her scent was intoxicating, her arousal perfuming the air.

"Come up here," I grated and gave her ass a light tap with my fingertips. She jumped slightly and giggled and walked up the bed to either side of me on her knees.

I put my arms around the outside of her thighs and pulled her pussy to my face, driving my tongue up inside her which I know wasn't much, but God I wanted her taste.

She tasted sweet, like fucking sunshine and the ocean breeze and I lived for it.

"Oh, *God*," she gasped and the rest of her breath left her on a shuddering sigh as I suckled lightly on her clit. She tried to rise up and I locked my arms over the tops of her thighs and wouldn't let her up. She buried a hand in the top of my hair and clenched her fist and I was vaguely aware her other hand she moved over her body, massaging her own tits as she gave herself over wholly to the sensations sliding through her.

Mm, I lived for the small noises spilling from her throat, the way she shuddered in my grasp, the way she gasped and shivered and yipped and tried to jump.

It was so raw, sexy, and organic. Fuck, she was so hot and she didn't even know it. She moved through life so meek and so beautiful and I didn't understand how I was the first man to really see the wonder that was her worth. Like I didn't know how to quantify this beautiful creature above me. It was like putting a value on something like starlight. She moved above me, sinuous, and I reached down to work at the front of my shorts to get my cock free because as soon as I made her come this way, I wanted her to ride me. I wanted to turn her the fuck on so much she let go and did whatever the fuck she wanted with me and I could tell that she was close.

She had this way about her, moving her hips a certain way, unbidden, just begging for that last little nudge with her body and without any thought. She wanted it, she wanted it so fucking bad and the only thing I wanted worse than her was for her to fucking have it and for me to be the one to give it to her. I teased her clit with my tongue and didn't give up, even after it got tired I just kept pushin' and I was rewarded by her crying out, bowing forward and her clawing at the sheets.

Fuck that was sexy, her body bowed low, arms outstretched, pussy practically completely in my mouth as she stretched and almost presented herself like a cat in fucking heat as she shuddered above me, her legs trembling her breath sawing in and out of her lungs as she tried to hold herself together while only flying apart that much more.

I loved, loved, *loved*, how I could make her fly apart and I loved it even more how it took another orgasm it seemed to put her back together.

"Fucking sit on my dick now, baby. I want to feel you."

"What? Oh! Condom? I don't want to get pregnant."

I chuckled. "Okay, but I got snipped after Lucia was born," I told her.

"Oh, in *that* case." She reached behind me and grasped my dick and I groaned. She walked back on her knees and put me inside her and *holy fuck*... I know that fundamentally wearing a condom didn't diminish the feeling *that* much but the sheer just... *fuck* being inside her raw was special. Was next fucking level. The psychology behind how much it turned me on so powerful I almost nutted right then and there like a teenage boy inside a woman for the first time, condom or no.

She put her hands on my chest, and took me all the way to the root inside her and biting her bottom lip, eyes closed, looked every inch the sultry little vixen I knew she harbored deep down inside but was too afraid to let her out.

She was out now, by God, and I wanted her to own that shit. I was just about to lightly smack her thigh and order her to get moving, to take her pleasure, when she started to move all on her own with a slow, sinuous roll of her hips.

"Oh, fuck yes, baby," I encouraged her. "Ride me. Just like that, you look so fucking beautiful."

Oh, man she just did it for me. So hot, so tight, so *wet* and silky, silky smooth where she was wrapped around my cock that I almost couldn't stand it.

"You ride me so good," I whispered, losing my damn mind until it was the only thing I could say on fucking repeat. She looked down at me and I swear to God it was like she'd tapped her inner goddess. I half expected her to suddenly become luminous or to be bathed in a physical light that radiated from just behind her. She was fucking *angelic*, and I saw wisps of light flicker at the edges of my vision with how hard I was trying to maintain control.

I was gonna come, and I didn't want to. Not yet, not until she had hers.

"Again, baby. Come for me again," I whispered, and I licked the pad of my thumb and delved it between us at the top of her sex. She cried out, throwing her head back as she picked up the pace, grinding on me, her body tight against mine, her pussy gripping me, I gritted my teeth, my spine tingling, my balls tightening, on the verge. So close, so very fucking close, until it hit me. She spasmed at the same time I did, both of us plummeting over that invisible edge, falling into space and time as our bodies took over and left our minds behind.

One. At once. At the same fucking time.

I don't think I'd ever had that happen before.

Fuck, I liked it.

26

*J*ustice...

I lay over the top of him, panting, seeing stars, his cock buried deep inside of me and our bodies a mess between us as both of us panted, desperately trying to reclaim our breaths.

He had his arms around me, holding me tight, one hand in the back of my hair massaging my scalp as I blinked back overwhelmed tears that were threatening to leak out of the corners of my eyes. Not like I was *crying*, per se... more like my eyes were involuntarily watering from such and intense and extreme orgasm.

"Fuck that was hot," he growled between pants and all I could manage to muster in reply was a weak, far away sounding, "Mm-hm."

"You good?" he asked, and I laughed a bit and found my voice.

"Oh, yeah."

He kissed my shoulder, the side of my neck, and finally the underside of my jaw – just wherever he could reach as we both fought to regain our breath and urged our frantically beating hearts back into a more sedate pace.

"We need a shower," he murmured. "And I need a change of clothes."

I giggled then boldly said, "Sorry not sorry," which made him laugh.

"Come on, get off of me," he said breathless all over again with his laughter. I obliged him, knees a bit creaky from my prolonged position on them and he bounced up and reached a hand back for me. I took it and he towed me along into the bathroom where he started the shower.

I pinned up my hair and joined him where we kissed lazily, letting our hands wander soap slicked over one another's bodies. Over ridges and planes of muscle, his hands gentle and sweet over the peaks and valleys of scar tissue riddling my side and back.

A fair bit in, Atlas called out from the other room, "Yo, yo, yo!"

"Yeah?" Radar called back to him and Atlas stopped inside the bathroom door and leaned a shoulder against the door jamb like we weren't just standing there naked, in the shower. I wasn't entirely sure I would ever get over just how casual these guys were around each other and nudity in general but as much as a frisson of anxiety went up my spine at having anyone walk in on me naked, it just as quickly disappeared as he looked at his phone scrolling down the screen not really paying any mind to us in the glass box that was my shower.

"The crew's stopping in NOLA tonight to party with the Voodoo Bastards, they say they'll be here by mid-afternoon tomorrow," Atlas said, and Radar made a rude noise.

"Pfft! I call bullshit. Ain't no way they're gonna party with the boys in NOLA and not be hung the fuck over in the morning."

Atlas laughed.

"We placing bets?" he asked.

"You wanna bet against me on that?" Radar demanded.

"Fuck no, what're you thinking?"

"Late tomorrow night, I'd be surprised if they rolled up before ten."

"Shit, you're probably right, man."

"It's not like I'm going to have this place packed up by then!" I cried incredulous.

Radar shook his head and Atlas looked up at me and grinned, "Ain't nobody expecting you to, baby. This is a full-service move. Our boys and girls'll help you get packed up and when we're done purging shit to the dump, we'll get a U-Haul and haul ass back to Florida."

"I still don't even know what to do about the house..." I said trailing off.

"That's tomorrow. We'll contact a real estate agency and get the ball rolling, it's no worries. We got you," Atlas declared.

"Not gonna let you fall, baby," Radar murmured and he pulled me down for another kiss.

I kissed him back, suffused with a warmth that had absolutely nothing to do with the steam of the shower water.

RADAR ENDED UP BEING RIGHT. The rest of the Kraken and their women that were able to make it didn't show up until late the next night. We made sure to have pizza and cold beer and had pushed enough furniture aside to lay out sleeping bags and bedrolls.

That was the last thing that La Croix and Collier helped with before they departed back to New Orleans. I hugged them both and thanked them for coming and for helping to keep me safe.

It was a veritable *whirlwind* of activity the morning after the Kraken arrived, though and it all started with Faith, Hope, and Serenity armed with serious looks and a clip board with fresh paper waiting for me to step out of my bedroom into the hallway.

"Decision time," Hope said seriously.

"What stays, what goes to the dump, and what do you want to try to sell?" Serenity asked.

Whoa boy.

It surprisingly, wasn't that bad... a lot of stuff ended up trashed or set aside because one of the guys wanted it – which was mostly to say part and parceling out Rodney's tools and tool boxes and garage shit.

The parts for his last work in progress car ended up *in* that car, and some of the legalities of ownership and what to do with the big things like vehicles still had question marks hovering over them but that was neither here nor there at the moment.

We focused on wrapping glass, taking things car and truck loads at a time to various Good Will and consignment shops and all within the first few days.

I marveled at the *family* the MC was to one another – I mean not how *my* family had been but rather what you imagined family should be.

There was a lot of discussion with the women who had been able to come about their lives and how they had come to the club and even though Faith, Serenity, and I were worlds apart in how our trauma had happened, we bonded over our mutual traumas, nonetheless. Weeping at times, laughing at others, and coping with some of the horrors through sarcasm and dark humor; mostly provided by Hope.

It was also Hope who was a steady and consistent reminder that we weren't ruled by our pasts and that the world was my oyster and there was only one way to go after hitting rock bottom and that was up.

On the fourth day, I got the call from Rodney's attorney to tell me he was dead.

I stood, all eyes on me as I stood frozen in the middle of the room, sinking to the floor to sit on my ass as my numb lips made words that I wasn't entirely sure what I was saying or what I was agreeing to.

"I don't understand," I said. "What happened?"

"Colo rectal bleeding. I'll spare you the details... just he didn't change anything about his will. It's all yours but you'll have to come in and..."

"I'm in the middle of moving," I said and there was silence on the other end of the phone. "Are you still there?" I asked.

"Yes, ma'am. I think that's a good thing, you moving on and all..." His voice droned in my ear and finally he got to the point. A date, a time, a place to fill out paperwork and fill in all the blanks of the etc. that went along with your estranged ex-husband dying in prison and his last will and testament still involving *you*, with no caveats as to a divorce which he'd never foreseen happening. *Because of course he didn't...* I thought. *You were supposed to be the one to die.*

I ended the call, looked up at Radar, and burst into tears and I didn't even know why, really… I mean, I wasn't sad that he was dead, was I?

I mean, I was relieved, right?

Right?

Shit.

I just wanted this rollercoaster to *stop*.

*R*adar...

 I was cuddled up to Justice, holding her tight. She'd stopped weeping a while ago and it was just me, her, and Atlas in her room which had been spared from the chaos the rest of the house was in.

She was awake, I knew that much, but nothing really needed to be said right now.

"I'm sorry," she whispered.

"It's okay," I told her and kissed the top of her head, holding her just a little bit tighter.

"We get it, babe. It's a-okay," Atlas offered. "You just feel all you need to feel."

"I don't know what I feel," she said honestly. "Just, nothing and everything all at once."

I nodded slowly and said, "To be expected."

"Is it, though?" She groaned and covered her face with her hands scrubbing at it with a frustrated sigh.

"K, out!" Hope cried, barging into the room.

"We got this one," Faith said, following her sister up.

"Off, you fuck!" Hope declared, shooing at us with her hands while Serenity was suppressing a fit of giggles behind her hands.

"The fuck is this shit?" Atlas asked.

"This is the girls putting themselves in charge," Faith declared and it was a night and day difference from when we'd first brought her back to Ft. Royal.

"Am I speaking alien translated into Greek?" Hope demanded. "Go!"

I looked down at Justice who was looking up at me her mind boggled and I chuckled and dipped my head to peck a kiss on her lips.

"Hope has spoken, apparently," I said, rolling my eyes.

"Boys are headed out on the town, Captain's orders," Serenity declared, and Atlas dragged himself to his feet on the other side of my lady.

"I hear you," I said with a nod. "You need me you call me, otherwise you ladies enjoy yourselves," I said with a wink at my girl as I untangled myself from her.

"I don't understand," she said, her voice faint with surprise.

"Only thing you need to do is tell us your favorite ice cream flavor," Hope said flatly.

"You're in serious need of some girl time to vent and get it together," Faith declared.

"No overbearing men allowed," Serenity said with a wink.

I smiled at Jussy and gave a nod. "You're in good hands, baby."

I blew her a kiss and stepped out, Atlas shutting the door behind us.

He and I both sighed in unison, a weight lifting off us as well. We both looked at each other and laughed.

"Man, I can't wait for the upheaval to calm it's fuckin' tits and to be back home," he said.

I nodded. "It's a lot in a short amount of time," I agreed.

He nodded and said, "I know it's starting to stress me out. How you doing?"

I thought about it, and I mean I genuinely thought about it. "I could use a break for a minute," I agreed.

"Word, let's go get one."

"Like Hope said; off, we fuck, brother."

"Off, we fuck," he agreed.

And off we did fuck, where or to do what I had no fucking idea, but hey… that was half the fun, am I right?

28

*J*ustice...

"Mm-mm." Hope shook her head and swallowed her shot and looked me square in the eyes. "Girl, enough of this sad bitch's shit, tonight? Tonight, we are *bad* bitches and you gonna need to get on board and start acting accordingly."

"That's right," Serenity agreed.

"We are *bad* bitches, not *sad* bitches," Faith declared, raising her shot glass and downing the contents.

I blinked and took my own shot and winced. I wasn't much of a hard alcohol drinker and certainly not shots.

"I should burn all his shit," I said off handedly. "That would be a bad bitch thing to do, right?" I asked.

"Fuck yeah!" Hope cried. "Now you're talkin'."

"Wait, what?" I asked.

"You're absolutely right," Serenity agreed. "You got anything around here still that'd make good tinder? Some of his clothes, pictures, letters? Anything like that."

"Um, I mean, um... uh, probably?" I stammered out.

"I'll help you look," Faith declared and she got up off the living room floor and pulled me to my feet.

"Like where are we even supposed to do this?" I demanded.

"Back yard, duh," Serenity said. "You got a barbecue or a fire pit or something?"

"I mean, a barbecue, but it's gas. The HOA doesn't allow charcoal grills in the neighborhood, the grass always has to be kept cut. A fire hazard they say."

Hope snorted.

"Fuck, he even had the HOA around to control you when he wasn't around, fuckin' loser."

"Well, I mean, I understand about the fire hazard..." I trailed off.

"Come on." Serenity wrapped her arms around my one and towed me in a general direction of where some of Rodney's shit might be located.

"Well behaved women rarely make history," Faith said, and that weirdly made some kind of sense to me.

We found my wedding pictures, which weren't really anything to super write home about. I mean, we'd been married by a justice of the peace at the courthouse. Me in a white summer dress and him in his dress uniform.

We looked so young, and if I could have barged in and told my younger self anything it would have been to run. Run screaming as fast and as far as humanly possible to get away from him. I would have some choice words for the younger Rodney too...

I sighed.

"It might have made my life so very different, sure but what about the next girl?" I wondered aloud as we stood around my big soup pot on the cement pad of my back patio, illuminated by the flickering flames inside.

"Do what now?" Hope asked, swaying on her feet.

"Oh, I was just thinking if I could go back and tell my younger self anything it would have been to run," I said.

"Ah, yeah, no... if I could go back and teach your younger self anything it would be how to kick his fucking ass and defend herself."

Faith nodded. "How to shoot him in the face."

"The bravery to cut off his penis as he slept," Serenity supplied and we all looked at her. "What?" she demanded. "He deserved it!"

"Where's the lie?" I asked with a sigh and dropped the photo in my hand into the pot.

"It's never too late to learn, sister," Hope said.

"True that," Faith declared, nodding. "Doesn't hurt that getting involved with the Kraken means never being hurt by anyone or anything again where there won't inevitably be some real consequences for the assholes that did it."

"Amen to that," Serenity said with a bit of a wobbly nod.

"It's easier to stand up for yourself when you know you got backup," Hope said. "And you got backup now for sure."

I watched the photo in the big metal pot be consumed by the flames and said, "You know. I still have that dress in the back of my closet."

Serenity grinned. "We should dye it black."

"Or let everyone throw paint on it," Faith suggested.

"Or get really kinky with your man, have him cut it off your body and rail you the way your husband never fuckin' could to your satisfaction."

I looked up at her and said, "I think I like that last option best."

"Yeah?" she asked.

"Yeah, is that weird and totally fucked up of me or what?" I asked.

"Hell no," Faith said, shaking her head. "Take it from me. My therapist says some of the stranger sexual desires I've had when it comes to Marlin is parts of my primal brain realizing that Marlin is *safe* and things trying to rewrite or reprogram themselves internally to heal from past trauma."

"What? Really?" I asked. "Because I feel like I shouldn't want anyone to ever get near me with a knife in a sexual context but the thought of Radar doing that? It's just… It's really hot," I confessed.

Faith nodded. "Maybe you should see my therapist," she said.

"Shit, you sell this place and you should have a decent amount to set aside for a down payment on a new place and the rest could front your therapy bills for a minute," Hope said.

"We're all really big advocates on therapy," Serenity agreed. "After

Stoker... he helped me find a therapist and it helped me a lot," she said and smiled.

"It's not like you have to see one forever," Hope said.

"You see one?" I asked.

She snorted.

"Nah, I'm the unhealthiest out of all of us," she said with a laugh. "My classic response is to just bottle that shit up until I explode and then have Cutter dominate and fuck the shit out of me until I feel like I have a grip." She shrugged. "Different strokes for different folks," she said and Serenity busted up laughing.

"You said strokes," she said and snorted and then for whatever reason the rest of us fell into gales of our own laughter. Probably because we were drunk.

"What else we got to burn?" I asked when we'd settled down.

"Now you're talkin'," Hope declared.

"Mm?" I stirred and heard a masculine chuckle beside me, a warm hand on my back. I sucked in a sharp breath and went to scramble to the other side of the bed away from the stranger but it wasn't any stranger at all, it was just Radar.

"Shh, shh, shh! Easy, baby! It's just me," he said, and I put a hand to my chest and panted.

"Oh, my God! You scared the life out of me!" I cried.

He chuckled and it was a rueful sound, he bowed and shook his head and asked.

"You still drunk?"

I blinked at his silhouette and shook my head stopped when the room swam a bit, and said, "Maybe?" in a querulous voice, knowing that I was in for it with a hangover in the morning – later today? I giggled.

"Oh, yeah. You're still drunk," he said, laughing to himself.

"Where did *you* go?" I asked and he got up onto the bed and opened his arms so I could cuddle in.

"You smell like a stripper," I complained.

"Well, I don't know how a stripper of my persuasion smells—" I smacked his chest lightly and he said, "Ow!" and shrank a bit, but I know he was making it up. I barely tapped him.

"No, like a *female* stripper, named Cinnamon or Diamond or something," I said.

"Oh, no, it was Bunny, actually and she was a Sacred Heart's club slut," he said with a shrug. I pushed off of him and leaned way back and asked a little wounded.

"Cheating already, huh?"

His look, what I could make out of it from the light coming through the bedroom door from down the hallway was dead serious, his tone even more serious. "No. Never. Flirt? Yeah, I gotta keep my skills up for you," he said. "But I'm not interested in anyone else. She came up, started hanging off my shoulder, propositioned me for the night and Atlas took her off my hands for me."

I stared him in the eyes and he searched my face right back. Finally, he leaned over and clicked on the bedroom light. I winced and closed my eyes, turning my head.

"Oof, babe, now is *not* the time to discuss anything, especially those texts."

"Texts?" I squeaked.

He chuckled and pulled me to him, and I went... I guess I believed him about the Cinnamon Bunny.

"Yep, you rest now," he said and sighed. He kissed my forehead and I melted. "You drink any water?" he asked after a moment.

"No," I said and it sounded small and meek even to me. *Wasn't I supposed to be a bad bitch, though?*

"Okay, stay right here, I'll go get you some."

"Noooo," I whined and he chuckled and disentangled himself from me anyway.

"Be right back," he said and I waited closing my eyes and laying back. The room spinning.

Oof!

He returned and sat me up pressing a tall glass of cold water into my hand. He held the back of my head and neck as I drank and urged me at one point to slow down. I handed the glass to him with an expectant look and he set it on the bedside table.

"Good girl," he muttered and smiled, glowing from the small praise. A look that changed pretty quick when my stomach rebelled.

"Ope, shit." He helped me off the bed and I barely made it to the bathroom sink – forget the toilet, sink was closer.

He came in the bathroom, and rubbed my back, held back my hair and muttered, "Damnit Hope..."

I never had anyone take care of me the way he did, cleaning me up, getting me bathed, handing me my toothbrush loaded with paste and wrapping me in a towel. Cuddling me to sleep in the great big bed that had been too expensive when my ex had wanted to buy it and how he'd opened a credit card in my name to do it because he couldn't open anymore in his.

I cried, embarrassed, a little scared, but Radar just chuckled, called me adorable, and told me to rest... that it would all be there in the morning to deal with just as easy.

"What did I text?" I asked, and he chuckled again and told me not to worry about it.

"In the morning, baby. In the morning."

❧

I DIDN'T WANT to deal with it in the morning. Not with the light of day lancing through my head, scorching out my eyeballs, and raking laser beams down the inside of my skull.

Once again, Radar was there, aspirin and water at the ready, and also ready to discuss these texts or whatever...

"Can I read them first?" I asked, and he grinned at me.

"I think you're gonna have to," he said and oh, my humiliation was complete. Oh, my *God*... they were so... *dirty*. Talking about cutting things off of me, fucking me against walls and in every hole and I shook my head, flaming vermilion and wanting to just pull the blankets over my head and *die* from the embarrassment.

"I am so sorry—" I started and his barking laughter stopped me cold.

He shook his head, eye contact boring into me and I felt my mouth go dry.

"Oh, no, baby girl... there's no take backs on these ones," he said. "I'll do everything you asked for and more – what I want to talk about isn't so much the texts as it is how can I get you to feel comfortable enough to ask me for these things that you want and you need *sober?* I don't want to have to get you drunk to find these things out, and ah—" he raised his chin and gave me a warning look when I went to speak. I closed my mouth.

"I really want you to *think* about these things, I don't want an answer now."

"Okay," I said quietly.

He nodded and said, "Good girl. There'll be plenty of time for all that kind of shit later. Right now, I'm tired of this fuckin' place and want to get you home."

"Me too," I said.

"Once everybody's back here, we'll look at packing up the rest of your shit and making a plan to blow this popsicle stand."

I nodded. "Okay."

He came over and kissed my forehead.

"Don't ever think you have to hide any part of yourself from me for my comfort or anybody else's," he murmured. "Those days are over. I'd rather you hurt my feelings and get it out in the open, babe. Now where's this dress?" he asked.

I colored beet red for an entirely different reason than from embarrassment and said, "The back of the closet."

He nodded.

"I'm going to take possession of that particular garment now, and when I think you're ready, I'll lay it out for you. Then I'm taking you out for a relaxing day just you and me, whatever you want to do... and then when we get home, I'm going to do what *I* want. You get me?"

I nodded mute; my breath stolen.

"Justice?" he asked and it held a slight edge of warning and heat.

"Yes, alright!" I said quickly. "I'd um, I'd like that, please," I said unsure what else *to* say.

He gave me a crooked grin. "We'll work on that, but yes, that's good," he said.

I smiled and he said, "Let's work on getting the fuck out of here."

I sighed, resigned. "I'm beginning to feel like we're never going to get anything but these stolen moments." The confession was out before I'd even realized I'd uttered it.

He paused and looked me over and said, "Thank you for telling me that," and then he stepped out of the room and he was gone.

I took my time getting dressed, pulled out the luggage from the closet and looked at my hanging clothes.

The rest of the house was either boxed, given away, or sold… it was down to basics and I wanted so desperately to be free of this miserable place.

29

*R*adar...

The back of the U-Haul's rolling door shuddered and the latch made such a satisfying fucking sound; *man...*

I sighed, this was it, we were almost fucking *out of here*.

I went back to check on her ex's truck and the trailer we'd rented for it, checking the tie downs on the bikes on the trailer.

"That's damn sure a fuckin' shame," Atlas said and sighed. I grinned.

"Only way to do it," I said.

"Yeah, yeah," he muttered.

The girls who'd ridden out here with their men were going to take turns behind the wheel of the U-Haul for the drive back. Atlas was going to drive the wasband's truck with our bikes on the trailer while I took Jussy in her car.

It was a nice truck, barely any miles on it, the payments not too bad, really; and for what we got out of the two muscle cars in the garage – both the completed one and the project car, if Jussy wanted to, she could pay the truck off and keep it.

She was still deciding on things and had expressed a desire to make those final decisions as far away from here as possible and so back to Florida we were to go so she could lose her mind and find her soul.

I just maybe had a stop or two I wanted to make along the way. Something all of my crew had no fucking problem with because hey, they not only got it, they were fucking great people and the *best* chosen-family a lucky fucker like me could ever hope to fall into.

"Right, we're gonna get on out of here," Cutter called and I gave him and Marlin a chin lift. Stoker came by and patted me on the back of the shoulder. "We'll see you on the other side." Cutter called and I nodded.

"Keep the shiny side up, brothers," I told them all and Justice found her way from the front porch to my side.

I smiled at her.

She'd given the first sign that she was gonna come out of all of this tougher and much stronger when some Karen from the homeowner's association had knocked on her door to try and fine her for having a fire in her own backyard and Jussy's response was to roll her eyes, and to ask the bitch, "Can't you see that I'm in the middle of moving out of here?" When the cunt had started to sputter about that not mattering and that Jussy needed to pay the fine, Jussy had told her, "Oh, fuck off, Cameron," and had slammed her front door in the woman's face.

That had been to a rousing set of cheers from the lot of us, and the plan was to give a one-fingered salute as we rolled past Cameron's house on the way out of the neighborhood.

Also, after that, we'd stopped being fuckin' polite and had parked our shit wherever we damn well felt like it. Wished we'd adopted that one sooner, getting the bikes in and out of the back was kind of a pain in the ass and by now it was clear whoever Rodney had tapped to fuck with his ex-wife wasn't going to do shit.

"You ready, baby?" I asked my woman and she looked over at me.

"You have *no* idea," she declared.

"Let's get out of here."

I got behind the wheel of her car and she slid into the passenger seat. We needed to swing by the real estate office on our way out of town and were going to catch up to our crew in NOLA at the halfway point… or so Jussy thought. I had some other plans.

What she'd said about stolen moments rattling around in the back of my brain the last day or so.

We rolled out, middle fingers held high, laughing about it and Jussy shaking her head blushing but she was smiling and I think it was honestly the brightest smile I had ever seen on her. It lit her up completely, made her glow from the inside, and I lived for it and to put a smile like that on her face every day for the rest of her life.

We'd spoken about it, in one of those stolen moments' sans anyone else. How we both craved a sort of home life stability. She confessed that she had always dreamed of being a happy housewife sort. Cooking, keeping house, making sure her husband had a safe and loving environment to return to.

She was brilliant, my girl. Creative, and driven. Built her business from nothing – learning Photoshop and drawing and the like as a side interest. Computers having always sort of fascinated her. She could keep up with both me and Atlas which was a treat and the more time we accrued just talking the more I found my sense about her was right on target.

We were practically made for each other. She was tough beyond measure; she was just in a fragile transitory make-or-break state where she needed to be shown her worth and just how tough she was.

The universe had seen fit to put her with me and mine for that, I was sure of it. Now it was time to take her out of survival mode and let her thrive.

"Where are we going?" She asked when I took an unexpected turn off the route on the GPS.

"Isn't that one of those Missions you were talking about?" I asked.

"Oh, yeah, but…"

"No buts. We only live once, and let's go have a look, yeah?"

She settled back in her seat and smiled, nodding, and said, "Yeah."

We toured the grounds taking pictures together and holding hands, unbothered by the oppressive heat for the most part just glad to be in each other's company.

"Oh, snap. I should get something for my momma," I said when we found the giftshop.

"I'm glad you have a good relationship with yours," she murmured.

"I'm sorry yours can't seem to pull her head out of her ass," I shot back and Jussy shrugged.

"She's my mom when it makes her look good or it gets her sympathy. When she wants to be…"

"Which is bullshit," I said and Jussy nodded.

"It is," she agreed. "But I don't care anymore. I don't want to waste any energy on anyone who can't be bothered with putting any into me, you know?"

"I do, and I'm behind you every step of the way on that. You know that, right?" I asked. She smiled and leaned in and kissed me.

"I do, and thank you," she said against my mouth.

I smiled and bought my mother a rosary made from pressed rose petals and another one to hang from the rearview of Jussy's car to make it smell nice.

We made it to New Orleans late that night, and I found us a nice hotel in the Quarter. Expensive as shit – but this was her first time to the city.

I made love to her that night, slow and sweet. We were both tired from the long hours on the road, and it just didn't feel like the time or the place to get any kind of freaky. Plus, that wasn't what any of this was about, anyway. I wasn't about to tell this woman how much I was growing to love her. Words were fucking cheap and I like to put my money where my mouth is so to that particular end, I would rather show her.

The next morning, we hit Café du Monde for their café au lait and fresh beignets waiting in line for a seat in the café and relaxing under the awning inside the railing and just watching the tourists and people of the Quarter go by, laughing as a trio of the Voodoo Bastards rode by. No, none of them were La Croix or Collier, but I did see Saint among them. Saint was a good dude and I'd been surprised that he wasn't with La Croix in San Antonio – those two were usually attached at the hip.

"I think we ought to spend the day," I said, sipping my coffee and Jussy looked at me.

"Really?" Her voice was excited.

"Yeah, why not? I ain't got nothing pressing back home and you can work from anywhere and were jamming it out so hard the last few weeks I'd like to hope you can spare the time."

She looked thoughtful and her smile said the jig was sort of up.

"You planned this didn't you?" she asked, laughing.

"Maybe," I said, nodding. "Cutter was actually the one to suggest a little decompress time before heading back to the fort," I said.

"Why *is* it called Ft. Royal?" she asked. "I didn't see anything there to indicate why."

I smiled, "Used to be, waaaay back in the day, an old pirate stronghold."

"Oh, really?" she asked, interested.

"Really, I can show you some of the old foundations and shit out in the water. Sea levels rose and some of the old town ended up under water. It makes for some good snorkeling."

She giggled. "I've never been. Knowing my luck, I'd dive and suck in a lungful of water."

"Just gotta remember to blow to clear the tube when you come up, like a dolphin or whale," I said.

She rolled her eyes, and said, "Should have stopped at Dolphin?" Then she gave a self-deprecating giggle. I briefly wondered if her wasband had ever gotten on her about her weight and if that was partially why she was so rail thin… it was an uncomfortable thought.

We held hands and took a walk through the French Quarter along Bourbon talking about what sights to see, different cuisine, and her lack of any taste whatsoever when it came to spicy food which I fucking lived for.

"I don't like to taste my endorphins!" she cried. "I like to actually taste my food."

I laughed and shook my head. "Spicy is a flavor enhancer," I argued and she shook her head.

"That's bullshit and you know it."

The banter with her was pretty fucking sweet.

We walked from the café to Jackson Square, then stopped through Pirate's Alley before heading further on up.

We toured the Lalaurie Mansion and had a late lunch before an easy stroll through Louis Armstrong Park to digest; finishing our day by taking a slow walk through St. Louis Cemetery no. 1 where Jussy left an offering of her Chapstick for Marie Leveau.

We hit a giftshop or two where Jussy mainly focused on a book or two about history and ghosts in our travels and she picked up a miniature of the Lalaurie Mansion.

I bought my girls a thing or two and a tank top for Jussy without her knowing about it in our travels and hailed a dude with one of those rickshaw bicycles to take us the rest of the way back toward our hotel.

Jussy groaned and flopped on the neatly made bed when we got back to our room.

"That was so much fun," she declared. "But my feet are *killing* me!"

I dropped into the chair at the room's little desk and wheeled it across the floor. "Gimme," I demanded and she lifted her head off the bed to look at me. I touched her knee and she lifted one of her slim legs where it was draped off the side of the bed. I rolled back and dropped her foot in my lap, working her sandal off and pressing my thumb into the bottom of her foot. She groaned.

"Oh, my God! That feels so good."

I chuckled.

"You spoil me," she declared with a breezy sigh.

"I should hope so," I answered. "Somebody needs to do it."

"Mm." She closed her eyes and I smiled. She was so beautiful. Even in her sadness before, she was lovely – but now that she smiled? Woof, she was gorgeous and the fact I was responsible for her smiles made me a thousand times the man I could ever have hoped to be. In her I felt a kinship. The world had cheated us both in more ways than I could count but in each other, we each found justice for those wrongs.

Some of it was bittersweet, sure, but could you really appreciate how sweet it was without the bitterness there to show you? Remind you, that it could just all be sour with no end in sight?

"I love falling in love with you," I said suddenly and she looked up, craning her neck to look down her lean body while I kept her foot in my hands.

"What?" she asked.

"You heard me," I said and her expression which had been sort of incredulous just a moment before, softened.

"You're in love with me?" she asked softly, as though she hadn't heard me right and if I wasn't, it certainly put me one step closer with the way she said it.

"Oh, I'm certainly getting there," I said with a smile. "You're adorable, you're kind, so soft and sweet. You're patient with me just as much as you profess that I am with you; and I know I haven't done the most awesome job at communicating all of the time, or given you a whole lot of reason to trust me – but you seem to. I'm grateful that you're here and that you're hanging in there with me. I know it's been hard."

She laid back down, her expression puzzled and I shut up and let her work whatever it was in her head out for herself.

She finally pushed herself up into a sitting position and took her foot away from me, but I wasn't done. I scooted a little closer, let her get adjusted, and pushy bastard that I was demanded the other foot. She gave it to me with a slight laugh and a shake of her head and said, "You make me lose myself, my train of thought."

I was quiet a moment and finally said, "Seems to me you could stand to get out of your own head a little more. There's a great wide world out here."

She smiled a bit and nodded slowly.

"You gave me that world, you know," she said softly.

I nodded slowly and looked up at her and dead ass serious said, "I'd give you more if I could. I'd give you everything."

"I don't want everything," she whispered. "I just want you, and *this*… I mean, whatever *this* is, whatever we're building here."

I nodded and smiled and said, "That sounds so fucking good to me, you don't even know."

She sniffed, getting a little misty eyed.

"That's all I've ever wanted, really," she said. "To love and be loved and to have someone as committed to me as I am to them who wants to *build* something with me. A life, a home, and I know it sounds so anti-feminist or whatever," she shook her head and looked away, swiping a finger under her lashes and I chuckled.

"Actually, if you stop to think about it – that's as feminist and rad as hell as you can get."

She looked at me and scrunched her cute little nose in confusion.

"I don't understand," she said.

"Feminism is basically the advocacy for a woman's right to choose her own direction, to use her own voice. That's what you're doing. Choosing what you want for you, for yourself, your own path – and fuck what anyone else has to say about it, anyhow. Right?"

She fixed me with an even stare and nodded slowly.

"Right. I mean, I guess so…"

"You're honestly the one with all the power in this dynamic, baby. Don't get it twisted. I may boss you around but you're ultimately the one with the choice to obey or refuse. The fact that you do obey is sweet as fuck and is so fucking hot to me, but yeah… just think about that."

She did, I could see it all over her face, and it was a lot of food for thought. Enough that she would be chewing on it for a while, which I was good with. I wanted her to know she had her own agency and the choice was hers… that no one could ever take that away from her again.

There was a certain power exchange at play in think kind of dynamic and I wanted her to discover that I wasn't here just to take hers and give nothing back.

Quite the opposite, in fact.

Quite the opposite.

I bent at the waist and kissed the top of her foot and then got up to go take a shower, leaving her to think and have a little space to herself, at least for a little while.

30

*J*ustice…

"Can I drive?" I asked and I know it was shitty, and I felt a little guilty, but it was a test.

Radar stopped midway around the back of the car, and index finger through my key ring swung my keys out around and caught them in the palm of his hand.

"Sure thing, babe," he said without missing a beat, and he came around to put the keys in my hand.

"Thank you," I murmured.

I didn't really want to drive, I just honestly wanted to see what he would do if I asked. I don't know why I expected him to say no, or argue… I guess I was just in a mood where I was doubting, and strongly at that, that this was real. That I was away from Rodney, that not all men… that I had been lucky enough to find one that was a fairytale.

Like, was that what this was? Was this going to be some happily ever after fairytale ending?

Ha, that's not how life works, I thought to myself.

"You okay?" he asked, breaking into my thoughts and threading his fingers between mine on the hand that I didn't have on the wheel, but was rather fiddling with my center console as I awkwardly fidgeted at a stoplight.

"What? Yeah!"

He chuckled. "You get too anxious or tired, you just let me know, babe."

"I'm fine," I said. "Just thinking."

"Want to talk about it?" he asked and I smiled and shook my head.

"No," I said simply and sighed. "Just being foolish is all."

"How so?" he asked.

I came clean, it was only right…

"I didn't really want to drive."

"Wanted to see how I would react?" he asked.

I nodded, staying focused on the flow of traffic as the GPS on my phone parked orders, taking us to the Interstate to head toward Ft. Royal.

"It's okay," he said and he brought the back of my hand to his lips and smacked a kiss to it.

"No, it's not…" I said with a harsh sigh. "It's toxic and rude."

"Yeah, but you know what else it is?" he asked.

"What?" I murmured.

"Understandable. You do what you gotta do to feel safe. You've got a good head on your shoulders, Jussy. It's one of the many reasons that I like you. This kind of thing is only temporary and asking to drive when you don't really want to doesn't hurt my feelings any," he said with a laugh. "I can drive, you can pull over whenever you want."

I shook my head and laughed a little and said, "No. I can do it for a while. We can swap when we stop for lunch if you want."

"All up to you, babe."

I glanced at him and then back to the road, satisfied that he meant what he said. There was no stoic repose, nothing was guarded or fake about his posture. His expression wasn't tight, but easygoing, his smile though small, was genuine. There was no tightness about him like a tightly wound spring ready to uncoil at a speed that could give you whiplash.

There was no danger about him.

It was refreshing to a degree, but I still couldn't quite manage to get myself to relax fully. I couldn't honestly say why. Guilt, maybe? I mean, I knew it wasn't right testing like that.

I was pretty embarrassed about it now, but I just couldn't help myself. The fact he handled it with such grace? I didn't deserve him.

No, you do... a voice in the back of my head declared and that? That was a comfort. Strangely, at first, but a year ago I would have batted the thought aside. Completely dismissed it. Two years ago? I wouldn't have dared think anything on my own. Not without Rodney's approval.

It was progress, and as I drove eastward, out of New Orleans toward Mississippi with every bit of progress I put beneath my car's tires in the direction of Ft. Royal, I felt hopeful. Hopeful that this new beginning would take.

I stuck to my guns and drove even past lunch despite Radar's offer to take over. About the time we pulled out of the other side of Mississippi to head through the little butt-flap of Alabama before hitting the Florida panhandle, Radar looked up from his phone sharply and said, "I booked us a night in the Calypso on the West End of Panama City. Driving straight through would be nice and all, but I want you all to myself for one more night."

I looked over and couldn't help the smile that curved my lips over that last part.

"Really?" I asked.

"Absolutely. Soon enough we'll be back with the rest of the crew, and my kid, and we'll be wrapped around the axle trying to figure out how to integrate our lives and forge a new home outta my house and I just want one more evening just you and me. A nice dinner out, a long walk on the beach, making love to you – all of it."

"Okay," I said after letting all of that sink in for the moment.

"Not that we won't get back to a lot of those things pretty quickly," he said, "but there's just something a little magic about the here and now."

"I agree," I said softly and he reached for my hand over the center console and tangled his fingers with mine, kissing them.

At one of the last rest stops before Panama City, he had me pull over and asked to drive.

"Easier," he said. "I know where I'm going."

I nodded and relinquished the driving duties a little grateful, I'd almost immediately regretted taking them up after lunch. Between my shoulder blades knotting with my grip on the wheel about twenty minutes in.

Panama City Beach's west end was apparently a little quieter, and not as crowded as the east side of town according to Radar. I had expected to pull into a hotel chain but was surprised when he pulled into a parking lot of what looked like higher end apartments or maybe condos.

"This doesn't look like a hotel," I mused and he chuckled.

"Condos," he said. "A lot of them are for rent, Air B&B style, I picked one up fairly on the cheap – I got lucky couldn't pass it up."

"How do you know about this place?" I asked, curious.

"Been out here before," he said quietly, in a way that felt... I don't know... for him, certainly shy.

"Old girlfriend or wife?" I asked softly.

He nodded. "Yeah, some of the best memories I have of her were made here. I hope it isn't skeevy or weird that I want to share that with you."

I smiled and shook my head. "Neither," I said. "Endearing, and very sweet is more like it."

Which it was, given that his last girlfriend, or old lady, or whatever the honorific or label might be for her, had passed away from cancer. There was no jealousy here. I mean, what was there to be jealous of or to feel weird about? We all had our histories and with as much as he'd put up with mine and the drama that had come out of it... this was a simple ask-without-asking from him.

We went up and stowed our luggage and I took the opportunity to freshen up with a quick shower and a change of clothes. Mostly because I had slaughtered myself with some ketchup and mayonnaise dripping out of the back end of my burger and had gotten not only my shirt but my jeans and for the last several hours, it was all I had been able to smell, you know?

Once out of the shower, Radar came up behind me to wrap his arms around my waist and kiss the back of my shoulder as I stood wrapped in a towel going through my moisturizing routine in front of the bathroom mirror.

"You okay?" I asked softly.

"Mm-hm, just checking on you."

I smiled. "Doing much better now that I'm smelling like." I checked my lotion bottle. "Citrus and ginger rather than ketchup and mayo," I responded.

"Either way you're good enough to eat," he said and nipped my shoulder. I giggled and cuddled back into him and he held me a little tighter.

"I wan you," he declared.

"What, now?" I asked.

"Right now," he said, pulling back on me a little. I laughed and let him drag me out of the bathroom and into the master bedroom with its king-sized bed.

My fresh clothes that I had laid out on it had been relocated to the love seat against the wall and had been re-laid out with such love and consideration. I smiled and turned in the circle of his arms and put my arms up around his neck. Confident, letting the towel slip to the floor.

He stooped and picked it up, laying it on the bed and said, "Get your ass up there, since you want to make good use of it."

I complied and he grinned wolfishly at me and jerked me to the edge of the bed so my ass was practically hanging off of it. I yipped in surprise and let out a peal of giggling excited laughter.

He didn't waste any time. He went to his knees, a heat in his gaze as he looked up my body and arms supporting me, licked me.

"Oh!" I shuddered in his grasp and he made this self-satisfied hum that ended on this deliciously dirty, dark and taboo little chuckle that made muscles I didn't know I had loosened in want and desire.

God yes, do whatever you want to me... I thought, and then finding a little hidden bravery from somewhere, I spoke those same words aloud exactly as I'd heard them in my mind.

His hands tightened on my hips and he *growled* in response and my whole body shivered in anticipation of what that sound would bring.

He teased my clit with the tip of his tongue carefully gauging my reaction, his deep brown eyes looking up the length of my body as I slid into the deep and even breathing reserved for just how much this man turned me the fuck on.

He teased me so sweetly, and denied me so devilishly in this carefully choreographed dance of lips, tongue, fingers and yes, even teeth in these delicate little nips to the inside of my thigh.

I laid back, tangled my fingers in the front of his hair when I couldn't take anymore and directed his mouth to where I wanted to be. He groaned and it was the hottest sound, almost doing more to edge me to orgasm than what he was doing with his mouth and his hands.

I closed my eyes and concentrated on all of the sensations and feelings he wrought through my overtaxed body that seemed to want to make up for all that time I had never been touched, or held, with any consideration. I was starved for this sort of contact, where I felt so loved without condition.

And God love him, love me is just what he did. Slow and with authority, building me up, and up, and up, holding me in the palms of his hands before with a sexy smirk that reached all the way into his eyes, he swished his finger like this and his tongue like that, and opened his hands to watch me fall.

I fell shrieking, body convulsing as the orgasm seemingly slammed into me from behind, carrying me over the edge of another, smaller cliff midway down. I don't know how many times I shuddered, and jerked, and crashed into the mattress beneath me, soaking the towel as he hung onto me and made a shining mess out of the beautiful disaster that was me.

I loved it. I lived for it. I never wanted it to end even as I pushed at him, frightened at the sensations that swept through me at the sweet prolonged torture he engaged in over, against, and inside my body which was more than enthusiastic to carry on without me despite my mind screaming at me to slam on the brakes.

Just when I was on the verge of panic, he let up and stopped, looking down at me, this pretty broken thing, whisking the towel out from under me and dropping it to the floor so it didn't have time to soak into the covers now under me.

He pulled off his tee over his head and dropped that as well, and the serious look in his eyes – I couldn't feel anything other than beautiful when he looked at me like that. I couldn't believe anything other than his reality which that I was desirable, that I lit a fire in his veins a match for what he lit in mine, racing like fire over a puddle of gasoline and burning twice as hot.

I bit my bottom lip and reached for him and he gave me that crooked grin. The one that said he had other ideas, the one that threatened me with a good time, that told me I was going to like this, as he wrapped his arms around my legs and hauled me back down the bed from where I'd tried to crab walk away in the throes of my prior orgasm.

He reached in his pocket and pulled out a foil wrapped square and tore it open with his teeth and I felt my mouth drop open.

It was a setup!

He winked at me, dropped his shorts, and I watched, hungry, as he rolled it down his length.

God, I wanted him inside of me.

I wanted him to fuck me until I came screaming around his cock, and by the way his smile dimmed into this all of a sudden oh-so serious and predatory look, I was about to learn the hard way to be careful what I wished for... except I trusted him, and it was *exactly* how I wanted it right this second.

"My turn," he uttered and I raised an eyebrow as he lifted my legs, and practically folded me in half, baring my pussy.

"For what?" I gasped, still not fully in control of my breath and beginning to lose it all over again with the look that he was giving me.

"To drive," he uttered and he drove into me from a standing position, the stroke deep, strong, and just this side of too much to handle.

I gasped, and arched, and raked nails down his exposed arms and with a vile, wicked grin that absolutely made my toes curl he threatened me with a good time.

31

*R*adar...

I drove into her with a little more force than I meant to, but with exactly the force that I wanted to because *damn* I was in a frenzy. Riding high off my desire for her, and equally pressed by a deep desire to make her *mine* in exactly every way that counted. I wanted to set her soul on fire, cool her with my kisses and soft stroking touches, and watch her transform from this soft creature that lay before me into something very much like steel. I wanted to help forge and unbreakable bond and ultimately, I wanted her to feel so empowered she didn't hesitate to stand up for herself with or without me by her side.

That started with proving to her that she had worth, and though it may not have been the healthiest method to bring about the lesson, I knew that making love to her, consistently, often, and letting her see it in my eyes and feel it in my touch would bring her around to at least start to believe...

I closed my eyes for a second, bowing my head, and just allowed myself to *feel*. Her smooth skin beneath my hands, the hot wet heat of her tight little pussy so snug around my cock. She felt like heaven and there was no place I would honestly rather be than with this woman in my arms, under me, clinging to me, holding onto me tightly as I railed her sweet ass into next fucking week.

I pulled her down again, having to readjust every so often to keep her at the edge of the bed where everything just felt so fucking good.

The way she reached for me, the way she stared at me through heavy-lidded eyes swirling with the magic combination of love and lust was such a fucking turn on it was everything in me not to come too early.

That spine-tingling, nut-busting, intense feeling building until I had to slow my pace, let myself come down a little, before edging both her and myself right on up the proverbial razor's edge all over again.

I danced with her on that fine gleaming edge between the solid here and now; just before the total descent into madness that was both terrifying and the best thing anyone could hope to achieve. At least for those few blissful shining moments... and I kept us both there for as long as possible.

She writhed beneath me, holding me to her, all inhibitions lost as we found this almost tantric rhythm, a back and forth, a give and take, a push and pull so powerful as to mimic the tides.

Her breathy moans pulling me to her like a siren's call. She could pull me down, down, down, to the bottom and I would die a happy man – At least I think one of the other guys had described it that way once and now I completely understood what he was talking about.

Like, *yes – drag me to Hell you beautiful, magnificent fucking creature!*

Sweat glistening, heat building, stars aligning, the cosmos stopping their orbit and spin at precisely that moment where she and I made eye contact and the universe exploded into a kaleidoscope of sight and the roaring sound of the blood rushing through my ears in perfect tempo and harmony of her thin, wailing cry of purest fucking bliss.

If ever there was a moment where a marriage of two souls took place, for me; it was this one right here – and I swear to fucking God, it was blessed by a choir of fucking angels... or maybe that was just the relaxed and satisfied sigh emitted by my woman.

To have and to hold... I thought to myself, climbing up onto the bed beside her and gathering her to my chest.

Forever and ever...

"HOW YOU DOING?" I asked her a couple hours later. We walked barefoot along the sand, the sky painted in dusky pinks fading up from the horizon to peaches and cream, to a faint yellow, creeping on up into a haze of white and finally a deepening blue. There wasn't honestly anything like a sunset on the Florida coast. Made the heat and humidity worth it.

"Hm?" she asked, bringing her head up and around, her deep thoughts popping with the delicacy of a soap bubble. She was so effervescent and expressive. So different from any woman I'd ever met before. Completely different from my last woman – but that was good. That was to be expected, too. There wasn't anyone like my Marisol and I didn't want there to be. There was honestly no comparison and as much as I loved them both, Sol was gone and though I would always hold her in my heart, Jussy's smile made it that much easier to set the pang of missing Sol and longing to hold her hand one last time a thing that was bearable.

"I'm fine," she said and beamed.

"You're just awful quiet is all," I said. bringing the back of her hand up to my lips.

"I think the word you're looking for is *content.*"

"Content, huh?" I couldn't keep the smile off of my face if I wanted to. "I like the sound of that," I said.

"Good, I'm glad," she said, and I spun her out and then in, and wrapped both of my arms around her from behind as she giggled and I swore that was one of the purest sounds in the world.

"Thank you," she murmured a little while later as the warm surf washed over our bare feet.

"For what?" I asked.

She sort of shrugged and murmured, "For helping me find some happy. For not running screaming?" She gave a sheepish grin and ducked a little, and I chuckled and pulled her in and put an arm around her waist.

One man's trash is another man's treasure... I thought to myself, and I *know* it was something that I'd heard Marlin say and maybe even the captain, too – but I damn sure wouldn't utter that in front of Justice. She was a fragile sort and there wasn't any point in causing any undue hurt or stress.

Instead, I simply shook my head and walked with her in a gentle stroll, finally, when I did speak, I didn't make it about her at all because honestly it wasn't. That was all her fuckin' ex's doing and that motherfucker was done and fucking dusted.

"I ain't afraid of old ghosts, baby. The past is past and you were doing your best to leave it in your rearview. You couldn't help it that the past didn't want to stay dead and it was coming up on you like it was. I'm just glad I could help."

"A real zombie slayer," she said with a crooked smile and I laughed, nodding.

"Not our first time – me and the crew. Not sure how much the girls told you."

I shook my head. "About themselves? A little, not a lot. I don't think they trust me yet."

I nodded and said, "Things are still pretty new. All intents and purposes, you're still an outsider. Give it time, they'll warm up to you."

"Honestly, I worry more about your girls," she said, chewing her delicate bottom lip.

"Nah, I wouldn't worry about them," I said. "Lucia already likes you – a lot, or she wouldn't have even, you know? Mari isn't home a whole lot, but she likes you too. She's said so. Plus, it's not their life and they know. Their old man hasn't been really this happy in a good long while. It's about time."

"I don't fully understand what it is I do that makes you happy," she said, mystified and I smiled at her.

"You do, baby. For a lot of reasons. Now I could list them all out one by one and get you all blushing and embarrassed like you do or you could just nod and take my word for it," I said.

"Aren't you scared?" she asked cautiously a little while later.

"About what?" I asked.

"Things not working out?" she asked.

I laughed a little. "No. I just have a radar for these kinds of things," I said. "Always have and always will. It's part of how I got my road name. That and I'm a bit of an amateur meteorologist… still. I have a radar for those things too. How bad a storm is going to be and if we should take cover or to what degree we should batten down the hatches," I said. I shrugged. "All intents and purposes, I knew that whatever storm clouds you had rushing up on you weren't all that bad and it wasn't anything me and mine couldn't take care of – and I was right."

She looked at me wide-eyed and stopped, I stopped with her and took her in.

"What?" I asked.

"That wasn't that bad?" she asked, and I could hear the shock in her voice.

"No, it wasn't that bad for *me*. It was plenty awful for *you*. Too awful, you ask me. You have every right to feel how you feel about all of it and I know it's going to take time and the like to come to an understanding with it all, and even accept that there won't be much understanding to be had in the end… but as for me? I've done a hell of a lot worse, seen a hell of a lot of shit and I'm not sure that for me that what I did to help you was the worst I've ever done… but that being said, there's a whole lot worse I would be happy to go through for you and to keep you safe."

"You keep saying things like that, I'm apt to fall in love," she said jokingly but I could hear the test of her words in the tremor of her voice. She was already there, just scared to say it - which I understood, so I took the leap first, pulling her into the circle of my arms and kissing her forehead, a lingering touch of my lips to her silky soft warm skin. I breathed in her scent, woman and flowers like a field of wildflowers in bloom and pulled back to look her in the eyes.

"I'm already head over heels in love with you, babe and I don't want to turn back."

She looked up at me and her face was so starkly beautiful in that moment. She looked stunned as well as stunning, her eyes misting as she cuddled into me and rested her head against my shoulder, looking out over the water. I didn't rush her, or this, I just held her and stood with her for as long as she needed me to do it.

Just soaking her in and this moment, until I was pickled in happy.

32

*J*ustice...

We slept in, enjoyed some sights, meandered our way down the inner coast stopping for lunch and enjoying ourselves, content in one another's company. Radar kept checking his phone throughout the day texting back and forth with Atlas about business and the need to get back to it and soon and I was alright with that. If anything, I felt guilty I had kept them from it for so long... even if I could recognize it was through no fault of my own.

By the time we got off the freeway and took the little side highways and roads leading to Ft. Royal, the sun was setting. By the time we reached the leading edge of town it was full dark. I was tired, and my heart sank just a little when Radar said, "Gonna stop this end of town and swing into The Plank, check in with the captain and the rest of the crew if that's alright with you." I smiled and nodded.

Really, all I wanted was to be home, with Radar, snugged up to him safe and warm settling into what I was hoping would be my new home for a very long time, but I was scared about that. Scared that after a week more, a month, six? That he wouldn't find me attractive anymore or that I would be too needy or too broken or that therapy, which I desperately wanted to seek out, wouldn't be enough and I would... I don't know.

I honestly never envisioned surviving my husband. Never envisioned having a future... and now he was gone, and I was here, and I was so scared. Scared about all of the what-if's and what-to-do-next's and I know that was some of the PTSD talking but... but... *what if?* What if his club decided that they didn't trust me or they didn't like me? What would I do then? How would I react? What would I do? Where would I go and how would I honestly survive having to start all over again?

Was this my life now?

Just picking up from one disaster after the next, forever and ever and ever? Not being able to have anything consistent or that was my own?

I huffed out a harsh sigh with how my mind ran away from me and Radar threaded his fingers between mine as we turned onto a road unfamiliar to me, just on the leading edge of town as we were about to dip down the boulevard.

The Plank was a nondescript bar with street parking only, but not street parking in the traditional parallel parking sense of the word. No, it had back-in angle parking all along its front. I knew we had reached the right place by all of the motorcycles parked out front, all shiny gas tanks and gleaming chrome where the overhead light over the bar's front door reached them, as well as the neon beer logo signs in the window.

There were wooden slat blinds behind the beer signs, and they were pulled down, the slats angled so you couldn't see in the front windows and I wondered if that was for safety or just aesthetic.

Safety, because my mind drifted back to a girl in the survivor's group that I had been in who had been badly burned when her boyfriend had some of his gang member buddies drag her out of her car outside her work, pour lighter fluid on her, and set her on fire. She said she always kept her blinds closed, always expected a drive by any day, even though her ex was locked up for ordering the hit on her and a multitude of drug charges as well.

Radar put my car into park and looked over at me, he frowned slightly and asked me, "What's wrong?"

"I…" he gave me a look of consternation and I closed my mouth swallowing the *'don't know'* that I'd been about to utter.

We stared at each other in the close dark of the car, and I said, "I'm scared that this is all going to fall apart, that your club won't like me and that this will all be over before it has a chance to start and I'll be left on my own to start my life all over again, *again* and I don't want to."

He nodded slowly, undid his seatbelt, and picked up my hand, kissing it and peering over it at me with such a grave expression.

"What?" I asked. "Please say something…"

"Come on," he said and undid my seatbelt for me. "You can't get to know anyone and let them decide if they like you sitting here."

I bit my bottom lip in a bit of dismay and nodded, gently slipping my seatbelt off of me and letting it retract into the door.

He was out of the car before I could think, say, or do, anything else. I took a deep breath and got out myself. He was waiting for me on the curb in front of the bar.

I looked at the plank of wood nailed above the door, beneath the light. The bar's name burned into the wood: *The Plank* and beneath that in gilded script, *it's beachy, it's manly, it's made of hard wood.*

I choked back a laugh at that, and he caught my attention with a soft 'hey' and his hands on my hips.

I tore my gaze from the front of the bar and turned them to Radar who searched my face and said with all seriousness, "They'll love you because *I* love you. That's how this works."

"I don't understand," I murmured. "I mean, that's insane."

"It's not," he said, shaking his head. "It's how this family works." He sighed and smiled up at me.

"It's not how family has ever worked for me," I replied softly, and he nodded.

"Fair, it's not how your family works, but it's how this family works and make no mistake, baby. This is your new family now."

His words were a comfort. I rested my forehead against his and smiled faintly.

"Thank you," I murmured.

"Anytime you need the reminder, you just let me know," he said.

"Okay," I whispered.

He led me to the bar's front door and opened it for me and as I went through a great shout and cheer went up, startling the shit out of me. I jumped as everyone called out, "Surprise!" and confetti poppers went off showering me with streamers and fluttery paper bits.

A big, home-made sign was draped in the archway that led to a back room that read, '*Welcome Home Justice!*' in big, bold, hand drawn block letters, flowers painted boldly around them making them pop. It was beautiful and touching and had clearly taken time along with all of the ribbons and balloons that filled the main barroom.

I put my hands over my mouth, totally taken aback, and turned to Radar who winked at me as Atlas came up and hugged me tight.

"Missed you, baby. Welcome home."

Next was Hope, Faith, Charity, and Serenity in rapid succession and then finally Cutter and Marlin.

Atlas took a beer from a nearby brother I hadn't met yet, who had eyes for Charity, and I thought that must have been the elusive Galahad that had been on shift both days of the beach parties I had attended.

"Radar!" Cutter bellowed over the music being cranked. "Welcome home, buddy! Gonna talk to your woman a minute, bro."

"Come on back with us, sweetheart," Cutter said to me, and he and Marlin flanked me and walked me back to the back room that the banner hung over.

In the back room there was an honest-to-God electric chair; or so it appeared – it could have been a replica, but I didn't think so.

"Have a seat," Cutter said and gestured to the chair. I blinked and went over and perched on the edge of it, delicately. He took one of the two chairs that Marlin dragged over, and they sat down in front of me.

"Just wanted to fill you in," Cutter said. "Your stuff's been put into a storage locker at the marina. Here are the keys, it's unit twenty-one and it's rent free for the first six months."

"Monty owes me a favor or three," Marlin said. "Sorry I couldn't get you longer than that."

I blinked at them, first one then the other stupefied.

"Why would you do all of this?" I asked. "I don't understand…"

"Radar explain you're family now?" Cutter asked, leaning back.

"Yes but—"

"But nothing, baby," Marlin declared gruffly. "You're fuckin' family and families help each other."

"Mine never did," I murmured, and Cutter shook his head.

"Fuckin' citizens," Marlin grunted and shook his head too.

"I'm afraid I can never repay you all you've done for me," I said, and Cutter shook his head a little harder.

"Another fuckin' citizen construct you'll have to forget about. It's fine, babe. That's not how this works, not how we operate, and you'll figure it all out given enough time."

"We're just here to tell you, you got a problem – any problem, with the town or anybody in town who's an outsider and Radar isn't around you call *us*," Marlin said.

"Forget 9-1-1 in this town, it's a thing for the citizens, but you're not a citizen anymore," Cutter affirmed.

"Just what are you two losers doing?" Hope demanded from behind them. I looked over the two men's heads and Hope stood with two drinks, one in each hand, next to a leggy blonde who was extremely tattooed.

"Letting the woman know where her shit's at and rolling out the welcome wagon," Cutter said over his shoulder. "And who you calling a loser, woman? I ought to spank that ass of yours."

His eyes sparkled as he said it and Hope's eyes lit up and she shot back, "I would love a good bar fight – bring it on!"

"Uh-uh," the tattooed blonde said. "Shut up and drink up – we're all here to have a nice time."

"Spoilsport." Hope stuck her tongue out at her.

"Anything else I should know?" I asked softly as Cutter upended one of my hands softly dropping a ring with two keys into my upturned palm.

"If there's anything else, it can wait," Marlin said and patted my knee.

"Welcome home, babe. We're happy to have you here," Cutter said, and I smiled.

"Thank you," I said, and he gave me a nod.

"You get this woman a drink?" he asked Hope.

"Yep! Right here." She handed him one. He took it and the other drink out of her hand, handed me one, and drank out of the other with a wink at Hope as she made a noise of protest.

"Neeeeeah!"

She lifted her foot and tapped him on the ass as he went by, and I nearly snorted rum punch out of my nose.

"What you need, Hossler?" Marlin asked the tattooed blonde.

"To say hi to my new girl," she said. "Why don't you go find your woman before Atlas sweeps her three times 'round the dance floor?"

Marlin grunted and got up. "He can do the dancing so I don't have to," he said and I smiled. Hossler came over and dropped into the chair near me.

"Welcome back, baby. I figure you maybe got some stories. Love to hear them." I smiled and she raised her glass and brought it forward I clicked mine against hers and took a sip.

"It's a long story," I said. "At least if I start from the very beginning."

She smiled and winked at me and said, "We ain't got nothing but time. Fire away, I'm here for it."

She raised her eyebrows and winked over her straw between her lips, and I laughed and sighed.

Oh, where to begin, though?

EPILOGUE

Six months later...

*J*ustice...
The rumble of pipes in the driveway made me sit up at my workstation in what used to be Radar's den but what had become a shared space of half his den and half my home office. I got up from my Mac and barely had the presence of mind to save my progress before I rushed to the garage door. I hit the button to raise the main garage entrance and bounced on my bare feet, breathless with anticipation.

The door rose painfully slow, and I bit my bottom lip.

Radar walked his bike into the garage past his Escalade in the driveway and parked it beside my little Kia.

He insisted I park in the garage, and for a time, also insisted for safety that I never get out of my locked car until the main garage door had finished closing.

I squealed in glee when he shut off the bike and I rushed forward.

"Watch the pipes!" he cried and I stopped and leaned way forward, throwing my arms around him and kissing him as he laughed.

"I missed you!" I cried and he helped me to lean back so he could dismount and come to me properly.

"I wasn't even gone a week this time!" he cried.

"I don't care," I murmured. He kissed me much better this time, growling into my mouth and making me swoon.

I giggled when he attacked the side of my neck with his lips and teeth.

"Mm! Bedroom, now," he ordered and who was I to argue?

I led him into the bedroom and delighted in how he walked me right up to the bed, wrapped his hand in the back of my hair and ordered me, "Bend over."

I bent at the waist, as he kicked my feet apart, and he held me down atop the mattress. I breathed deep, already glowing, already sliding into that space where I could unwind and let go and let him use my body to my heart's content and I *loved* that. I loved giving myself over to him and letting him use me. Loved listen to him as he softly praised me in that deep and sultry voice. His Cuban accent to his Spanish so sexy and smooth as he told me suck deliciously dirty things.

Like how he loved me, how he couldn't wait to be inside of me, how much he loved my tight little pussy snug around his cock and how he was going to make love to me for hours.

He wasn't always so gentle, but then again, I didn't always want him to be. Now, though? Now it was perfect.

He worked his jeans open and slid his hand from my hair, down my back, using both hands to ruck up my long skirt and groaning in appreciation as my pussy was bared to him.

"I'm going to fuck you so good, my good little girl," he muttered, and he slid the head of his cock up and down my pussy lips, teasing me.

"You like the thought of that?" he demanded.

"Uh-huh," I said faintly, and he smacked my ass. I yipped and he chuckled.

"You like the thought of that?" he asked, and I smiled and like the brat I had been evolving into, I said, "Mm-hm!"

He smacked my ass again and I laughed, a full-throated thing.

I had loved this part of our relationship, working through some of my likes and wants in therapy, understanding that the things I liked were normal and to enjoy growing into them and understanding them. It helped that Radar not only enthusiastically was willing to explore with me, but that he was patient, sweet, loving, and kind.

He communicated clearly, he held me when something didn't work for me and I wept, and absolutely nothing was a deal breaker or off-limits. If I wanted to try it, even if it wasn't his thing, he obliged me.

If I didn't like it, even though it was sort of his thing, he never begrudged my not wanting to do it and I never begrudged him when he was really in the mood for it. We talked, and it was a beautiful give and take and every time I shared my body, my hopes, my dreams with him we grew that much closer.

He was more than just my lover. He was my best friend... and I know, I know, so many couples said that, but this was the first and last time I wanted to experience it.

"You tell me what I want to hear, and I'll give you what you want," he said, bent over my body, his voice low and rough in my ear.

I giggled and he slipped against me, and oh fuck I wanted it. I wanted what he was offering so fucking bad, but the game we played was a fun one. His domineering nature so sexy and so in control and my need to test, to feel safe and understood dynamic in my occasional bratty-ness.

"Tell me what I want to hear, baby..." he murmured playfully.

"I want your cock inside me," I said breathlessly. "I want to feel you – *please?*" I begged.

"That's my good girl," he murmured, and he thrust inside me, hard, my hips barking against the edge of the mattress, the slip and slide of him against my walls making my knees weak.

His first few thrusts were hard, and deep. Absolute in a way that screamed that he owned me, and he did. Heart, mind, and soul – our bond growing stronger every day.

"Mm, you feel so fucking good," he declared, and I very nearly melted from the praise.

"Yeah?" I asked, breathy.

"Mm-hm, I've been thinking about you all fucking day, baby. Just like this, balls deep inside you," he whispered, his body flush against mine, his cock moving inside me as he ground back and forth against me.

Oh, God, yes! I lived for when he did this. His cock hitting all the right spots, edging me closer and closer.

"You like that?" he demanded.

"Yes!" I gasped. "You know I like it, you know I love it!"

"Yeah, I like it too, I like it when you write for me, I like it when you moan for me, tell me you were a good girl while I was gone and I'll make you come for me," he said.

"I was a good girl!" I gasped after a moment or two of just indulging in him, feeling him, reveling in having him home and inside me.

"Were you a good girl?" he teased.

"Yes!"

"You drank your water?"

"Yes!"

"You ate your meals?"

"Yes!"

"You touched yourself?" he asked.

"Ye- No!" I cried, falling into his trap.

"Yes?" he demanded.

"No!" I cried.

"Yes?" he asked again.

"No!"

He laughed and bowed over my back and leaning over me, hand back in my hair, hand delved down deep in front of my body between me and the bed he touched my clit.

"That's my good girl," he growled and he drove into me, riding me, and teased my clit with his fingertips in just the way I liked until I came wailing, trembling so badly I would have surely fallen had he not been holding me up against the bed with the press of his own body.

God, yes! I lived for these moments. I lived for these times we were together. I lived for doing the whole domesticated bliss thing with and for him. For learning how to cook his favorite things from him in the kitchen, just like his mother used to make. For laying against him on the couch as he vegged out after a long day at the computer tracing criminals. For being patient with him as he worked on withdrawing from the whole bounty hunter thing and turned toward his passion which was private investigation. For being his rock at the end of the day as much as he was mine each and every day.

I lived, I laughed, and I loved every moment of this with him and with his club – the extended family I had always wanted but had never had.

I loved how after he made me come this way, he stripped slowly and lovingly out of his denim and leathers. How he stripped me carefully and sweetly out of my own clothing, and how he took me all over again, fucking me slowly, sweetly, teasing another orgasm from me, before taking his own.

Finally, it was my everything to lay beside him, limbs tangled, head on his chest, listening to his heartbeat and the tale of how this last manhunt or investigation went.

It was everything to have him play with my hair, to kiss my forehead absently during the retelling, and listening to the soothing comfort of his voice as he made me laugh, made me quiet, and made me think things through and figure out the little puzzle or lesson held in each hunt.

"What about you?" he would always ask. "What did you get done?"

Six months and he never asked me for anything except to pay off the things that I needed to – from the credit cards my *was*band, as he liked to put it, racked up to making sure that I had more accrued in my savings, to planning a vacation for us, just us two, for our one year together. Which I was still working on that.

I would tell him any of my accomplishments big or small, and he would always kiss me on my forehead and praise me. Even when I didn't really do anything at all, he made me find value in myself.

I was hopelessly in love with this man and with each passing day? The fear of imminent disaster faded.

"I got shit done like a bad bitch," I said laughing and he laughed with me. He always thought I was adorable when I tried to act all hard because hard, I was not – however, neither was I as soft as I had been. I could stand up for myself now... had a few times since moving here. With my mother, with my father, and even with Rodney's family who were somehow upset with me for moving and getting rid of his shit – the same shit I had given his brother close to – no, *over* a year to come and collect.

"Aside from covers what did you get done?" he asked.

I smiled and climbed onto him, straddling his hips, looking down at him and said, "I got the final payment paid off on Rodney's truck."

"Your truck," he corrected. I grinned.

"Lightning's truck," I corrected, and he grinned.

Lightning had taken over payments and at the end of that fucked-up rainbow, I was to sign it over to him – which I had. Boy did he love that truck and I was happy it made him happy.

"Nice, good deal!"

I nodded.

"And I went and looked at new cars for me," I declared. "I hate the Kia and I was hoping you would come with me to kick some tires."

He grinned. "What did you have in mind?" he asked.

"Something small and sporty," I answered.

He grinned. "What like a Miata?" I laughed.

"Very fucking funny!" I cried. "No, like something that actually suits me," I said, and he rolled his eyes.

"A Miata *does* suit you, babe."

I rolled my eyes. "No, it doesn't! Something with balls suits me." He pulled me down on top of himself and forced his mouth against mine in a deep kiss that was filled with good humor and a deepening and abiding love for me.

"I got the biggest set of balls you'll ever need, and I'll be the ride of your life, babe."

"For the rest of my life?" I asked and he grinned at me.

"Wouldn't have it any other way," he affirmed.
And that was more than alright with me.

The End

ALSO BY A.J. DOWNEY

Christmas with the Brotherhood

Indigo Knights

1. Her Thin Blue Lifeline

2. His Cold Blue Command

3. A Low Blue Flame

4. His Wild Blue Rose

5. Her Pained Blue Silence

6. A Cold Blue Call

7. Her Reluctant Blue Cavalier

8. Forged Under Fire

9. Under A Blue Moon

Sacred Hearts MC Pacific Northwest

1. Over the High Side

2. Wind Therapy

3. Apex of the Curve

4. Low Sided

5. Eating Asphalt

Paranormal Romance (with Ryan Kells)

1. I Am The Alpha

2. Omega's Run

3. Hunter's End

Indigo City Darker (with Jared KingPacal Lain)

1. Triple Threat

2. Double Shot

Standalones

Synchronicity

ABOUT A.J. DOWNEY

A.J. Downey is a Pacific Northwest girl living in an East Tennessee world who finds inspiration from her surroundings, through the people she meets, and likely as a byproduct of way too much caffeine. She specializes in real and relatable romance stories featuring that real-life kind of love that everyone craves.

Stalker Information:

Website
www.ajdowney.com

Sign up for her newsletter at
http://eepurl.com/dkQiIH

Facebook Group - AJ's Sacred Circle
https://www.facebook.com/groups/authorajdowney/

facebook.com/authorajdowney
twitter.com/authorajdowney
instagram.com/ajdowney
bookbub.com/authors/a-j-downey